Range of Light

Range of Light

Valerie Miner

ZOLAND BOOKS
CAMBRIDGE, MASSACHUSETTS

First edition published in 1998 by
Zoland Books, Inc.
384 Huron Avenue
Cambridge, Massachusetts 02138

PUBLISHER'S NOTE

This book is a work of fiction. Names, characters, places, and incidents are either the product of the author's imagination or are used fictitiously. Any resemblance to actual events or persons, living or dead, is entirely coincidental.

"Dragonflies Mating" from *Sun Under Wood* by Robert Hass. Copyright © 1996 by Robert Hass. Reprinted by permission of the Ecco Press.

The John Muir quotation is from Elizabeth Stone O'Neill, *Meadow in the Sky* (Fresno: Panorama West Books, 1984). The Virginia Reed quotation is from "The Donner Party," an *American Experience* film written and directed by Ric Burns, PBS, 1992.

FIRST EDITION

Book design by Boskydell Studio
Printed in the United States of America

05 04 03 02 01 00 99 98   8 7 6 5 4 3 2 1

This book is printed on acid-free paper, and its binding materials have been chosen for strength and durability.

Library of Congress Cataloging-in-Publication Data

Miner, Valerie.
    Range of light : a novel/by Valerie Miner. — 1st ed.
        p.   cm.
    ISBN 0-944072-86-0 (acid-free paper)
    I. Title.
    PS3563.I4647R36   1998
    813'.54 — dc21   97-45794
                                              CIP

FOR HELEN

Acknowledgments

I would like to thank the Rockefeller Foundation Study Center at Bellagio, the Banff Center for the Arts, the Blue Mountain Center, the Virginia Center for the Creative Arts and the Heinz Foundation at Hawthornden Castle for providing me with residencies during the years I was writing this novel. Thanks, too, to the McKnight Foundation, the University of Minnesota and Arizona State University for grant support.

Over the years I've walked a lot of Sierra trails and studied many books about these mountains. I won't reproduce the entire bibliography, but in particular I want to express admiration for *Meadow in the Sky* by Elizabeth Stone O'Neill. Also of special help were *The Mountains of California* by John Muir, *High Sierra Hiking Guide, 4* by Jeffrey P. Schaffer and Thomas Winnett, *Indians of the Yosemite* by Galen Clark, *Yosemite Wildflower Trails* by Dana C. Morgenson and *Native Trees of the Sierra Nevada* by P. Victor Peterson and P. Victor Peterson, Jr.

I am very grateful to the people who read *Range of Light* in various drafts and provided valuable response: Paulette Bates Alden, Judith Barrington, Martha Boesing, Maria Damon, Janice Eidus, Pamela Fletcher, Jana Harris, Elizabeth Horan, Helen Hoy, Ruth-Ellen Joeres, Deborah Johnson, Amy Kaminsky, Myrna Kostash, Helen Longino, Victoria Nelson, Martha Roth, Karen Rust, Sue Schweik, Gretchen Scherer, Peggy Webb and Susan Welch.

I owe much to the generous research assistance of Kristin Bolton, Nancy Hellner, Nancy Kool, Scott Muskin, Gretchen Scherer, Rebecca Pierre and Andrea Weiss.

Finally and most importantly, I thank Helen Longino for many years of loving partnership and adventure, including a decade hiking together over these glorious Sierra trails.

Probably more free sunshine falls on this majestic range than on any other in the world I've ever seen or heard of. It has the brightest weather, brightest glacier-polished rocks, the greatest abundance of irised spray from its glorious waterfalls, the brightest forest of silver firs and silver pines, more starshine, moonshine, and perhaps more crystal-shine than any light poured into them, glow and spangle most. And how glorious the shining after the short summer showers and after frosty nights when the morning sunbeams are pouring through the crystals on the grass and pine needles, and how ineffably spiritually fine is the morning glow on the mountain tops and the alpenglow of evening. Well may the Sierra be named, not the snowy Range, but the Range of Light.

—John Muir, 1869

Never take no cut offs and hurry along as fast as you can.

—Virginia Reed, twelve-year-old survivor of
the Donner Party, 1846–47

The people who lived here before us
also loved these high mountain meadows on summer mornings.
They made their way up here in easy stages
when heat began to dry the valleys out,
following the berry harvest probably and the pine buds:
climbing and making camp and gathering,
then breaking camp and climbing and making camp and gathering.
A few miles a day. They sent out children
to dig up bulbs of the mariposa lilies that they liked to roast
at night by the fire where they sat talking about how this year
was different from last year. Told stories
knew where they were on earth from the names,
owl moon, bear moon, gooseberry moon.

—Robert Hass, "Dragonflies Mating," 1996

Range of Light

1

Kath

WE WERE DRIVING through the dry, August slopes of the Coast Range this afternoon toward the glacier-skinned Eastern Sierra. Inhale this mountain air, I reminded myself, relax. In the passenger seat next to me was Adele, Del, my oldest friend — still dark, elegant, secretive. And just now, tense from her plane journey across the country.

To me the Sierra was the backbone of California imagination and possibility. The mountain water irrigated the great San Joaquin and San Fernando valleys. From the Sierra you could see miles across California to the Nevada border and you couldn't comprehend that range without an awareness of the nuclear tests done so close by or without understanding the water wars that flooded glorious Hetch Hetchy. Most people thought of the Pacific Coast as the California frontier, but I was much more drawn to this mountainous spine. I dreamt about its music: rivers rasping with snowmelt; thunderstorms pouring succor and threat. I'd always been struck by the sheer white boulders, the clarity of light shining back from Tuolumne Falls, the fiery sunsets you could see from Lyell Fork, the long, clear mountain nights of mid-June and the shooting-star lottery of August. Here we were in August, my favorite month.

This afternoon my excitement mounted as we headed east through the hills, past the energy-efficient windmills at Altamont Pass. Strange, miraculous, to be with Adele. For years now I'd pictured our next encounter would be after death. Me attending her funeral. She, as the lucky one, would be the first to go and there I'd be, a crone at her casket lugging all the questions, all the guilt. Now we were leaving the oleander-trimmed freeway — lusciously delicate pink and white daphne — behind and driving on a two-lane road bordered by fruit and nut trees. Cherries. Pistachios. Cashews. Slowly. Breathe. Enter this world carefully, completely.

A rearview mirror inspection: I was short, thin, blond, a confident driver. Most people also found me taciturn in comparison to gregarious Adele who had turned blessedly quiet during the last few miles. I'd grown used to taking this road alone and our present silence was a relief. While I had enjoyed catching up with Adele on our nonstop chat from the San Francisco airport, I needed a breather here. Selfishly, cantankerously, I wished I were alone. For one thing, I'd have left Oakland at 7:00 A.M., before the heat set in. No, this year wouldn't bring the peace of my annual solitary trek. It wasn't going to be the break from other humans I needed after a year of budget cuts at work and disintegrating parents on the home front. Of course, as a newly unemployed person I had plenty of time ahead to be alone.

Still, a week in the Sierra was bound to restore me. If I let go now. I'd have to set aside, far aside, those questions about going back to school. There was a big difference between obsession and meditation. I'd walk and reflect and rediscover some optimism and if Adele wanted to do the same, that was fine. If not, there were daily buses back to the Bay Area.

What did we remember? What did we imagine? What did we see? That first night, back in 1965, I sat in camp, enjoying the warmth of evening sun on my weary back. It had been a long drive and none of the other girls felt confident about the curving highway. The air was rich with smoke and pine oil. Adele sat at the picnic table beside Nancy, sculpting Reynold's Wrap around the large, cold, solid baking potatoes.

"Isn't it great to be able to eat whenever we want?" Nancy yanked her orange hair into a braid. "Are you sure you don't want a little dinner preparation music? I found a great station on my transistor when you guys exiled me to the bathroom last night."

"No radio," called Donna. She was helping Paula assemble the tent. "Music's all around. Birds, crickets, wind."

I covered the potatoes with red coals, pretending to ignore the conversation, to be above the topic, when I simply didn't want to get caught between my friends.

Adele nodded. "Revolutionary, the idea you could eat any time you were hungry instead of when time said you were hungry."

Emerging from the tent, Paula straightened her long, thin frame and shook her masses of black curly hair. "We did it!"

The second person out of the tent looked less certain. But doubt always shadowed Donna like a birthmark. A dark line ran between her brows and across her tanned forehead. "We'll be OK if it doesn't rain, I guess."

Another memory from the next day, several days later? It was late afternoon, I know that, and I was walking alone toward camp when I spotted Adele propped up against large, white boulders, sketching a clump of mariposa lilies. Her black hair shone almost purple in that intense light. Mom thought Adele looked like a movie star, "one of the Hepburns, maybe both" with her dark eyes, fair, fair skin, long legs and elegant gait. From anybody's perspective Adele was the most womanly of us five girls. Who knew what would happen to her when she defected from California and went to Radcliffe that next fall? I stood still, observing the way Adele's long fingers held the pen, watching the swift, brusque strokes as the flower appeared in fragile vitality. I felt amazed by my friend's skill, by the grace of her body, by the attentive tilt of her head. Sometimes in class I'd have the same awe of Adele: a mixture of admiration for this exotic creature and longing — perfectly futile — to *be* her. No, it was more ineffable. It was as if we were creatures from different universes locked in a startling, terrified magnetism.

Now I glanced sideways at my familiar, unfamiliar middle-aged passenger. Reassured that Adele had brought the right clothes. An L.L. Bean model in her cotton pants and hiking boots. Maybe during the lost years she had become Mountain Woman. You had to be prepared for surprises with Adele. Again, I promised myself not to get preoccupied with her. I should've called off the trip after the others canceled. It was one thing to have a woodsy reunion among five old pals. Something else to be stuck alone with a best friend who had deserted you two decades ago. For years I thought I'd never talk with her again. Not that Adele knew she had deserted me. She might even say *I* had betrayed *her*. Happy camping ahead.

I could've kicked myself for attending that sappy high school anniversary. After a little wine and a few life stories, we were all laughing about our long, lost time in the Sierra. Someone suggested we go again. Nancy was saying, "Kath, you were in touch with Donna, right? Why don't you get her to come with us?" For some reason, maybe because Nancy looked so happy after all those years of rotten men and booze and breakdown, I found myself saying yes. Yes, I would try to find Donna. And by implication, yes, I would join them next summer in the damn mountains.

So suddenly this was "next summer." In a couple of hours this stranger and I would camp at the Meadows. Lay our bodies beside one another in my extremely small tent.

This dry heat had intensified with the altitude. I rolled down my window.

"When is Nancy's surgery?"

"Wednesday morning," I answered. "I told her we'd call and wish her luck. But she said, no, wait till after the operation." Gripping the steering wheel, I knew I shouldn't have caved in when Nancy insisted we go without her. "She said otherwise she'd worry we were looming around her like spirit vultures."

"Oh, she'll be fine." Adele stretched for nonchalance.

Even after all these years I could distinguish her natural and unnatural voices.

Nervously, she continued, "I have two friends who had mastectomies this year and they're fine."

"They say it takes five years to be sure." I felt doubtful.

"*Sure* is a word I've folded in tissue paper and stored with other remnants of my youth."

Was I one of her youthful remnants? She probably didn't mean to condescend. She was just anxious. We fell silent and after a while I pulled into a small town. "Gas," I explained. "And I thought we could get some fruit."

"Isn't this Malga?" Adele grinned with satisfied, satisfying recognition. "The place where Paula got the strawberry milk shake?"

We laughed.

"Which she proceeded to vomit all over Donna and Nancy in the backseat!" I added, "Good memory. Is that why you became a historian?"

"Either that or a complete incapacity to deal with the present." Adele shrugged.

I leaned the hose into my gas tank, feeling the sweat dripping from my armpits down the sides of my breasts. Damn, it would be hot as hell until Crane Flat. Amid the putrid fumes, I speculated on the life span of gas attendants. Greasy, nauseating smells.

A rusted ivory pickup pulled in and idled next to us. The hunky, gray-bearded driver jumped out puffing a cigar. Maybe we'd all go up in flames. Maybe this was the descent into Hell and the Sierra was Heaven. Returning from the cashier, I considered my grouchiness. Normally by Malga, my mind was calmer, easing into the mountains.

Adele was washing the windows.

"Afraid I made a mess of it." She threw up her hands and plopped the filthy squeegee into the bucket of gray water.

"Better than it was." I laughed. Once behind the wheel, I saw she'd left wide streaks across the dusty front window. I switched on the automatic windshield cleaner and we drove through hot, dry Malga with soapy water arching over our windshield like liquid fireworks.

Billboards promised a Burger King and a Taco Bell. Malga was a one-story, one-street town. A few people strolled along the sidewalk but most had the good sense to stay inside in the midday heat. *The Bear* was playing at the Malga Bijou Theatre. Actually, I had enjoyed most of that silly romantic film but didn't feel ready to admit this to Adele.

Each year as I trespassed in the Sierra, I counted on the mountains to clear my spirit. Driving along now, I inhaled the sweet-sour aridity, reminding myself that most of California, like most of the West, is really a desert. I loved the fierce, ever-buzzing, every-dying California earth. I longed for these mountains of conflagration, destruction and generation. I didn't understand people who sentimentalized California landscape as serene and restful. But insofar as the landscape continued, it did provide courage. Sputtering down the main drag of Malga together, Adele and I were headed back to that common land.

2

Adele

Monday / Malga to the Sierra

MY BODY RETURNED GRADUALLY as we followed the asphalt from
the airport to Malga. Nonetheless, I was fairly wiped out. Perhaps Kath
had been right to propose a night in the Bay Area. It was crazy to step
off a cross-country flight and streak to the mountains. But I hadn't
wanted to stay at her place on the first day: I preferred neutral territory.
Terrifying to have a history of intimacy with someone you no longer
knew. Besides, I needed to get to the mountains. If I had stayed overnight at the coast, I would have felt compelled to call Father.

So far the drive had been more fun than I had expected, refreshing
in a way. Actually, when I'd agreed to join my friends, I had imagined
being able to back out at the last minute, had thought that the cultural
studies conference at Stanford would interfere with — rescue me
from — my impetuous pact. But the meeting had been moved ahead a
week, so I couldn't refuse. Nancy had been so eager — keeping in
touch with all of us, making the site reservation, photocopying catalog
pages about camping gear. Lou insisted I could never finish the bibliography this summer, attend the conference *and* go camping with old
friends for God's sake without eating into our family fishing holiday in
Maine. Go on ahead with Taylor and Simon, I said, and he was shocked
at the prospect of opening the cottage without me — as if I were taking vows of chastity and antimaterialism, joining Mother Teresa in
Calcutta. Calcutta or Bombay? I really needed to pay more attention
when I read the paper. I thought Mother Teresa was a very bad thing

regardless of where she was stationed, running around the world as a front woman for Catholic imperialism, but of course it did matter whether it was Bombay or Calcutta. When Lou heard about Nancy's cancer, he was sure I would withdraw because Paula had dropped out for a film project and Donna had disappeared years ago.

Now, Kath and I pulled into Malga, ingesting the scorched air. I tried to imprint on my brain the image of golden hills undulating against a brilliant sky. On the far end of town, the roadside stand we visited was crowded with melons, tomatoes, scallions, celery, pearly white corn, bok choy, endive. Covetously I compared the array of produce to that available in Cambridge. What insanity: a quarter century exile from this glory. My self-imposed exile.

"Oh, look," Kath called in her high, clear voice.

I turned toward the lithe girl and instead found a handsome middle-aged woman waving two apple juice Popsicles.

"Remember these?" Kath was smiling broadly.

"Yes," I laughed. "Let's get some of these, too." From behind my back I flourished a plastic sack of succulent, dried apricots and I could already taste the rich sourness.

"Absolutely." Kath tossed them into a red plastic grocery basket. "I'm sure they're deadly. It's the sulfur in the curing process."

"If it's a choice between dying from chemicals or expiring from boredom, I'll take chemicals." Why had I thought about dying twice in the last twenty minutes? In some ways I never believed that I would survive the twentieth century. Perhaps Nancy was on my mind; of course Nancy would be all right. She was relatively young — we all were — and she was a fighter.

As we carried the brown bags bulging with fruit to Kath's car, I wanted to drive. However I was so exhausted from the plane trip; look at the mess I had made of the windshield. Returning to my passenger seat, I unwrapped an apple juice Popsicle for Kath and another for myself, a gesture that marked me as both motherly and wifely. No, no family associations this week. I needed a break from Lou and the boys, literally and metaphorically, and they could probably use a little vacation from me.

Kath sucked noisily on her Popsicle, then navigated back to the highway.

We drove contentedly, silently, higher and higher toward our week together in the mountains.

"Vista Point." Kath glanced at me. "Should we stop and get some perspective?"

"Sure." I sat straighter and looked out the window. The idea behind this holiday was to camp outside my head for at least a short time.

Out by the guardrail, Kath did two deep knee bends. "Fresh air! Beautiful country — all these yellows and reds and browns — it's like the land turns *plaid* between Manteca and Priests Grade."

"Yes." I let California pour over me, avoiding a long look at the dammed water below. The sun was high, strong, hot, but already I felt cooler than in Malga.

Kath hopped over the guardrail and peered down a dry, grassy hillside. "Good drop," she called over her shoulder.

I held my tongue but imagined phoning her parents from the hospital, a vaguely familiar yesteryear voice. Be careful, I prayed. Slowly I grew conscious of swimmers, waterskiers, houseboats.

Kath was being uncharacteristically loquacious. "Picture living on those boats. Madonna beach towels. Dirty dishes. Sex on the soft, lapping water at night. Breakfast at the seasick restaurant."

I closed my eyes and heard the long ago voice — flip, ironic, the short, sharp sentence fragments spitting from her tough wit.

"Can't you just imagine the soft hum of midnight radio over the shuffling of the pinochle deck? I mean, I could see enjoying the houseboat for a couple of days. Then I'd go bonkers from confinement. Know what I mean?"

"Yes." I nodded.

We stared at the water together.

I was hurting from a deep, old loneliness for the friend who had disappeared and also frightened of our sudden closeness. Tears rolled down my cheeks.

"You OK?" Her arm reached over the guardrail for my shoulder.

"Just jet lag."

"Right," Kath answered dubiously, guiding me to the car. "Must have been a Boeing. They're notorious for lancing tear ducts."

I sniffed and smiled.

"You could be feeling the altitude. I mean, we've climbed a couple of thousand feet." She looked worried.

"It's so good to be in California," I murmured.

"Nice to have you."

In the car, I closed my eyes, hoping Kath wouldn't press further, not now. She had been a complicated, flinty girl who walked a fine line between bluster and delicacy. I seemed to be one of the few people who saw her fragility. With her gentle movements and an aureole of blond hair, she was by far the prettiest of us five. Often I was puzzled by my best friend, awestruck by her sureness and independence, perhaps a little scared too. Not that Kath would ever turn on me. The amorphous fear had always been about myself, perhaps that I would never measure up.

I remembered our first visit in complete scenes — people talking, laughing, pondering with all the inspired, arrogant certainty of youth. I remembered one afternoon particularly, how rain showers drew forth seductive smells in sequoia needles and willow bark as well as the stronger, musty odors of moss, mushroom, lichen. I made my way through the woods tentatively at first, as if rain carried contagion. "Don't get your feet wet," Mother had admonished a thousand times. But there was nothing to be scared of on a short jaunt to the lavatory. The temperature was in the high fifties, low sixties. The precipitation was soft, summery — for it was August and among the many things Mother did not distinguish between were summer and winter rains. I took a shower every day and I wasn't going to be afraid of sprinkles.

Drops, gems, sparkled in the bushes, despite the sleepy sky. Even in that fathomless gray, I savored the subtle play of shadow and light. In the lavatory, the cold concrete blocks felt like an igloo. I put paper on the seat, although Kath insisted you couldn't catch anything worth catching from a toilet. How did Kath know so much? How much did she invent? The seat was damp. I watched goose bumps rise on my thighs and I imagined that in a different stage of evolution, feathers or coarse dark fur might emerge from the bumps to warm me. Wind whistled through the ventilation holes in the eaves. I was alone in the bathroom. The other campers either had more disciplined bladders or used the piss pot technique, which Paula and Donna advocated but which Nancy had vetoed as too gross. Perhaps Kath had been wise to go for one last solitary hike, because she was probably a lot happier than the four of us in the tent.

I could hear Paula complaining as I turned into our campsite. Opening the tent flap, I located the source of irritation: our canvas chamber reeked of nail polish.

"Fingernails are one thing . . . ," Paula argued.

"Actually, they're ten." Nancy smiled, concentrating on shellacking her toenails purple.

Donna glanced up from *Travels with Charley.* "Who's going to admire your pudgy toes in the mountains anyway?" Donna usually sided with Paula, as I often found myself agreeing with Kath.

"You never know, romance has been found in stranger places."

"What does romance have to do with toenails?" Paula suppressed her smile.

"Foot fetishism is a sign of enormous sophistication." Nancy sniffed theatrically. Zasu Pitts doing *Marat/Sade.*

Presumably the nail polish was the cause of Nancy's watery eyes. Donna and Paula were right, of course, this stink was an imposition in such a small place. Kath might find us all asphyxiated. If Kath were here, she would simply insist that Nancy complete her left foot outside, when the sun shone.

"How about it, Adele?" Paula leaned forward in her sleeping bag. "Three to one, right? Democracy requires that she cease and desist."

"Well . . ." I didn't see how five more toes — I studied Nancy — four more toes — would make much difference. I shrugged, then concentrated on finding my page in *The Song of the Lark.* Nancy waited until Paula returned to her letter. Paula was always writing to friends in France and Japan and Australia. Mother said Paula had "a lot of energy" as if she suffered from a disfiguring disease.

Drip, drip, the rain persisted. Nothing to be afraid of, I told myself. Just a benign drip, drip. And the occasional very distant roll of thunder. Kath would be fine. Her ugly black boots had impermeable soles. Kath was, of course, completely prepared for the outdoors in her cheap and hideous army surplus gear. Nancy had brought clothes for sunbathing. Donna, in her own distracted way, had packed nothing but her normal Saturday jeans, T-shirts and loafers. Not even tennis shoes. Paula and I had shopped together at Magnin's sportswear and while we were stylish, we were also getting much wetter than Kath. I began to doze, waking occasionally to find the afternoon proceeding in a luscious, slow, lazy way with Paula writing, Donna reading, and Nancy primping for her long, lost lumberjack.

"What's going on?" Kath opened the flap. The cool, fresh air made me realize how sleepy I was. She looked like a yellow gentian in her nylon raingear. Her cheeks were rosy and her blue eyes wide with amazement.

"Smells like someone has been experimenting with toxic gases. What is this — a wax museum?" Kath caught sight of Nancy, who had fallen asleep with her feet propped up on the ice chest. "Oh, I get it, the Queen of Sheba!" Laughing, she tied open the other front flap of the tent.

Nancy sat up.

"I'm starving," Kath declared. "And I did the last quarter mile smelling coq au vin. Must've been the neighbors. What's for dinner, guys?"

Donna leaned forward with a finger in her book. Nancy set down her mirror. I ran my hand over the pleasantly rough texture of my sleeping bag, waiting. Paula spoke up. Brave girl. "We all found it a bit *froid* and wet for gourmet preparations, so we thought we'd drive over to the grill for hamburgers."

I smiled at Kath's astonished face, then teased, "Or perhaps you were planning to trap a few squirrels for us?"

We settled on beans and franks. Each of us took turns tending our fire in the light evening drizzle and everyone except Nancy agreed it wasn't so cold outside after all. She made her social contributions in the form of the fudge, cookies and cream soda her mother had tucked into her care package. And she promised that when dark came, she would prove to us beyond a doubt that her killer nail polish truly was iridescent.

Often I questioned my attachment to those six long ago sylvan days. All the same, at night when I was anxious, I would deliberately recall moments from the vacation to calm me down, to help me fall asleep. Of course the memory, like the body, adapts over years. And the past survives in pieces. Remembering is like looking at a stained glass window; already constructed in shards, the image shifts with light and time. What shards had Kath preserved? Did we feel the same about the other girls — particularly about our admiration of and fears for Nancy? — or perhaps we were more distant than I had imagined. I really shouldn't have been so surprised and hurt by our separation in college. Yet I chafed over that rift, ashamed about some unseen transgression on my part, angry at the way Kath abandoned me in painful times, confused about whether I was making too much of it. Lou, hardly a defender of Kath, nevertheless always said I exaggerated her desertion. Yet if the separation had not been that much of a trauma, if we had always been wholly autonomous individuals, why did I continue to dream about her?

As Kath and I passed through Big Oak Flat, elevation 2,803 feet, where the saloons are not *nouveaux* but have been around forever, I thought how much I enjoyed old Western towns. People drank hard liquor and real beer, none of this sissy wine cooler stuff. As we moved from the village into the dark forest, I had this ridiculous impulse to name the greens — chartreuse, kelly, lime, logan, emerald. Was this desire a perverse academic symptom — naming as prelude to owning — or was it simply a tentative, urban-bound approach to understanding? Such hectic cerebration reminded me that I needed to slow down, that within twenty minutes I would be landing on the moon.

"Funny," Kath said, reading my mind, "how the Europeans raced across this continent, turning countryside into city, and now we zip back again, hoping to catch a glimpse of some spot our ancestors left untouched."

"So many of us" — I laughed — "that we have to reserve a spot in the High Country a year ahead of time."

What I remembered most about his place was the lunar quality: the sheer, silver rocks, ghost white boulders, daunting slabs of stone, reflecting, unforgiving sunlight. Cars, trucks, RVs, motorcycles sailed beside us, higher and higher into the altitude, along the ribboned road. To be alone was why I came here and not to be alone for one summer week. I wondered how many of the city habits of obsession, calculation, time hoarding, self-defense I could release in seven days.

"Welcome to Yosemite," read the sign.

"Don't worry," Kath said. "Most of these cars are going to the Valley. They don't even know there's a High Country."

"Good." I sensed she was nervous too and this relieved me.

Kath turned, attempting a smile. "We made it."

Subdued by the caravan of cars, I smiled back. Of course it hadn't been this crowded all those years ago. I had brought a different range of emotions — more excitement then; more trepidation now. In any case, I loved these mountains. I longed for physical exercise. It was ludicrous to worry about Kath. Somehow during the last few decades I had grown less prepared for the mountains and for life. But it was too late to turn back.

3

Kath

Sunday, the day before / Oakland

I SLEPT LATER than I meant to. Baffin was usually up by now, nibbling my ear or making a racket in the backyard. But it was 7:00 A.M. and my gray cat lay sound asleep beside me on the chenille bedspread, purring in her congested way.

"What a morning to fink out, Baffin. I've got hundreds of chores." Running a hand over my head, I cursed myself for forgetting the haircut. How was I going to fit that in? I rushed into my miniature kitchen and put on the kettle. Then back to the bedroom to slip on running clothes. No sense skipping the run. The rest of the day wouldn't be worth a damn if I didn't exercise.

"Here, Baf, here you go." I filled the cat's bowl with fresh kibble and canned fish. Disgusting smells. Amazing the sacrifices you make for love. Sixteen years of early morning tuna. "Come on, Baf, that's a girl. Breakfast." I poured the coffee water through the filter, an elaborate contraption that my sister, Martha — who preferred those instant flavored coffees — laughed at. I listened to a couple of items on the radio. Still, my sweet cat didn't stir. She liked to sleep in sometimes; maybe she'd been roving last night. So much for my jogging companion. I loved the gaping stares of people who ran with Labrador retrievers and Irish bloodhounds. Your cat jogs? they shouted. Why not? I shrugged, gleefully stumping the dog chauvinists. But Baffin deserved her days off like anyone else.

*　　*　　*

This morning the West Ridge Trail was cold, damp. Dew dripped from the branches. Of course the fog would lift at noon; still I found the morning veil depressing. Although I'd lived my whole life in Oakland, I couldn't get used to gray summer mornings. Maybe what I loved most about the Sierra was the brightness right after dawn. Yes there was the occasional thunderstorm, but I could count on at least three crystal mornings each week.

Rushing through my stretches, I reminded myself that the point was to prepare for the day ahead. Meditate. I entered the trail. Slow down your mind. Speed up your legs. You do this routine every day. Gulping the clean, luxuriously moist air of the Oakland hills, I checked off the tasks: pick up tent and make sure patches are watertight. Stop for groceries. (Would Adele mind I was vegetarian?) Visit Martha to make sure everything's arranged for Mom and Dad. Fix Señora Castillo's refrigerator and remind her I'd be gone for a week. Pack food, camping gear, clothes. Call Nancy and wish her well on the surgery. Move the last remaining boxes from the office. Instruct Carter about feeding Baffin. The muscles in my thighs and calves stretched and contracted, stretched and contracted.

"Hi. Where's Tiger this morning?"

I looked up to find the nervous stockbroker who liked to chat me up during stretches.

"Sleeping in!" I called back, alarmed by my spontaneously friendly voice.

"Have a good one." He grinned, heading back to his car.

Inhaling the eucalyptus-scented air, I began to run. Listening for jays, mourning doves, I felt lucky to live so near the trails. Why worry about starting a little late? Everything would get done. The golden hills had an eerie, winterish cast in this fog. Morning mist kept down fire danger.

Sweaty and relaxed, I climbed into my car. Might as well get around to moving the boxes from the office. I'd been ready for a week now, but couldn't bring myself to make the final transfer. There'd be a sentimental scene if I hauled them out during the day. And I'd been too exhausted all week to go in the evening. No one would be there on Sunday morning — at least not at 8:45. I switched on the radio to accompany the transition from outdoor paradise to urban disappointment.

Broadway, downtown Oakland, looked deserted under this still, milky sky. Three buses snuffled together at the transit shelter. Outside

Capwell's Department Store, a cop car idled. Two ragged men — one black, one white — picked up cans from the trash bin at the BART stop. On the corner, a clutter of ageless, sexless people huddled under blankets and newspapers. I drove with my gaze ahead, as if avoiding eye contact would make me invisible.

I had heard Tom was living on the streets again, and this made me sad and scared. Sure the remorse was way out of proportion. We'd been a sixties romance, only a few years together. I'd cherished him for who he was hoping to become, his boy's hands filling into man's hands, working magic at the garage, with his guitar, in bed. In fact, Tom became someone unimaginable after the war. Surly. Brutal. Hard to believe this sweet, ironic guy could turn that violent and angry. His playful face had grown tight and his eyes darted anxiously. Hard to believe I stayed with him after a dislocated jaw and broken arm. These were accidents, I told myself, he didn't know his strength. But the accidents continued, and despite a dozen attempts to get him into a rehab program, despite all the years between then and now, I still felt sorry, responsible, still kept a spare twenty dollars in my pocket in case I saw him on the streets.

The office parking lot seemed creepy this empty, this early. Conjuring reassuring weekday noises of squealing tires and honking horns, I parked a yard from the door. Once inside the multilocked office, I'd be fine. I'd dump my boxes on a dolly and be away in two or three trips.

Opening the glass door to the third-floor office, I flipped on overhead fluorescence. The light buzzed loudly, filling the vacant room with loss. I'd miss my friends here, people I'd spent all day — sometimes evenings — with for two years. Did they count as "relationships"? There should be songs and poems about losing people on your job. My stomach clenched as I passed Verna's desk. Verna, who laughed at all my jokes and brought cookies for the office every Wednesday morning. And Carter — whose foul music was always seeping out of those faulty headphones. Carter, who had sat with me in the hospital after Dad knocked Mom down the first time.

And the kids. Slowly, I removed photos from the board over my desk and put them one at a time into the manila envelope. Marcie and Yolanda and Dina and Hortense and Clarice and Esperansa and Samantha and Amy. "The Miss Pregnant Teen Gallery," Carter used to laugh. I'd miss these kids and their kids. And the ones who'd have followed if funding hadn't evaporated.

Our office was permeated with that funny Monday morning odor of disinfectant and floor wax. The fluorescent light had hit high soprano now. I pulled pens and pencils from the top desk drawer, puzzling about the familiarity of this packing ritual. All my life I'd hobbled from one job to the next. Each of them funded on soft money. Each of them sinking into a lava of extinguishing ideals. Head Start. Inner-city tutoring. Environmental lobbying. The free clinic. And the last decade, counseling and educational programs for teenage girls. All the jobs had been useful; most had been quixotic. At each of them, people who were less experienced than I rated promotions and better pay because of their degrees.

Three times I started back to college, even though I knew I wouldn't learn much. And three times I quit in frustration with academic games. What a ruse — to get a degree to find a better job. Like medieval Christians buying indulgences to enter Heaven quicker. Clearly my intelligence and hard work were more important than initials after a name. But in the end, it was always the same: soft money. Short-term jobs. Packed boxes. Now I grabbed three more NorCal cartons from the storage room, the same blue and white cartons I had brought here two years before. The same goddamned boxes. It was so quiet I could hear the clicking furnace and the buses rumbling outside. What was alive and irritating and hilarious as an office during the week was a square room with four walls, shabby cubicles and filthy windows on Sunday morning.

One by one I'd watched my friends lift off, with their houses, kids, cottages in the country and now — this was hard to fathom — their retirement portfolios. Maybe I was, as Martha kept instructing me, just not facing reality. For such a smart person, she said, I didn't show much foresight. Was I always going to rent a one-bedroom apartment at the back of an ancient widow's house? Well, Señora Castillo was eighty-seven and doing fine. I smiled. Probably I wouldn't get evicted any time soon.

Samantha. Amy. Hortense. One by one. Photos for my album. Another job, another album. This was a perfectly reasonable record of a life. A perfectly reasonable life. And yet, as Martha would ask, what was I waiting for? The lottery? The Virgin of Guadalupe? What had I expected? Here, this is what I'd expected: that if I worked hard, proceeded with conscience, I would make progress. A modest presumption. Progress. Not success. Just perceptible change. OK, I had seen *that*. I should be grateful I had more choices than my parents. An easier — if not better — life. Mom, who had been so proud of my scholarship, had never understood why I dropped out of college. Ever since, she'd fretted about my measly prospects: no husband, kids, steady job. Great, I'd given my mother twenty years of worry. Maybe I didn't know how to organize my life. But I could organize boxes. Look at this. Four cartons on the dolly in the first load. I'd be out of here in no time.

The drive to Martha's house in Pinole wasn't long, yet I only made the trip two or three times a year, taking Mom and Dad out at Christmas, Easter, a birthday. I had reasons for staying away, hated this stretch of Highway 80; I'd seen too many mangled cars on the shoulder. And my heart seized up whenever I drove this deep into the suburbs. Martha would ask, "What's wrong that you don't want to be with family?" For years I tried to answer this question. I tried to explain that while I liked people individually, I felt suffocated when the whole family converged. Martha would have none of this. "You work in an itty-bitty office two feet from the same people all day. Don't talk to me about claustrophobia." (It was no small source of satisfaction to her that, despite two years of college, I had less job status. She was now assistant manager at the salon.) Only in the past year had I come up with a clearer answer to her question. Finally, I understood that what Martha meant by family was her *own* family — herself, Bob and the kids, and since they had grown up, *their* spouses and kids. The more I tried to explain my phobia about large gatherings, the more upset Martha became. I knew I should, as Mom would say, leave well enough alone.

I'd managed to obsess about Martha all the way from Oakland to Pinole — a good eighteen miles and twenty minutes. Parking the car, I lectured myself: Martha was a good person who worked hard, did volunteer work, got and gave pleasure with her embroidery and singing. She'd made a lot of her life. She was a decent sister.

At the door, I drew a long breath and knocked.

Martha answered in seconds. "There you are. We were wondering when you'd show up."

"Are you going out?" I was confused because Martha had said to drop by anytime Sunday.

"I wish. No, Bob's plugged himself into TV sports for the next six hours."

"I'm not late or anything?"

"Who said you were late?"

"Oh, nothing."

"I bet you haven't eaten. I've saved some pancakes. Come back to the kitchen."

I sat at the counter staring at the stack of blueberry buckwheat pancakes made from scratch. On the wall above the counter, she'd hung a new embroidery: a spray of glistening California poppies. No doubt about who inherited the artistic genes.

"Syrup or jam?"

"They smell terrific, Marth, but . . ."

"Come on, one won't hurt. You look more like an adolescent beanstalk than a mature woman."

"One, then." I grinned. As I ate, Martha caught me up on all the news about Kirsten and Sam and the grandchildren. This was fun. One relative at a time. I felt comfortable, involved. Admiring Martha's layered haircut and the new frost job, I knew I should have worn a scarf over my own rangy mop.

"Mom and Dad," I began.

"You were going to bring Dad's pills or something."

"Yeah, here's the refill. He knows how to take them . . ."

"I guess he does." Martha played with a manicured pink thumbnail.

I took a breath and continued. "And this is Hilary's number. The friend who works at Elder Services."

Martha pretended to be confused, to cover her annoyance.

"In case — as I told you — Dad gets out of hand again."

She stiffened.

Martha hated it when I talked about Dad knocking Mom around. She insisted that Mom just lost her balance once in a while. This was important, so I pressed. "I told Hilary about things, and she's more than willing to help if you need her."

"You mean you told a stranger about private family troubles —"

"Hilary's not a stranger. She's a close friend."

"Kath, you floor me." Martha picked at the grooves in the counter tile. A good way to ruin her manicure, but she was beside herself. "Don't you have any dignity? Even if you're right about Dad — and I think your ideas are very farfetched — you keep these things in a family. Where's your sense of loyalty?"

Loyalty! I held back. This was Martha talking, Martha who never had time to visit our parents but proclaimed that they were fine where they were, that they didn't need a residential facility, that Dad was not knocking Mom around. It was selfish, a betrayal, Martha said, to "deposit them in a nursing home." Maybe Martha had too many conflicts here in this house to see what was going on between Dad and Mom.

I explained once again that I wasn't suggesting a nursing home but some kind of comfortable senior residence with activities, medical care, supervision. Martha would have none of it. Mom and Dad had a right to live out their lives in their own home — just as she and Bob intended to do.

Abruptly, Martha began to empty the dishwasher, clattering knives and forks into a drawer. "So you're off on your vacation alone again this year?"

"No." I brought my empty plate to the sink. "I'm going with Adele."

"Adele?" Martha said blankly, wiping the pristine counter with a two-toned blue sponge.

"Adele. You remember. My best friend in school."

"Oh, yeah, that girl with the pompous mother." She kept her voice neutral. "The girl who left for college back East. Whatever happened to her?"

"She became a professor — of art history, film history."

"A professor of movies?"

"Not exactly." I laughed.

Martha frowned, studying me. "How long is this trip?" She set aside the sponge and stood with her hands on her aproned hips.

"A week," I answered warily.

Again, she looked perplexed. This time for real. "What on earth will you talk about?"

During the drive back to Oakland, I tried to keep my mind on Mrs. Castillo's errands. Martha had a point. What *would* Adele and I talk about? I could tell her about my career as a failed hippie in the Haight. About my series of dramatic roommates in the Castro. About my 101 jobs. About what happened to Tom. About the five years with Anita. What would Adele talk about? Her trips to Europe. Her sons' hockey team. What a fool I was to have agreed to this damn trip. Well, I could get sick. Adele wasn't leaving Cambridge until tomorrow morning. I could phone with a bad case of the flu.

No, this was my one week in the mountains. As much as I was nervous about talking with Adele, I'd be more resentful of her for stealing my precious High Country vacation. There was no other time this summer. No other time when I could get Carter to take care of Baffin and Martha to look in on Mom and Dad. Besides, I *had* to start job hunting soon. Martha had almost exited my mind when I stopped at Whole Earth Access to pick up the door latch and batteries for Mrs. Castillo.

Although it was 12:30 by the time I fixed the fridge and I needed to start packing, Mrs. C. insisted I eat an enormous sandwich. Of course, since I was going to be away for a whole week, we had to sit down for a chat. During each of the last eight summers, I'd sent my landlady a postcard from the Sierra, and she now looked forward to the stories.

"You are not afraid of bears?" Mrs. C. shifted her bulky form on the creaking kitchen chair. She wore a pale cornflower blue dress with red roses on the cuffs and open collar.

"No, Señora. We leave each other alone."

"You brave to go by yourself — a girl by herself."

I laughed, for Mrs. C. voiced this same doubtful admiration every year. And next to Mrs. C. I did feel like a girl.

"This year I'm going with a friend."

She watched me closely.

I noticed that the always-on TV set in the living room was showing M∗A∗S∗H. What did Mrs. C. make of Klinger?

"Adele," I filled in. "A woman friend." I paused. Well, I could hardly say, "my former best friend."

Mrs. C. nodded approvingly.

Nine years ago, when Mrs. C. had interviewed me for the apartment, her only condition was "No mens overnight." I never knew what Mrs. C. thought of Anita. Maybe she, herself, was a dyke at heart. Certainly Señora Castillo had had no mens in her life since César died in World War II. There were many things Mrs. C. and I didn't talk about. Still, we seemed to talk enough. She took comfort in my presence nearby and in our brief chats. I took comfort in her daily salute: "Take it easy!"

"Adela. Is a nice name."

"Yes." I nodded hopefully. "A nice person." Staring at the crucifix over the spotless sink, I tried out these sounds on my tongue, "My oldest friend."

I shook my head as I walked back to the cottage, marveling how I always felt so much better after being with Mrs. C. — certainly better than after those expensive visits to the shrink Anita had sent me to.

∗   ∗   ∗

Something was wrong. I could tell the minute I opened the door. Baffin was sprawled on the rag rug next to my bureau, jerking slightly. Mewing softly. I lay next to my friend, caressing her head. Jesus. My eyes flooded. Instinctively, I knew there was nothing to do. Some kind of stroke? Part of me said, Call the vet, it could be food poisoning, but I knew this was the end. I sat down petting the dying cat, whose eyes were filled with longing, shaped by hardness. Why had I been gone so long today? Why didn't I notice she was sick this morning? If I hadn't been so preoccupied with this damn trip, with damn Adele ... I stroked the cat. Sixteen years was a substantial life. Baffin's pulse had stopped. Still, I talked to her — about our runs and our long Sundays in bed and about all the good times we had since my roommate Gerard had won her as a consolation prize in a drag queen contest. "A female feline," Gerard had reported with mock distaste. "Much more up your alley than mine." Baffin and I became inseparable. Now I reminded her that I hadn't traveled much, but when I could I always took her with me — even camping in Canada and Mexico, savoring the subterfuge of smuggling her across international borders. Maybe Baffin understood I had to leave her home this time. What else could I do? Adele had always been allergic to cats. No, this wasn't my fault. Baffin had lived a long life and now it was simply her time to go. Something Mom would say. I was turning into my mother. Slowly. Indiscernibly. Irrefutably.

In the backyard, next to the flaming bougainvillea, I dug a small grave and buried my old pal. I wanted to take a long walk, had a yen to go out to Point Reyes, one of Baffin's favorite spots. But there was no time. A more spontaneous person, a more passionate person, would have driven to Marin and held a memorial or something. I could hear Anita complaining about my reserve as if I were practicing for a diploma in rigidity. God knows I loved Anita and tried to change. But Baffin would understand. I knew this as I dug her grave. Baffin didn't need a schmaltzy send-off. She knew how much she meant to me. That's why we had lasted sixteen years together.

Christ, suddenly it was 4:00 P.M. I had to pick up the mended tent, borrow Carter's cooler, shop for groceries ... And I did accomplish all this plus a call to Nancy, who acted plucky about the second operation and giggled about the pleasures of being off chemo for a while. Pleasures: eating, sleeping, keeping your hair in your head. Nancy was what

Mom would call "a brick." Did this passing of words and phrases always occur automatically as one generation slipped to the next? Was Mom slipping, would she die soon?

Sitting down with a plate of pasta, I switched on the TV. Maybe I observed the evening news the same way people observe mass, dutifully at the outset, yet increasingly distracted. Usually I already knew all the stories from the afternoon papers and radio. But TV was company. I put down my plate and reached to pat Baffin, then felt a dull, heavy stab in my chest.

After dinner, I sat out on the back step enjoying the perfumes of five different tomato plants. Summer evenings in the backyard were my favorite retreat. Jasmine and honeysuckle in the air. This year I had planted basil among the tomatoes. And mint and lavender by the side of the house. I liked to detect each scent individually, then enjoy the aromas mingling together. Now looking out at Baffin's grave, I began to sob.

In order to pull myself together, I thought about the next evening, when Adele and I would be in the mountains. Did Adele have a garden? Did she watch the evening news faithfully? What *would* we talk about? If a cat had nine lives, how many rounds did a friendship have?

Face it: we'd become close when life was more promising. All you did in those days was choose. And now, well, sometimes I felt I was choosing to stay alive. No, it was simpler. I was choosing not to die. I closed my eyes and thought about those walks Adele and I took home from school, arriving an hour after the bus would have deposited us. Dad thought I was crazy. Good exercise, Mom said, even though she worried about our walking in winter darkness. But we didn't notice time or exertion as we planned jaunts across Europe — where Adele would be writing on the Adriatic Sea, on the exotic, Yugoslav, coast. Rides across the Sahara — where I'd be working as an aid officer. Maybe as a nurse.

That first summer out of high school we had made a lot of plans too — about husbands and babies and vacations together in the country. Then so much happened: my abortion, Tom's craziness, Adele's sister Sari's suicide, Mrs. Ward's death. It was easier to think of it in a list like this — as if one grief canceled or at least assuaged another. Somehow, then, neither of us had been able to reach out. What lunatics we were to plan a week together in the mountains now. I walked over to Baffin's grave, said good night, farewell, and went to bed.

Of course I couldn't sleep. Instead, I lay there, thinking that the roads had separated, my car going one way and Adele's another. I rolled over, trying for comfort in the enormous bed. We'd both lived through the same social events, if at different edges of the continent. The War. The women's movement. Ten years of Republican cutbacks. The roller coaster of nuclear armament and disarmament. In Massachusetts, Adele had probably also taken meditation and yoga. I wondered if we'd talk about these accessories and interruptions to the lives we had planned. If we could congratulate or blame or console each other. If we could forgive. I pictured this trip — insofar as we had each agreed to continue after the others dropped out — as an attempt at a truce. It was too bad that treaties weren't usually signed until bodies were piled high. Well, middle-aged frailty was more susceptible to forgiveness than youthful immortality. I reached over for Baffin.

4

Adele

TENAYA LAKE shimmered in a basin of silver boulders: a mystery, not a lake, in its clear, blue darkness. The water was guarded by trees and hemmed with a thread of beige sand. An impulse to touch the surface, to enter the mystery in some small way, surprised me.

Kath's voice: "How about here for a picnic?"

Getting out of the car was the last thing I wanted. I could continue sailing for hours in this thin air. We were two balloons released from our strings, bobbing into one another as we spiraled higher and higher, far from the gravity of our daily responsibilities. Of course we should rest. Kath must be depleted from driving and I should really eat something to orient my body to West Coast time.

Out on the suddenly choppy lake, wind teased waves toward the deck of a lone boat. Weather was so changeable up here: hot, cold, misty, dry. An emotional barometer for our friendship. The spirit of this breeze had succeeded in claiming the water from a half-dozen people who had scuttled back to shore and were busily packing their campers and cars. But two parkaed boaters — male? female? — bloody arrogant human beings — persisted as ticks on the neck of a bear. Good for them.

Tenaya Lake. One of the most Indian-feeling places in the Sierra. The name of course — Tenaya, chief of the Yosemites. The size of the lake — large enough to actually sustain people. The glorious location — you could imagine humans living there, on the side of a great mountain, on the shore of that vast, rocking water. You could imagine but not see. The Indians had to be removed before you could imagine. Depending on who you were. Tenaya Lake. Blue, deep, clear, reflecting the sequoias from one side and the sheer white rock from the other.

Together we spread a dark green plastic garbage bag on the sand and huddled under ancient yellow and orange afghans made by Kath's older sister, Martha, who always, unfathomably, hated me. Proceeding wordlessly, automatically, Kath sliced tomatoes and cheese while I poured steaming milky coffee in red tin mugs. Closing her eyes, Kath exhaled the highway fatigue.

I zipped my sweatshirt tight and pulled the VIVE QUEBEC scarf closer over my ears. Cold. No, chilly. In Massachusetts, I had discovered wet cold, ice cold. This was cool. A luscious, cool mountain retreat. Lifting my left hip, I flicked away a stone and sank back on the crackling plastic. Yes, moist, fresh air. Yes, the plane had landed. Oakland, Castro Valley, hot, hotter, Manteca, Stanislaus Forest. Cooler. Welcome to Tenaya Lake. Cold. I was here, safe with Kath, despite the prickle of apprehension along my neck, safe with my oldest friend.

"Mustard, lots of it, right?" Kath spoke with that California slowness that I found both trying and seductive. "And just a taste of mayo?"

I nodded, touched yet unnerved by her retentive memory. Had I changed so little in a quarter century? How well did this other person know me? How important were mustard and mayo? Here I was allowing Kath to do the navigating, driving, feeding. Well, I would revive with this lunch and insist she sit back as I drove the remaining distance.

"Do you have any plans?" Kath asked as I bit into my sandwich.

"Plans?" I paused, reluctantly, between chews. Plans were what I had come to escape for one week.

Kath bit her lip. "About where you'd like to hike?"

"Oh, yes." The food was clearing my head. Now for the dried apricots. I wanted to lose five pounds before Stanford, but a little fruit was harmless. We would be doing a lot of walking up here. "Yes, I'd like to go back to Lyell Fork. And Gaylor Lakes and — what's that — yes, Mono Pass."

Kath nodded, swallowed. "That's what I thought, too" — her voice rushed ahead — "we can do the backpacking near the end, once we've built up a little stamina."

"Backpacking." I gulped, then realized she wasn't thinking in heroic proportions. We had discussed this on the phone and I had seen the modest packs in the trunk. If nothing else, backpacking would help me slim down.

"Yes, just some mild hikes — maybe up to Vogelsang and down to Glen Aulin."

"Sure." I tried for confidence. "The High Sierra Camps. Nancy sent me a flyer."

Kath nodded, satisfied.

Perhaps Lou was right about the journey being sentimental, but I could hardly withdraw as the trip had initially been my own impulsive, drunken suggestion. I had been unhinged by seeing my classmates after all those years. I might have missed them altogether if Father's seventieth birthday hadn't guilt-tripped me back to California. During that long, "festive" week, the class reunion provided one of the few legitimate excuses to escape his house. I was so happy for the break from Father that I forgot to guard against the consequences of time travel.

What a macabre scene: the class of 1965 convening at Father's country club in 1990. Closed to Blacks and Jews when we were in school, the Lazy Hills Country Club now boasted a late-twentieth-century foyer mural celebrating California multiculturalism. In the dining room, bright lights buzzed off garish purple and gold crepe paper decorations. At first I was startled by how fit people seemed. A number, myself included, I trust, looked better than we had in high school. Our faces had settled into individuality and reflected some degree of personal history rather than the mindless optimism or terrified panic of our adolescent years. Generally the women looked younger than the men, and it took me a while to realize this was because most women didn't go bald and most men usually didn't dye their hair, wear tummy-suck panty hose or use makeup. I marveled about my own vehement protest against makeup in graduate school. Ah, for the return of that fresh-faced certitude.

Nancy, who had gained fifty pounds, recognized me the minute I entered the glittering, ethnic mosaic vestibule. A member of the organizing committee, she knew that Kath and Paula also had made reservations. No one had heard from Donna in years. Nancy had saved a table for the gang and filled me in on her life in Tucson as we waited for the others. Paula arrived next, her classy black suit draped in gold jewelry. She was a consumer reporter for a network affiliate in L.A. Not exactly the *60 Minutes* job she had targeted, but very high-powered. Nancy told Paula she'd seen her on the motel TV when she'd taken her four daughters to Disneyland. She had thought about phoning but felt embarrassed by the twenty pounds she had acquired. She hoped maybe they would meet at the fifteenth reunion but didn't attend because she had gained another ten pounds. She had missed the twentieth for the same reason and decided she had better go to the twenty-fifth while she could still fit through the door. We laughed with her. Nancy had always been a good sport.

Over our tediously inoffensive chicken and rice dinners, Nancy and Paula and I exchanged news and photographs of parents, siblings, husbands, children. I was unabashedly pleased by their admiration of Simon and Taylor — the snapshot where they were clowning in their hockey outfits. Jesus, I had contracted the my-kids-are-cuter-than-your-kids virus. Pathetic, although old friendships do make for the best rivalries. We waved across the room to eerily grown-up versions of our classmates and drank too many glasses of chardonnay. All evening I kept wondering what had happened to Kath. Together with Paula and Nancy, I watched with mild, petty disappointment as the prizes were awarded for "most changed," "least changed," "farthest traveled," "longest married." Just as in high school, we were not part of the winning circle.

After dinner Paula left to talk to Mr. Barth, the lecherous drama teacher who now looked long past any danger. Nancy and I watched the couples dancing to Bobby Darin and Beatles and Beach Boy songs. I was glad Lou hadn't come — he never flew to California anymore — because he would have been visibly bored, whispering snarky comments. Nancy was drinking a lot and telling me about her year with the Moonies, her breakdown, her return to the Church. Her recovery from the Church, library school . . .

I spotted a woman twisting with Michael Bagley and — his boyfriend? — Stephen West. Suddenly it dawned on me why Michael had been so tense and distant all those years before. I had an impulse to tell Michael about my article on homoeroticism in *Film Noir* but settled for smiling at my earnest desire to persuade him how cool I was. Gold crepe paper was sagging lower and lower, artificial rays from the fluorescent lights melting down the walls. The room pulsed with the hot noise of second-rate music and fermented conversation.

Surely the woman was Kath. You could tell, even from the back like this. Something about the way she held her shoulders and the good time she was having with Michael and Stephen, oblivious to the rest of us. The old hurt welled up. Why hadn't she come looking for me? How long had she been at the reunion? Did she plan to leave without saying hello?

Enough wounded pride. The Lazy Hills Country Club was never a backdrop for healthy memories. And after all, a year had passed, we were at Tenaya Lake together. Carefully I packed up the lunch things. "Why not let me drive the rest of the way?" I suggested.

Kath looked doubtful.

"I'm refreshed now." I sat taller.

"No, it's OK, I'll keep going."

"But you must be wiped out."

"If you're sure?"

"Absolutely."

Still reluctant, Kath handed me the keys.

Higher and higher we climbed in the old Chevy. The shimmering boulders reflected sunlight and transfigured trees, grass, dirt, pine needles. 8,600 feet: the sign for Tuolumne Meadows. I had prepared myself, but who could be ready for this vast expanse of field — so richly earthy after the silvery lunar rocks — for this warm lap of land hugged by highway and shouldered by snowy peaks? I was pleased by Kath's abrupt gasp.

We held silence until I turned our car into the campground.

"Crowded," Kath apologized.

I shrugged. "We have a reservation, we have a place to sleep, and tomorrow we can strike out on our own." On our own, I reconsidered; I was spending a week alone with Kath. Scarier than spending time with a stranger because she knew all my early vulnerabilities and none of the complexities of recent years. How much could I tell her about Lou's sleeping around? I really did believe him that the affair was over — and one affair is not "sleeping around" — so it was pointless even to think about it. Perhaps she would be curious about the boys. I wouldn't deluge her with all the pictures at once, just show her one or two and then the rest if she looked genuinely interested. Nothing more boring than the oblivious matriarch flashing a prodigious photo album. Still, I wanted Kath to appreciate my metamorphosis. No one else was quite as able to see through the pretense; she could tell me whether the changes had truly taken.

What different ways campers had of colonizing these sites. Some spots were modestly settled with pup tents and cars. Others were civilized with several large tents, plus another screened contraption for groceries. Laundry hung from ropes strung between trees. Every site had a night food locker and a charcoal pit. Kids played Frisbee or listened to the radio. Adults gossiped around early campfires. Decompress, I warned myself. See the people relaxing, you can do it. We unpacked and prepared dinner — a quick pesto fusilli that was slightly too al dente for both of us.

Then, still caught up in the freeway's momentum, we drove over to Tuolumne Lodge, where Kath showed me how to sneak into the showers. After washing off the sweat and dust of our long trip, I rang home to say I had arrived safely, to make sure Lou and the boys were well. Lou could have talked on and on, but I kept the call brief. Expensive, I explained. Sipping a glass of cabernet from the lodge, I waited for Kath outside on the warm boulders by Miller Cascade. Brown and green and foamy water coursed downstream over gradually diminishing rocks. If I sat here for a millennium, this handsome stone might turn to sand filtering downstream to the ocean. Perhaps I was being drugged by the high altitude. I wished the name didn't remind me of a beer commercial.

The sky edged from coral to pink, but the rocks by Miller Cascade were still warm. It wasn't cold enough for the heavy green sweater that Lou had bought me on the Isle of Harris the previous year, but I loved its fuzzy security. He was right, why get upset about one indiscretion. It happened in "the best of families." Everyone had been tempted. I sniffed the deep red wine and listened to water coursing over rocks. I wanted to think it was snowmelt, but this was too late in the season. Rather the stream was the remains of the storm Kath had mentioned. Water rushed through fallen branches, spitting into the warm evening. Lou had noticed that storm front on the Weather Channel. Oh, don't worry, I said, remembering the apparition of Kath as a nylon gentian years before, I was perfectly capable of wearing a poncho. After all, skin was waterproof. Not chillproof, he parried, tucking the Harris pullover in with the jeans and turtlenecks. Hugging my sweater now, I inhaled the luscious lanolin scent. I hoped my woolly benefactor continued to bleat in a misty pasture with a new coat of her own.

"Hey, look," Kath called. Then a high-pitched squeak next to my knee. I glanced down at the small, striped creature and could hear

Lou's hyper warning, "Watch out for the rodents. Even the cute ones carry rabies."

"Belding ground squirrel," said Kath. "He's a tame little guy."

I grinned at Kath's wet, sleeked back hair, which looked almost brown. Her fresh face shone; she had so few wrinkles it was hard to believe we were the same age.

"But" — Lou's scrupulous, engaged voice emerged from my mouth — "why do you call the squirrel 'he'? Could be female. We always do that to animals." I paused, musingly, to take the sting from my criticism. "Call them 'he.'"

Kath pursed her lips. "Except spiders."

Sipping the wine, I glanced curiously from the squirrel to Kath and back again.

"Hey, look, up there."

Peering, I saw nothing.

"Marmot," whispered Kath. "See, a yellow marmot, that groundhog-looking animal, ducking in and out? See her between the rocks?"

"Yes." I nodded, although I saw nothing. Tomorrow, I promised myself, I would open my eyes.

5

Kath

Monday Evening / Tuolumne Meadows

SITTING WITH ADELE on the boulders by Miller Cascade, I felt we'd always been friends. So easy now, to talk and laugh together. Still the same people, just scuffed and polished here and there. Adele seemed softer. More assured. I suppose I'd developed something resembling a sense of humor. Really, this was completely natural, like we'd seen each other every week during the last twenty years. Also eerie, like those decades hadn't happened. Over the next week I'd be asked to explain my life, my failures, my accidental but not yet fatal course.

"How was the phone call? Are Lou and the boys doing OK?"

Adele's face washed with pleasure, suspicion. Honest, I *was* interested. Saying this would be begging the question.

"Fine, fine. Watching TV together in the backyard. It's one of those sweltering Cambridge nights. Humidity is something I don't miss about the East."

I was curious about what she did miss and if she was lonely for them already and whether she found me so boring she might cut the trip short.

"But they all seem to be coping splendidly, eating ice cream and watching *Star Trek* on cable. Lou is spoiling them while I'm away — maybe to make me feel guilty. It's not going to work: I deserve this holiday. I need it."

That was better. "Tell me about the boys."

Adele grinned and, as if her smile were too heavy for her face, she bent her head back on that long, pale neck. "Totally different. Simon's ten. A sweet, relaxed kid. Bright as his dad, and with a temperament from some other universe, at least some other family: gentle, noncompetitive, confident."

"And Taylor?"

"Taylor." She paused, thinking. "Taylor is a year younger. Assertive, nervous and also very smart. Carrying neuroses from both the Wards and the Joneses. A complicated, fascinating boy, but too burdened for his age."

"Sounds familiar."

"What do you mean?" She was actually puzzled.

"You were a pretty burdened youth," I tried cautiously.

"Me? You mean Sari. I was the lucky one."

We were going too fast. I wasn't ready for painful memories of Adele's sister, Sari. For any painful memories. Why had I said anything? Because I was jealous of Adele's kids. Not so much jealous of her for having kids but jealous of them for having her. How could I get out of this? I didn't have to.

She saw warning lights and asked, "How are your parents, Kath? I often think about your mom. She was . . . I mean, probably she still is . . . so warm, loving. Your place was such a refuge after my life in the house of a thousand swords."

I shrugged. It was coming back now, how Adele had never understood my family, had always idealized them as simple people with good hearts. Well, this wasn't the time for analyzing Peterson pathology. "OK, I guess. But Dad's developing a sort of senility, and that's hard. Harder on her than him." I kept my voice even. Later, maybe, I would tell her about Mom's bruises.

"I'm sorry." Adele looked at me with those huge brown eyes. "For all my troubles with Father, at least his mind is intact. How tough for you!"

I nodded. "Maybe we can talk about it sometime later this week. When we're not so tired." Shivering, I wanted my sweater. Night had dropped abruptly. "Maybe we should get some rest?"

"Yes, yes, of course." She gulped the last of her wine.

"Sorry, I didn't mean to rush you."

"Lou says hi." She stood with the empty glass.

"Oh, right, good. 'Hi' back — next time you talk to him." What else could I say about this man I had despised forever? Who had despised me. Adele had always been skillful at social niceties. So much more mature, a better, kinder person altogether.

As we passed the meadows, I imagined how they'd look in winter. Quiet December with sun glinting off the ice. Long, dark tree branches scoring shadows across the white blanket. Every pawprint visible in snow. This summer evening, the meadow simmered with the scavenging, courting music of nocturnal critters. Baffin had loved the meadows. I wanted to talk about my cat, but even thinking about her choked me up. No, I wasn't ready.

Despite the dim light tonight, I spotted deer, jackrabbit and hawk. Adele saw a ground squirrel. We both smelled the skunk.

Adele entered the tent first. I stayed outside, surrounded by aromas of dying trees and camp dinners, listening for night sounds, watching the sky in hopes — dashed — of shooting stars, waiting, waiting for the courage to crawl back into the tent with an all-too-familiar person. The fear was ridiculous. We were grown women, with separate lives. Adele beamed the lantern, and the tent became a lavender firefly poised in the cool mountain darkness.

She didn't look up as I entered. I saw she was reading *Lantern Slides* by Edna O'Brien, and I felt excluded, but also relieved because I was surprisingly shy about undressing. Finally in my sleeping bag, I got fixated on Edna crashing our party.

"I hope Nancy's OK," I said. "Pretty scared, I guess."

"Sure." Adele set aside the book. "I'm sure she's terrified. Still, she has a lot of confidence in that surgeon. And the girls are there."

"All four of them?"

"Yes, Clare flew in from Panama."

"I bet Nancy was — is — a great mother. Maybe also a little overwhelming."

"What do you mean?" Adele's voice stung back.

"I mean she doesn't let go. You know the way she stayed in touch with us all these years."

"I think that was nice."

"Oh, I do, too." I couldn't help but consider that I would be enjoying a restoring, solitary mountain retreat if Nancy had been less persistent. "I admire it. I don't know. I just don't see where she found the time — the energy — to phone, write postcards and send those annual Christmas letters. In comparison, I'm a complete hermit."

Adele laughed, a deep, lying down, gurgling laugh. "You are a recluse."
That felt all right. It was true.

"But don't you see, Nancy enjoyed it. Remember how her family always had those big New Year's parties."

"I remember Mr. Decker, fetal position under the piano, purring like a cat." I grimaced at the memory of silly Mr. Decker, who at the time seemed a happy contrast to our overserious fathers.

"And to Nancy, our friendship meant a lot."

I felt the wind exit my lungs. "Are you saying" — I was on edge — "that it didn't mean a lot to me?"

"No," Adele responded quietly. "No, I don't think I'm saying that."

I lay there in silence, aware of Adele's soft breathing, of the scents of her herbal shampoo and sandalwood soap, my eyes closed.

"I'm just saying that Nancy was intent on celebrating friendship — through letters, at the reunion, with this trip. In contrast to family events, like weddings and anniversaries, there aren't many rituals for friendship."

My lids opened. "Yeah, family always comes before friendship."

"So do lovers. I mean, friendships are women-women things, or between men. They lack the commodification of sex appeal." Adele backtracked nervously. "Of course there are nonromantic friendships between men and women and romantic single-sex relationships, if you know what I mean . . ."

"I know what you mean."

"So friendship is a kind of accessory to life." She stared at the nylon ceiling.

"The detachable sidecar," I said, approaching danger.

"Yes." Abruptly, she diverted us. "And Nancy knew — she always had a talent for friendship — that self could be constructed beyond family."

From the next campsite: the sound of our neighbor unzipping his compact tent. I felt a twinge of envy about his uncomplicated, independent camping trip.

"No, not without a sense of family," Adele continued. "I suppose her father's incest, well, shaped her irrevocably."

"So friends were a safe port."

"More like a raft. Because she went on to create her *own* family. And those girls, they really have become the center of her life."

"Hope it's a long one."

"Yes." She was subdued, tired.

We fell silent. Time passed. Tentatively Adele whispered, "Shall I turn out the light?"

"Sure." But once the lantern was off, I needed to resume. "I used to be so scared I would die in my sleep, you know" — why was I rattling on like this? — "that I would say to Mom, 'Good-night-see-you-in-the-morning-I-love-you.'"

"That's sweet." Her faint voice was distracted.

"No," I felt compelled to explain. "It was a superstition. If I said it, I wouldn't die."

"That was a lot healthier than Sari. When we shared the upstairs bedroom on Wharton Street, she used to recite that twisted prayer, 'If I should die before I wake, I pray the Lord my soul to take.'" She sniffed.

"Yes." My voice was muted. Sari was still one of the many hard topics ahead.

"Well" — she steadied her words — "good night."

"Good night."

She added, "See-you-in-the-morning."

I could smell the earth beneath us. It had been a long day. Time to sleep. But I was speeding on an overdose of altitude and anxiety. The mountains were a dangerous place, where the long, clear vistas create an illusion that you could see *life* clearly. Any minute now, I would step over a precipice.

Adele's breaths grew even. Poor woman must have been wiped out. What a life she had racing all over the country. Lecturing. Teaching. Writing books. Raising two sons. Adele was so much more grown up than I. Sophisticated. Accomplished. Her breathing sounded more content now. What did I have to contribute by way of conversational topics? The condoms preferred by North Oakland teenagers? The challenges of providing pregnancy counseling to teens in public schools? The state's lousy administration of soft money funds and how politicians had manipulated the agency for electoral ends? My own choice right now between taking another quicksand job and going back to school?

Ridiculous to even think about spending that kind of money for tuition with my parents the way they were. No point getting a degree at a time of wholesale layoffs. Going back to school had more to do with some ancient vanity than with job prospects. Still, I needed to prove that I was different from the rest of the Petersons, that I had belonged in that advanced high school class.

Our campground was quiet, except for the occasional roar from the highway or the swish of an anonymous small animal inspecting pots and lanterns. Or an intermittent hoot. Baffin had hated owls. How could anyone find them cute? Maybe the brilliant eyes distracted people from the menacing claws and beaks. I'd always been petrified by their patient vigils, by the eerie, soundless swiveling of their heads.

Here I was, Kath Peterson, age forty-four, continuing to worry whether I had been put in the right high school track. Here I was, lying in a tent with an old friend who had traveled thousands of miles to a new life, had suffered through a major family tragedy, had a national — who knew? international — reputation. This trip had to be one of the silliest things I had ever done. Why had I gone to that idiotic reunion?

In fact, I wouldn't have considered it — I had already thrown out the sappy invitation — if Michael and Stephen hadn't ambushed me at the Pete Seeger concert. I knew they had always wanted to go to the Senior Ball. ("A gala named for fags," Michael had insisted way back then, even before Stonewall. I wondered who I'd been protecting in high school by not telling Adele that Michael was gay.) And this reunion would sort of make up for missing the festivities years ago. Still, they needed support — at least one friend who would stay on the dance floor with them. And they couldn't take a chance waiting for the thirtieth reunion, when people might be more liberated. Who knew what would happen to two HIV-positive queers in five years?

It took good old Nancy to drag Adele on the dance floor, where, after hugs and nervous kisses all around, we bopped to "I Heard It Through the Grapevine" until my ankles ached. Then Nancy commandeered a guitar for Paula, and half the class of 1965 — Vietnam vets, Berkeley radicals, gay fathers, corporate executives — were moaning after Charlie on the MTA. ". . . his fate is still unlearned. Poor Charlie, he may ride forever . . ." Of course, vital Adele sang the loudest, the longest.

My back settled into the sleeping bag, and my sleeping bag settled into the uneven earthen floor. We were trying to sleep beside one another. (Above ground. Before the funerals. With so much left to say.) Physical senses being safer than emotions, I concentrated on the pine needles scrunching beneath the tent. Maybe one reason Adele's presence unsettled me was that I would now have *this* memory to replace the other. I was happy enough with the past, with the way I had shaped and shaded it over the years. Maybe I resented Adele for being real. I didn't want to know how *she* remembered those years. I wanted them all to myself.

Gently now, I lifted the small window flap. Yes, I thought if we pitched the tent at this angle, I would catch a glimpse of tonight's moon. There — a lucent slice of melon. Mid-August was the season of shooting stars. Searching my swath of sky, I was disappointed to find everything holding firmly. Adele's breathing continued slow — in . . . out, in . . . out — and steady. My arm grew tired of holding the flap. Soon the rest of my body would surrender. Soon.

6

Adele

Sunday, the day before / Cambridge

I WOKE from the half-light. The anxiety. The snoring. Sometimes Lou's attitude about snoring was comical: he simply refused to believe he did it and insisted I was dreaming or projecting. Well, snoring could be soothing, in and out, in and out, like the rhythms of a ceiling fan. I could get used to it. Just as I always worried those ceiling fans would fly off and decapitate me, I imagined Lou's snoring into spluttering coughing fits. Actually, I was lucky to have this smart, sensitive man snoring beside me. Noise was a small price. Well, the schedule was too jammed this morning for the semiotics of nasal expression. Quietly, I slipped out of bed. No, I hadn't disturbed him. In and out. In and out.

I pulled on some underpants, then threw a long T-shirt over my relatively fit (of course I'd be able to keep up with Kath) body and tiptoed into the study to sort out papers for the trip. One week in the High Sierra and one week at Stanford. My carpool buddy Clara said this dichotomy was hilarious, very Western. I acknowledged the looniness of swinging from the rugged backcountry to Palo Alto's manicured groves, a huge emotional and physical shift. But I had a whole day between events. Time now for a shower and a thorough rereading of my paper. Thank God I had managed to avoid adding a visit with Father to this volatile mix.

On the way to school last week, Clara praised my adventuresomeness with dubious enthusiasm. "Mountain climbing! Backpacking!" she declared as if I were hitting the Oregon Trail solo in a covered wagon.

Carefully, I placed my conference paper in a new green file folder. This way I wouldn't fret about not having it. I could always look in my briefcase and see that it was there. What a first-class neurotic I was. Next to the file I slipped a copy of my new book, which, I had learned, was always worth carrying. A conference program. The letter from the dean at Berkeley. Why was I taking *that*? To memorize on the plane? To keep Lou from finding it? Of course Lou didn't rifle through my desk. I had an overly dramatized superstition about the letter. Click. Click. Click: our automatic coffee machine seduced me into the kitchen with the sharp, sullen aroma of fresh mocha java. As the gleaming brown drug filled the glass dispenser, I thought about what a virgin I had been in that first year of grad school. I didn't smoke pot, didn't drink coffee. Now I poured myself a mug and returned to the study.

As I ingested the caffeine, my attention was drawn as it was almost every morning to the old postcard of Half Dome at sunrise. I had carried this sentimental relic from office to office over the years. The article was almost finished, really, but I had promised myself one last edit on screen before I printed it out. This was the eighth draft; it should be ready. Lou would laugh if he knew I were still working on it. He had always been able to complete projects in two or three drafts. Startled by a rap on the glass door to my study, I turned to find Taylor.

He was a short, handsome boy whose fierce determination reminded me, at times, of Father. Since the kid had spent hardly any time with his grandpa, I was afraid that genes account for a lot more in human development than I had reckoned on. Something else I hadn't anticipated was how my love for the boys would expand with each phase of their lives. When Taylor was an infant, I thought he was perfect. And yet, as the months and years allowed him originality, volition, culpability, my heart ached more deeply for him. People didn't think enough about children as individuals. Adults spent too much time worrying about kids' needs and griping about the impositions they created and not enough time rejoicing about their very individual contributions. The aggrieved expression on Taylor's face forced me back to the present.

"You're up early." I smiled, holding open my arms, encouraging him to relax.

Taylor nestled his head into my shoulder and my chest expanded with pleasure.

"Yeah, we have the kayak race today, Mom. And I know Simon is going to dawdle."

"Dawdle?" Where had he picked that up? A word his grandpa used often.

He moved away and I had to restrain myself from pulling him back.

"So will you get on his case? Will you make him hurry?"

I glanced out at the Bavarian clock on the living room mantel. It wasn't even 6:00 A.M. The clock was Lou's most romantic acquisition, something he had picked up in Munich during our junior year abroad — to put on our mantel when we settled down. My breath had been taken away by the expense of it, but Lou had insisted it was a sound investment. Never once during the last twenty-three years had it needed repair.

"Taylor, your van doesn't leave for an hour!" I held out my hand, but he had turned skittish, wary of contact. Gently I added, "Let your brother sleep in. If he's not up in half an hour, you can go wake him."

He stood there looking at me through Sari's gray eyes.

"But . . . OK." Taylor pouted with superb nine-year-old self-right-eousness. "As long as you promise — thirty minutes."

"I promise. Sweetie, I promise."

In fact, we did have to wake up Simon, but he was dressed and ready at five minutes to seven, which was more than you could have said for his father, who still slept soundly, yes, snoring.

"We should get the old bear on tape." Taylor rolled his eyes.

I laughed, appalled and delighted by his irreverence. "It's OK, I'll take you."

I scribbled a note to Lou and set it on the dining room table. "All aboard."

After making sure they were safely on the Camp Wildriver van, I stopped off at a copy center in Cambridge, bought a postcard for Father, and settled down for a cappuccino at Nick's. Actually there was time between faxing the article and getting my hair cut to go back home. But it would be a trek, and Lou liked having the place to himself occasionally. The postcard revealed the Charles River in summer splendor, a couple reading on the banks. "All well here," I wrote. "Working hard on summer projects. We go off to Maine in three weeks. Hope your back is better. Love, A." I would mail it today. Send another when I returned from my trip, and he would never know I had been in California. I used to feel terrible about such behavior, but, as

Lou said, people needed survival strategies. Lou had been such a psychological refuge over the years — not just a base of security but a voice of sanity, reassuring me that, yes, my family was a bit gothic and yes, geographical distance was healthy. A stronger person wouldn't have needed such absolution.

Cambridge was at its most vibrant in the morning with people rushing between bookstores and copy shops. Even on Sunday there was a refreshing hum. Sure, I missed the old Sundays when everything was closed and Lou and I would walk along the river or drive up the coast. But now I didn't know how I would get everything accomplished if shops were closed on this day of rest. My capitalist sabbath was a tune-up day, gearing me for the week ahead. I kept telling myself to cut something out. For instance, Lou thought I spent too much time volunteering at the shelter, but then he did his own political work for Greenpeace. Probably I needed to concentrate better. And if living in Cambridge was an invitation to frenzy, it was better than being marooned in the suburbs of Wellesley. I did some of my most inspired thinking at Nick's Coffee Shop, scribbling in a notebook. Was it odd that I was addicted to caffeine while Mother and Sari had craved downers?

Occasionally at Nick's in the summer, I pretended to be sitting in Berkeley or North Beach. People walked by slowly in the heat. They dressed in a way that was *almost* indistinguishable from Californians. Not quite so many sandals. But for most of the year, I felt the geocultural differences keenly. In Massachusetts, one was always conscious of who had arrived first. In this stratified social system, I was still an outsider after a quarter century. Among Californians, most white families, at least, were relatively new. Everyone had reached the edge. People dwelled in the present and the future. My schizophrenia wasn't helped by the fact that people on each coast harbored mutual antagonisms. To Bostonians, Californians were New Age narcissists. To Californians, Massachusetts people were thin, rigid, bloodless snobs. To compensate for the misery of frozen weather and crumbling buildings, Easterners shrugged off California as a failed paradise crowded with brain-dead people who shoot each other on the freeways.

Despite the caffeine and the early morning start, I was almost late for my hair appointment.

"Usual color and cut?" Barbara inquired in that hectic, upbeat voice. During the last ten years I had come to trust Barbara to shape and paint my hair. In fact, I had no clue what color it actually was — Winter Black, Jet Evening, something like that.

"Going on a trip?" Her voice, rich with the busy texture of Dorchester.

"Yes. To California."

"Vacation or one of those conferences?"

"Both," I said, leaning back into the basin. I flashed on Mary, Queen of Scots, laying her neck on the guillotine: the perfect simile for spending a week alone with Kath.

"Where's the vacation? Lying on a beach somewhere?"

"No." My shoulders tightened. "A week hiking in the High Sierra."

"Taking the kids?"

"No, just a friend and I. An old girlfriend." I sat up stiffly as she toweled my hair.

"Sounds like a good break."

I nodded with tentative satisfaction.

"You must know her pretty well to want to spend a week in the mountains together."

"Well, we're old friends. Since fifth grade. That's thirty-five years."

"Oh, you'll be fine. People don't change that much. I have a friend from the eighth grade, and we still hang out together. Same dynamics. She's the bossy one. I'm the rascal. You'll be fine."

"Yes," I murmured distractedly as Barbara teased my roots with a little green brush. Was she getting it dark enough this time? So hard to tell when wet. I closed my eyes. Kath would never consider coloring her hair. Of course gray didn't really show in blond hair. Still, I would die if Kath knew I had spent the day before our trip in a beauty salon. Barbara could be very wrong about us getting along; there were so many differences in our lives now. Occasionally I imagined Kath reading one of my articles. But where would she come across *Representations* or *Genders* or *Signs?* I had once thought I'd dedicate my first book to Kath — but that would have broken Mom's heart. And the next one had to be dedicated "to Lou and the boys without whom . . ." Besides, what would Kath make of a gendered reading of fifties Western films? Was Kath a feminist? Of course, she was the first feminist I had ever met — at age ten.

"There you go. All set for the dryer," Barbara declared.

"Looks as if I've been through a mudslide." I wondered at my squeamishness today.

"Preview of your trip!" Barbara laughed heartily.

Adjusting myself under the dryer, I picked up a copy of *People* magazine. I read it in the compulsive way I ate potato chips and then felt vaguely nauseated afterward. But there was something about the rag — it was as if the gossip held out promise and admonition about how to live and not live one's own life: Princess Di was binging again; Garth Brooks was having throat problems.

From the outside, from the point of view of many people, I had an enviable life. Look at this story about an Ozarks woman with nine kids who was mayor of her town and also held down a job as a telephone operator. I was very lucky — I had worked hard and used my advantages as best I could, but I *had* those advantages, and compared to this woman in Arkansas, my life was vanilla pudding. I recited the reassuring litany to myself: Finished grad school in five years. Married. Did a year of adjunct teaching. Landed a job at Wellesley. Published a book. Got tenure. Had two healthy children. I was what I would have considered a wild success story twenty years ago. Clara praised me for keeping my ego in check. But my children, my partner, were gifts of fate. And I knew that my career was a fluke, that I had stumbled on my aptitude as I moved along — the inadvertent academic. Once, I had thought I might get a master's degree and marry a bright, handsome man, settle down in the Bay Area and exchange child-rearing stories with Kath.

Yes, that had been the plan, almost a pact.

How did I get here — a forty-four year old college professor, mother, wife, writer. Or mother, wife, writer, professor. What was the order? The priority? This is how — a combination of activated desire and restrained imagination.

Driving home, I gobbled a slice of pepperoni pizza — not the healthiest lunch, but it was quick and would save me from creating an elaborate meal with Lou. I couldn't believe that some of my colleagues cooked for their families every night. Lou had always been great about that. He was introducing his sons to the kitchen already. Simon could make a mean omelette, and Taylor's gingerbread was terrific. There — he wasn't a bad mate at all. I was the rotten parent for, unnaturally, selfishly, I sometimes ached to be free of the guys and I would go up to the Maine cabin a week ahead of the family to write or sketch. Lou was good about these respites, but the boys complained they missed me. I finished the pizza and switched on the radio, realizing that I hadn't heard news today. Perhaps I could bring my Walkman to the mountains. No, Kath would not approve.

Of course I hadn't got here — hadn't claimed this relatively balanced life — without some sacrifices and compromises; it wasn't all serendipity. I still felt pangs about turning down grad school at Berkeley. But Lou really needed to be at Yale for divinity school. And Rutgers had a perfectly good art history program. What else could I have done? I didn't want to be in California, that was part of the truth. As much as I missed the West, I didn't want to be that close to my parents. So choosing Rutgers hadn't been sheer accommodation.

Strange to have his map of life darting before my eyes now. It was as if I were preparing some kind of defense for Kath. Ludicrous to worry this way; so what if she didn't approve of all my choices? What did it matter?

Likewise . . . oh, shit — a truck cut in front of Lou's Saab. Damn, I was always more afraid of getting into an accident in his car. A chorus of honks erupted from the hot irritable drivers. My own horn blasting among them. Ugh, Massachusetts summers were so sticky and tempers short. Likewise . . . it had been a completely mutual decision when we chose Cambridge over Seattle to settle. I had to decline a tenure-track job at the University of Washington to take a temporary appointment near Lou. He was right that I would get a better post soon. Still, I did occasionally find myself reading articles here and there about the San Juan Islands. When I shopped, I still looked discerningly at raincoats.

Lou was sitting at the dining room table eating cold roast potatoes from last night's dinner, engrossed in the Sunday *New York Times*.

"I put out your green parka. It was in a hall closet and I thought you might forget it." He studied my hair. "Nice cut."

I kissed the top of his lush, curly mane. "That's sweet of you." The archetypal southern gallant, he never commented on my shifting hair color.

Now I sat beside this man who was affable, hardworking, socially engaged, able to juggle fourteen things at once and still have spare energy. One infidelity does not a marriage break. As he said, although Sonia was a younger woman, she wasn't a student but a colleague from a different department. No hint of sexual harassment or even inappropriateness unless you were running for president. I mean, how could a sixties woman get unstuck over a little sex? Sex, not infidelity. Infidelity was an arcane concept. That affair with Sonia was over last year and forgotten as far as he was concerned. Sure, I had a right to be pissed off. But it was just a blip in our long, steady marriage. Nevertheless, it reminded me how we had both changed over the last twenty years. We had grown a little bored with one another. Resting my elbows on the table, I told myself that compared to most marriages we were doing fine, emotionally, materially.

"The coat. That's very thoughtful of you, especially since you don't want me to go camping." The irritation slipped out.

"It isn't that I 'don't want' you to go. Rather the expedition strikes me as one more obligation in a life overcrowded with commitments." He leaned back, stretching his muscular arms above his head. Dark hairs peeked from the sleeve of his white T-shirt. I could almost smell the familiar, arousing sweat and taste his salty skin.

We were on different planets. He didn't understand my tie to the West, to Kath. I didn't completely understand it either, but he couldn't even *see* it.

Lou continued, "I think you'll regret not working on the bibliography this week. I'm worried about you being exhausted by the time you get to the conference. And frankly, I think you got yourself into this thing on a sentimental whim. Since the others have backed out, you should feel free to cancel, too."

"Nancy didn't *back out*. She has cancer surgery."

"The others." He addressed the magazine, which reeked from one of those deadly perfume ads.

"Kath is going."

He was silent.

"And the fact is, you don't like Kath."

He stroked his recently-trimmed black beard. "I met the woman briefly a lifetime ago. I don't like or dislike her. I hardly know her. *And the fact is,* neither do you."

Furious, I held my temper because I had no emotional elasticity for a fight right now. I cleared the table of the boys' breakfast dishes, then drifted into the bedroom to continue packing.

My open suitcase yawned demandingly. The idea that I didn't know Kath! Was it "sentimental" to think I knew Kath better than anyone in my life? I felt a twinge of disloyalty, for I did, indeed, feel as if I understood Kath more completely than I knew Lou. Last night he had rented *The Third Man,* and we watched Holly's incredulity grow and diminish as Harry sold watered-down penicillin. (A classic story of friendship betrayed: is this why Lou had selected it at the video store?) We watched Holly killing his old pal. I could still hear the zither music. Was Kath Holly or Harry?

I folded a succession of T-shirts and placed them on the right side of the suitcase. This was the only way I could cope: one half for the Sierra, the other side for Stanford. Lou was partially right: I felt obliged. The trip was some kind of penance for not keeping in touch. Of course I hadn't heard a thing from Kath after Sari's death. Or after Mother's.

I was angry with Kath. I felt contrite. Lou understood my reasons for going on the trip were unformed. Perhaps it was some sort of foolish menopausal pilgrimage — back to the West, up to the mountains. Perhaps it was a way of returning to Kath, to myself. Perhaps it was a chance to think about the Berkeley job. An opportunity to assess who I was becoming before it was too late.

The Sierra side of my suitcase filled, I got up and stretched, catching a glimpse of my dark hair in the mirror. Shame and relief: I always felt a mixture of the two when I had my hair done. How easy it was to ignore my principles for vanity. While I didn't think I was sexually objectifying myself, I probably was age objectifying. No, that wasn't fair either. These political terms were so sterile and judgmental. Perhaps I was just trying to look as young and competent and able as I felt. What was I supposed to do — refrain from jogging? Surrender to middle-age paunch? Stop tweezing the tiny hairs sprouting from my chin? Let myself go gray? All in the name of natural aging. What was a little masquerade in this era of constructed identity? I was simply dressing to fit the part of the vital, imaginative scholar I was. I had achieved the crest of what I hoped would be a long, wide, productive plateau. I was just coming into my own as a thinker and teacher, so I wanted to dress as the self I knew. Career posed enough uncertainties. I wanted to recognize this person in the mirror.

The Stanford side of my suitcase I packed with crushable skirts and a cotton dress. I tossed in a couple of sweaters for the necessary layering, although I suspected it would be consistently hot and dry on the Peninsula. And I would carry a trench coat over my arm. On the dresser, my eye caught sight of the Midnight Sparkle nail polish I had bought to send Nancy. I would mail it with a priority stamp this afternoon. A silly hospital present, an alms, an insurance policy.

I zipped the bag and checked the bedside clock. One o'clock. Never in my life had I finished packing for a trip eighteen hours before take-off. I supposed this was good, because the missing items might rise to my consciousness between now and tomorrow morning. Was I meta-morphosizing into an efficient person? Or was I simply frantic? Well, I had time for a jog. The boys wouldn't be home for another three hours.

"Going for a run?" Lou glanced up from his magazine. "Good. Shake off some of that tension. You'll sleep better tonight."

I shot him an irritated glance and said, "Sometimes you can be a pa-tronizing ass."

He feigned affront, then shrugged. "Well, admirable people need fa-tal flaws in order to remain sympathetic."

Always the last word.

In spite of myself, I called, "Cheerio!"

He waved almost shyly. So I had hurt his feelings.

I donned my Camp Wildriver headband, a birthday gift from the boys, and set off. Outside, the Cambridge streets were muggy. The stink of dog shit rose from the pavement. Traffic was loud, congested, and the air thickened with exhaust. Spring in Cambridge can be vi-brant, but by mid-August every living thing is bedraggled, defeated by humidity. Would my lungs explode from all the fresh air in the Sierra? I found the hill to the park pleasantly easy, and sooner than I expected, I was completing my first lap.

I felt more like thirty-five than forty-four. Maybe even thirty. It was as if in the last ten years my muscles hadn't aged but rather found their stride. The vehicle was in good condition but low on fuel. Was it possi-ble for a whole life to evaporate while one wasn't looking? My spirit was dormant, in a jar somewhere. Perhaps that was the nature of aging: one's nerve endings died, one learned to compromise sensibility as well as principle. Ten years ago I would have been horrified at the way I was now able to finesse a response to a politically volatile question. What I said and felt had less and less in common. Hardly ever did I answer anyone directly because I never knew what would get back to whom. I talked this way for the administration, that way for my women's stud-ies colleagues. I spent so much time guarding against misrepresenta-tion that occasionally I even forgot what I thought. And I wound up in the most surprising places. Downhill now, I was halfway through my run, sweating profusely but not puffing. I'd be OK in the mountains.

How had I wound up in the still male-centered culture of academia? Here I was, so determined to escape my mother's experience as benumbed chatelaine. Propelled by feminist principles to carve out an independent life of social contribution, of professional and domestic satisfaction, here I was surrounded by men. Abandoned by Sari and Mother and Kath. Left with my father, husband and sons. To some degree — conscious and unconscious — that was my choice. I was naturally better at being close to men because you couldn't get too close, couldn't merge as you did with women, because the men in my life hadn't deserted me. Anyway, the eighties had flashed by and I looked up to find myself with the boys. A privileged, coveted place. But lonely.

Dinner was my favorite: pasta primavera. Lou had bought a special bottle of Chianti.

"Boys, do you know how sweet your father is?" I caught myself absentmindedly peeling the familiar label off the bottle.

Simon and Taylor were competing to see who could get more spaghetti on a fork at one time.

"Well," I continued to my imaginary audience, with the uncertainty I often had in the classroom: anyone listening? Lou was listening. I was saying this for Lou and myself.

"This is the same wine we drank on our wedding night."

Simon nudged Taylor. "That was before us."

I laughed.

"Yes, it was the convention then." Lou took a gulp of wine. "Children came after the wedding."

"'Convention.' Mom, what's 'convention'?" demanded earnest Taylor.

"Ask your father. It's his word."

Lou missed a beat. Only one. He had been drinking too much, and I realized how distressed he was about my trip. "Look it up in the dictionary. And let us know what you think I meant. It has several connotations."

"Taylor," I said. "Tell us more about the kayak race, sweetie. Were you scared out there by yourself?"

7

Kath

Tuesday Morning / Gaylor Lakes

THE WOODS SMELLED RIPE from fungus and decaying bark. An ambitious hawk sailed above, scrutinizing us. Adele shivered in the early morning damp. We were both well enough covered. She wore a parka over her cotton turtleneck and Scottish sweater. I had a flannel jacket and two layers of T-shirt. I hoped Adele hadn't noticed the holes in my left hiking sock this morning. I had meant to get a new pair before leaving town. Jesus, I was getting self-conscious. Concentrate on the real, the practical, the present. She carried our lunch in the fanny pack. I carried a canteen of water, glad that she wasn't squeamish about sharing the same bottle, pleased by this small intimacy. The hawk circled lower, lower.

Adele trudged up the steep trail without a break, taking it too fast, as if she had something to prove. Still, she seemed OK. I turned my attention to the wildflowers, profuse for this late in the season: Gray's lovage, daisies. You had to look closely. Subalpine terrain was like ocean or desert the way grandeur could obscure subtlety. And you had to be careful not to take grandeur at face value. There was an intricacy in the dimension of those mountains. Just as there was compressed power in flowers like the fairy lanterns. A third of the way up. So far so good. We were adding 800 feet in elevation as we climbed from road to ridge.

Two yards ahead of me now, Adele finally paused. I caught up with her, and together, inhaling the dry lodgepole scent, we looked out on

Mount Dana, Mount Gibbs and Mammoth Peak. Closer, just below us, the white boulders scattered across Dana Meadows made that flat, grassy expanse look like a haphazard cemetery.

"Wonder what it would have been like to be an Indian here three hundred years ago?" I said, flinching as a sudden wind froze sweat to my skin. "OK to summer in the High Country, but come late September, early October snow, I'd want to be on a raft, off to visit my cousins at the coast."

"Yes." Adele smiled. "My fantasies are set in Victorian London, and I'd adore the long dresses, but not the outdoor plumbing."

I laughed, nervous about how she was going to enjoy backpacking in a few days if she was fussy about toilets.

"I never imagine myself as the maid ironing dresses or the Indian woman tending a newborn, gathering food and pounding acorns all day." Adele removed the parka but hesitated at the sweater.

I passed her the canteen, then took a sip myself. We headed higher. Steeper now. Harder to breathe. Soon we'd reach the saddle and it would be joyfully downhill. Each year I was struck by my all-consuming awareness of the trail, of the hours involved in getting from one place to the next. Of how the route and the map temporarily overwhelmed everything else, even your most serious worries. Hiking forced an urban speed freak into the present. This was so much more immediate than writing a grant for your salary to be skimmed by bored government bureaucrats. Hiking was a form of meditation. But you could grow obsessed with the route itself. That was no more transcendent than obsessing about work. Soon the walking would be flat, unless we visited the mine we'd explored as kids. Kids, I fought the label then, and it seemed crucial now.

At the ridge, Adele waited again. We faced the elegant giants: Unicorn, Coxcomb, Cathedral Peaks. I wasn't big on churches, but the spired architecture of Cathedral Peak always made me feel kind of reverent. Wind here was tight, strong. The sun warmed my shoulder muscles. Suddenly I was twirling in a pirouette.

Adele watched me, fiddling nervously with her long, black ponytail.

"I do this every year. A three-hundred-sixty-degree turn. Gives me a sense of hope, a reference point for the next twelve months. I mean, there I am at some infuriating board meeting and I tell myself, 'Just look at that view inside your head — Unicorn, Coxcomb, Cathedral — keep some perspective on these assholes.' It helps."

Adele sipped from the canteen.

Since the descent could be a little tricky, I struck out ahead of her. The trail down to the water would be shorter. Middle Gaylor Lake was at a higher elevation than Tioga Pass Road. The route down was scattered with scrubby, gnarled trees. What different trips we must be making — Adele comparing the temperature, humidity, foot traffic to a quarter century ago and me making comparisons with last year and the year before. One July first, I couldn't make it to the mine shaft because of the snow.

At the base of the hill, Middle Gaylor Lake was a deep blue. On the far side walked a solitary hiker in a red windbreaker. If it hadn't been for Adele's sleeping in, we would have arrived ahead of the Red Windbreaker. Disgusting competitiveness. There was a difference between experiencing the land and owning it. I had to remind myself of this each year as I returned from the city. The Red Windbreaker had a right. The mountains didn't belong to me. If I was lucky, I'd reach a state where I belonged to them. I glanced back to watch Adele gingerly climbing downhill. I proceeded in a careful side step to protect against slipping. Behind us, the hill grew taller. Dana Meadows had disappeared.

Standing in the spacious valley, I thought of those lakes hidden to the south. Would Adele remember?

"The Miner's Hill," she said breathlessly. "Up there, to the right, isn't it?"

I nodded. Side by side we walked, and I imagined Nancy, Paula and Donna hiking behind. No snow this year, but it hadn't melted long ago. The new, spongy grass made me uneasy.

Adele grabbed my elbow, pointing.

About eight feet away, a large marmot observed us. The gray and brown creature stood her ground, staring ahead defiantly. Like the idea of us gave her a migraine.

"Not so welcoming." I grunted. Her clan had probably survived the Ice Age, fortified by all that fur and tenacity.

We waved to the animal and walked up the hill toward a disintegrating black cabin. Looking back, I saw the marmot holding her ground, as if defending young. Or maybe she was simply put out by two more trespassers this morning. Mountain summer was short — just enough time for most animals to mate, reproduce and start raising offspring. Too bad for them this was also the season of thunder-footed, Velcro invaders.

Adele stepped into the dark, moldy structure. Hesitantly, I followed. Moisture shined on the walls.

"Did the miner die in this fire or do you suppose he reached that saddle above Middle Gaylor Lake to find his home in flames?"

I was alternately charmed and irritated that she thought I had answers to such questions. Shrugging, I watched her imagination accelerate.

"Did he have a wife? Kids?" Adele asked as she ran her hand along a wet beam in what might have been the kitchen.

"A mining company, I think I read," I offered. "Probably a couple of guys here. Maybe it wasn't a house but some kind of shop? Who knows when it burned? Maybe after they left?"

"No family." Adele surveyed the view through the doorway. "No, I feel more a solitary spirit. Perhaps someone who traveled across the country looking for gold and silver. The optimism of that. The hubris."

I watched her carefully.

Adele held on to the doorframe.

Awkwardly, I extended the canteen. "Fire can make a person parched."

She gulped the water.

"How about going to the lower lakes?"

Adele nodded, although I suspected she wanted to stay longer and summon dead miners. Was there any silver left in the veins under Tioga Hill?

"This way," I called, directing Adele cross-country. Reluctant to meet the marmot's gaze, I skirted the trail. We bounced over springy grass and scrambled around boulders. Here and there were bouquets of white columbine. Every twenty yards, I glanced over my shoulder to check on Adele.

"Wouldn't this be a cozy place for a bear and her cubs, shaded by these enormous rocks, with rivulets of water?" she asked in a light, amused voice.

"Yes," I agreed. "Perfect place."

Turning, I watched her flinch as she realized I wasn't kidding. She swallowed, then quickly recovered equilibrium.

For some reason, I thought about when I taught Adele basketball in the fifth grade. Weeks and weeks passed, and she couldn't grasp the concept of guarding. It seemed rude to her, standing in someone's way, waving your arms about, when the game should properly be a test of who was the most skillful at shooting baskets. Finally, it occurred to her that guarding is a different kind of skill. And she became better at it than I was. Our exchange was more than fair. That spring, Adele gave me my first diary, and over the years maintaining a journal had kept me sane. Martha had never liked Adele, and it took years before I understood she saw how Adele was pulling me away from the family. Martha, who lost touch with all her school friends even though most had stayed in the Bay Area, always viewed friendship as some sort of threat to the family center. And I was the opposite. I saw friendship, especially Adele's, as an escape hatch from family entrapment. Friendship seemed more profound because you chose which friends to love and they could leave you, as Adele had left me. Concentrate on the land, I scolded myself for the tenth time today.

What I liked best about Granite Lake was how so much of it was obscured during the long walk across the valley. Suddenly the water appeared, startling me as much as it had when we were girls. Did Adele remember that initial surprise — Paula saying, "It must be around here," and then, "Voilà!"

"Whoa!" Adele cried with pleasure at the lake's precise reflection of mountains and sky. Stubby clouds floating on deep waters. "Whew," she said, removing her fanny pack, absorbing the beauty.

Adele had always had this talent for savoring. Oh, I enjoyed the glory of this place, but I couldn't chew on it as Adele could, couldn't roll it around on my tongue in front of someone. Not even in front of Adele. Maybe especially not in front of Adele.

She edged toward the lake to rinse her hands. "Ooooooh." She pulled back. "Now that's *glacier* melt. Forget snowmelt."

I walked forward, knelt beside her and felt compelled to keep my hands in longer than Adele had. What was going on, why was I behaving so macha? I needed the protection of a clear line between us. I should live in the pleasure of this rediscovered closeness, but even stronger than this pleasure was my grief about lost pleasures of twenty-three years' estrangement. How long could we pussyfoot around before we confronted the hurt we both felt? Maybe we could avoid it for the whole week. A deep, cowardly part of me hoped so. I'd rather tackle a bear than "deal with" the anger and grief between us. On the other hand, I needed to know, at least, that Adele felt this pain too.

Adele didn't seem to notice my icy hands display. She had opened the fanny pack. "Cheese sandwiches are intact." The tomato was whole, sweating sweetness into her palm. And the orange we'd brought for extra moisture oozed tropical fragrance.

A chill sliced down the back of my neck. What was the marmot doing? Certainly not worrying about us.

"Good sandwich," I said between bites. "It's nice of you to humor my vegetarianism. But I don't mind if you pack a meat sandwich."

"No, I'm fine with cheese." Adele smiled. "And I saw all the luscious avocado and sprouts and tofu in your cooler. How could baloney compete?"

I stretched out on the rocks. "I mean, if meat's what you're used to . . ."

"No, in fact meat's what Lou and the boys like, and it's crazy for me to fix separate meals for myself. I'm sure your diet is much healthier, more principled."

Too early in the day, in our trip, to start talking principles. Urgently needing to keep the conversation light, I said, "The Indians ate acorns, pine nuts and manzanita berries." I contrasted the discomfort of the boulder and the pleasure of the sun soaking into my skin. "Also wild cherries and Sierra plum. Now *that's* healthy."

"Sounds good to me," Adele said. I could hear her tearing the skin from the orange, splitting the globe in two. She handed me half. Closing my eyes, I sucked the golden juice.

"I remember from school, how your mom used to cut your oranges in half," Adele said.

"You remember that?" I turned my head and stared into the dark pool of Granite Lake, wishing it was swimming temperature.

She laughed. "And I remember your mom always made you Velveeta sandwiches on white bread with mustard. Mustard with horseradish."

"Del, Del." I sat up, pulling my knees to my chest and smiling at the old nickname.

Adele cocked an amused eyebrow.

"Del, what else do you remember?"

"I remember Katherine Peterson planned to go around the world with UNESCO. Or the Red Cross."

"You used to tease me, call me a missionary."

"I was jealous."

"*You* jealous?" I objected. "Miss Success, who could draw like — what's her name? — Mary Cassatt. Miss Success, who won all the school writing prizes."

"Yeah. You were the one who was going to change the world."

So it had always been a problem, I thought. "Ambition! You wanted to become a writer. The next Willa Cather, they said at graduation breakfast."

"You remember that?"

"I remember a lot about you."

Blushing, she approached the water, knelt down and splashed her face. Adele was a shapely, graceful woman, even in hiking gear. In comparison I was a gawky adolescent. Martha was right on that.

"The only trouble" — she paused and moved toward me, frowning — "is that I didn't have anything to write about. I didn't know anywhere the way Cather knew Nebraska."

"You knew California." Surprised by my volume, I softened my voice. "And you found plenty to write about."

"Art history. Criticism," Adele demurred. "Theory. It's not the same thing as real writing."

"That's stupid." My father's anger. I could feel my jaw jutting out. My father's style.

"Stupid, that's what I think sometimes too. I spend my whole life writing books about ideas."

I waited.

"Eight years writing one book. Ten years writing the next two" — she flung her left arm wide, northward — "and now three years compiling a bibliography that will be read by — what? — ten people, twelve if I'm lucky."

I inched over to her. Hands on my old friend's neck, I began to massage. Reaching under the heavy green sweater collar — how could she stand this hot wool? — I kneaded her knotted muscles. "At least thirteen," I whispered.

Adele laughed. God, that wonderful, long, low, gurgling laugh from so many years ago. I could feel her shoulders lower and release. Still, I kept my hands there.

Adele relaxed in the fresh, early afternoon air, and the vibrations from her back felt like purring. I tried to ignore my sadness about Baffin.

"Remember how we used to gossip at the lockers?" Adele asked softly, like she was talking to herself. "Remember how we talked on the phone every night? How we were going to be friends throughout our adventurous lives?"

"Yes," I answered, longing and fear pulling me toward her, away again.

"Maybe we always *have* been friends, despite the distance and the differences. A conversation on hold. Or do you think that's sheer sentimentality?"

I was afraid it might be. But I didn't have to answer.

Adele was crying in quick, jagged sobs. Terrified, I lifted my hands from her neck into the dry mountain air. The only comfort I was capable of offering was the canteen. I heard myself say something as foolish as "Wet your whistle?"

We were walking southwest now at a more even pace, Adele's energy returning. Silently. More comfortably than this morning or last night. Each less aware of the other person. Finally able to accept the land as a companion.

I enjoyed the long, downhill strides you could take toward Lower Gaylor Lake. What a perfect place to camp, but the grassy meadow was so fragile and the supply of wood minuscule. I'd love to sneak in here on my own some night. I'd be careful. No one would know except that old marmot up at the cabin. I wondered sometimes about my fantasies of being alone. I had always had them. As a child, before I fell asleep at night, I often imagined myself in a turn-of-the-century Pullman coach. I was surrounded by burnt purple velvet, watching out the window for the moon. Lulled to a peaceful sleep by the rocking of the train going somewhere, anywhere, away.

The sky shone a bright blue, completely deserted by morning clouds. Stripping as we walked, I shed down to my last T-shirt. When I glanced back at Adele, she had tied the sweater and parka around her waist. Tomorrow, she'd have a better idea of what to wear.

"You've come closer to achieving your vision," Adele mused.

It took a minute to realize she was continuing our lunch conversation. "Oh, sure," I answered, "driving an ambulance through war-torn Europe?"

"No, I mean . . ." She pulled out a pack of sugarless gum and offered me a stick.

"No thanks."

"Mouth's dry," she explained. "My boys taught me this. On our hikes in Maine."

"Do you guys get up there a lot?" That's it, I said to myself, talk about her family. A natural topic between two women. Would she think Anita was a natural topic? No, Kath, keep it predictable.

"Not enough." Adele sighed. "Two weeks in the summer. Thanksgiving. Maybe Easter. It's really a sin, when you think about it, that the house goes empty most of the year." She stuffed the pack into her jeans' pocket and grinned at me. "No you don't! You can't shift the topic that easily. We were talking about you."

"Hmmmmmm."

"See, you always wanted to do something to help, to change the world."

"Right in the center of revolution, I am."

"That's right," Adele said seriously.

"Laying in sandbags against the end of the world."

"But at least you're *in* the world — working with kids around AIDS, pregnancy, drugs, literacy. It's completely consistent with what you always wanted to do. You may not be careening around in an ambulance, but it's important work."

Was important work. I couldn't bring myself to talk about the layoff. I felt ashamed, as if I'd dropped out of school once again. Of course the funding cuts had been political, not my fault at all. I'd done some decent work. Look at Luna almost finished at Laney, and Betty, who was now a dental hygienist. The program *had* made small differences in some lives. OK, I had to talk about being unemployed sooner or later. The longer I postponed it, the harder it would be to tell Adele. But not yet.

I concentrated on Lower Gaylor Lake, where I would remove my boots and hiking socks and undersocks and settle my feet in the cool, cool waters. I wanted to leave problems about family and lovers and job and school behind. We were getting close to the lake now. Two California gulls circled. Was that a spotted sandpiper along the shoreline?

8

Adele

Tuesday Evening / Lyell Fork

FISH LEAPED IN THE STREAM, casting circles on the mottled water. My tired ankles waded in shimmering, sweet-smelling grass. As sun edged toward the horizon, our shadows lengthened across the boulders and Kath's baseball hat gave her silhouette a rakish quality.

"I remember the sunsets here," I whispered, manically chewing gum to clear my breath, "also those clouds — so wild and fiery — what were they called?"

"Cumulonimbus."

I smiled at the rhythm of vowels, at our companionable memories. To the west, sun splashed flames on Mount Dana. The pink eastern sky washed down to the hills, the grass, the creek. Water whistled past us, streaked with blue and coral. Once I planned to write my dissertation on the Luminists who came to paint the Sierra. And, although Frederic Church's work was the most famous, I preferred the paintings of John Muir's friend, William Keith. This place had a powerful hold on Scots. Perhaps it was the Ward in my blood that drew me here.

"There," Kath said suddenly, pointing to a large gray rock twenty yards from the trail. "Let's sit."

After sunset Mount Dana and Mount Gibbs seemed even more imposing in the rosy sky. A sliver of moon was rising over Kuna Crest, whispering into the shoulder of the mountain as it ascended.

"OK." I followed warily, for although I coveted this moment of twilight, I knew that it couldn't last. I had spent half my life trying to make permanent what was not and perhaps the other half trying to make the inextricable relationships, such as those with my family, simply transitory ones.

Kath's voice woke me. We sat close enough to feel each other's warmth in the cool night. "We could float from here to the ocean."

Yes, I thought, and around the world. "Oh, right"— I caught on — "this is the beginning of the Tuolumne River. Now where does it go from here?"

Her face lit up. Although we both cherished this place, her connection was deeper. I felt a little jealous of her passion for the High Country.

"Well, water comes from Mount Lyell and Mount Dana, threads through the meadows, navigates downhill to Waterwheel Falls and the Grand Canyon of the Tuolumne and ends in O'Shaughnessy Dam." Her face took on that intense earnestness I remembered from high school.

I nodded attentively, affectionately.

"From there it's stored in San Pedro Reservoir to irrigate the Central Valley. The rest mixes with the San Joaquin and flows out into San Francisco Bay."

"Which is why we have desert on one side of the Sierra and farmland on the other." I nodded, imitating the lispy voice of our unfairly maligned sophomore science teacher, Mr. Cummings. "Human engineering."

We laughed.

"Sometimes when I'm hiking alone," Kath mused, "I wonder if I'm more afraid of people or bears."

The first time I stayed overnight at Kath's we were eleven. By the sixth grade, I had visited a lot of my friends' houses, but Kath's place was distinctive, exotically decorated with her mother's ornate Quebec crucifixes and turquoise statues of the Virgin Mary. Kath told me her father drew the line at Catholic school. Enough that they should go to church, he had protested to Mrs. Peterson, but he wasn't going to have his daughters study a peasant language like Latin. Everything was different about the Peterson place — the random, lumpy furniture, the always-running TV. There were no paintings, no bookcases. The living room walls were hung with metal-framed family portraits and a church calendar. Everyone sat in front of the TV — Mr. Peterson whittling. My mother would have imploded at the sight of those tiny balsa chips on the carpet. But Mrs. Peterson just got out the vacuum at the end of the night and, presto, the mess disappeared. Dinner was starchy and ample, and there was a big bowl of buttered popcorn on the coffee table with a giant bottle of Pepsi from which we filled our green plastic glasses. My memory of that first sleepover was almost as vivid as the recollection of my mother picking me up the next morning. She seemed to sniff the doorway as she formally thanked Mrs. Peterson. In the car, she asked me, "What does Mr. Peterson *do?*"

Another childhood scene: the following year *chez moi*. We sat on my bed, giggling, pretending to do a jigsaw puzzle. Mother, now resigned to Kath, served us corn bread and apple juice. As soon as Mother left, we continued confiding about sanitary napkins and belts and those tampons some of the wild girls were using. Kath exhibited stoic courage about her cramps. I listened with envy and embarrassment, impatient for my first period. Examining my girlish room — daintily decorated with pale pink walls and rose trim, lace bureau scarf and pillowcases, Princess telephone, vanity lined with dolls of six nationalities — I ached to be the woman Kath had become.

Lyell Fork was disappearing around us into a vague territory of shadows and noises. Now the nocturnal animals would take over from us creatures of the sun. I imagined the night world to be gentler than the harsh daylight land, as if seeing in the dark were a sign of holiness. Wordlessly we turned back toward camp. Perhaps night was a preparation for death, an instruction in humility and surrender. Soon primitive evensong would commence. An urge rose from within me — a noise, an old, obstinate question.

"I wish we had stayed in closer touch." I said "we," accepting some responsibility.

"Yeah." Kath quickened her pace.

I followed her gaze to the stream. One, two, three fish. Jumping, darting in aquatic ballet.

Selfish to disturb her reverie. I felt as if I had barged into church belting out "Only the Lonely." However some instinct, some perversity, pressed me forward. "I've been so comfortable with you these last two days. I mean, it's like when we were in school. It's just that . . . I don't know . . . it would have been wonderful to share more of each other's lives."

I paused, conscious of Kath's jaw setting, her gaze shifting to middle distance. I shouldn't have blundered into this, I should have planned it carefully. After all, my disappointment and grief had been welling up for two decades. Kath might have equally strong feelings. As much as I feared her emotions, I desperately needed her to care. This familiar spot seemed to invite intimacy, as if we had returned to our private sanctuary. No, of course, many people had watched this evening waterway before — Indian grandmothers, European sheepherders, Transcendental hermits. Our friendship had always taken place on some well-beaten path, and it was ludicrous of me to fetishize either the relationship or the place as private refuge.

I watched her posture stiffen.

"You," she began softly, too softly.

I leaned closer.

"You're the one who broke off." She walked faster.

"But"— I hurried to catch up — "I wrote you from Scotland every —"

"I'm not talking about Scotland —"

"Every week for three months." I insisted on finishing the ancient complaint. "I phoned, left messages, four or five times."

"You left long before that. You went to Radcliffe. You never intended to live your life in California."

"I went away to a good college, a perfectly normal American choice." We were walking even faster now — whether to get back to camp before it was pitch black or to escape the intensity of this conversation, I couldn't tell.

Kath held herself in, peering through dimness at the elusive trail.

"I came home on breaks."

"You didn't after the first two years." She walked faster. "You started a whole new life."

"I just went away to school," I repeated, flabbergasted.

Deliberately, she continued, "You know, this is a funny country. You grow up with someone, go to school together, hang out, assume you have the same options. Then a few years later they come back with a Ph.D., a BMW and a new accent. And you're still looking for a steady job."

"I intended to come back. Remember how we were going to be neighbors and baby-sit for each other?" Despite the anxiety in my gut, I had to smile at our precisely timed life blueprint. Nowadays there seemed to be *no* time left because I had lost the youthful sense that there was a time for *everything*. I felt Sari's death now, as I always felt it in California. Why had I thought I'd be able to avoid it this time? Because Kath was with me, because we could rewrite the whole scene together, resurrect her from the dead? All these years later it was hard to admit that I couldn't have stopped her. It was *Sari's* death, Sari's suicide, Sari's exit from the family. Perhaps I could even feel grateful for her that she had found a way out.

"I left my family." I stopped, struggling to hold Kath in my gaze. "I didn't leave California. I didn't leave you."

"Leaving is an action." Kath's eyes grew wide. "It's not an idea. You can't pick your audience."

I concentrated on not crying. If I abandoned anyone it had been Sari.

"Look, Del, I'm really, really sorry about what happened to your sister. It was tragic." She walked faster now, speaking into the wind, and it was difficult to hear. "I liked Sari a lot. It was a terrible waste. And so hard on you!"

I stared at her expectantly. The wrong note, for Kath did not like demands. "Yes," I said simply, concealing the degree of my wanting before it was too late.

She looked behind her at the trail and continued. "Still, long before her death, you were gone for good. Once you went to your Ivy League college, you were on your way up and out."

I could see Kath trying to hold herself back, but the banks had crumbled. "You made your choice."

Her words were a fist in my stomach.

"Don't you understand? Don't you see, I was leaving home. I wasn't leaving *you*."

"Home." Kath glanced out at the stream as we walked over the bridge. "Wasn't I part of home to you? A close friendship — 'a best friendship'— and you walked away."

"Kath, be reasonable."

"I guess friends aren't that important. People have lifetime attachments to their parents, spouses, kids. But friends are expendable."

"For Christ's sake," I shouted into the mountains that now seemed to surround us like shadowy judges, "I just went to college."

She persisted with infuriating calm. "You just went to find yourself a new life."

She was right, of course, although I still pretended not to understand. I *had* left Kath. And I had left the West. I was a deserter in the undeclared civil war. Lou thought Western identity was a joke, but to Kath and me California was nourishment and refreshment. I had never been sympathetic to patriotism, but I had always felt remorse about leaving the West. Remorse when Canadians complained about their friends defecting to the United States, when the Scots talked about the brain drain to England. In Boston, I inveighed against the provincialism of Easterners, but Kath was right, I had become one of them. Tonight I was too tired, too angry, too petty to tell her I understood this, that I was sorry, that I didn't know what else I could have done. Instead, I declared, "Well, how about *your* disappearing act?"

A jay barked loudly from the stand of lodgepole pines. Those Steller's jays were notorious camp robbers, but I loved their sauciness all the same, and I concentrated on the birds' shrieking.

Kath produced a flashlight. "It's stupid to stay out this late," she grumbled. "I should have been watching."

9

Kath

1965–1967 / Western California

WELCOME KATHERINE PETERSON, read the fuchsia cardboard sign on the door to my dorm room. Thrilled and mortified by the public attention, I knocked hesitantly. That first night at U.C. Davis was a bad Carol Burnett skit. There was Dad lugging my high school graduation present luggage that he had won at a union raffle. Mom trailed behind us with an iron in one hand and a shoe box of chocolate chip cookies in the other. My legs were sticking to my jeans from our long, hot car ride. My new roommate, Judy, greeted us with a broad Princess Grace smile, dressed in white shorts and a baby blue blouse, the perfect fashion for 100-degree Sacramento Valley weather. Not that there was anything snooty about her, really. She acted more friendly than I had expected for someone from Anna Head School. Amazingly eager to meet me.

As Mom and Dad entered the modern dormitory cell, they looked shorter, older, worn. After a few awkward exchanges, Dad said, "Well, it's a long drive back to Oakland. We better get started."

As Judy and I ate cookies and talked about Orientation Week, I veered between excitement and exhaustion. That night, lying in my twin bed four feet across the tiny room from her, I found it hard to sleep; the day's events swirled wildly in my brain. Then there was Judy's snoring. I didn't know girls could snore. Neither my sister nor any of the girls on the camping trip snored. Well, I would get used to it. I would get used to everything. Still, I couldn't sleep.

*   *   *

That first morning of orientation I stood, sniffing the brand-new smell of my books and studying the blond, blond girls and guys bicycling around the green, green campus. Davis felt like a science fiction movie. What the hell was I doing here? No one in my family had been to college. Martha and I were the first ones to finish high school. I didn't have a clue how to be a coed. My stomach turned. Well, these bicyclists had all been new at some point, too. I would learn. The Orientation Week would be fun, filled with movies, hayrides, dances and lectures.

Perching on a bench in front of Freeborn Hall, I placed the expensive books beside me. Here I was, finally, at college. This strange place. Alone. My mind hadn't quite arrived. That was the problem. I had spent so much time getting ready to come, finishing up my summer job at Roos Atkins, packing, convincing my parents again and again that college wasn't an absurd idea. I was an average American girl. Look at Adele, Paula, Donna and Nancy. Going to college was the next step. But my parents hadn't taken these stairs and even *I* wasn't sure they led anywhere. That day, surveying the eerie academic stage set, I felt very scared. I didn't know how to behave in a lecture, whether you wrote down every word or tried to memorize the stuff as the professor went along. What if I didn't make any friends? What if I was in the wrong place? Martha said I was living in some *Mademoiselle* magazine fantasy. Mom said a secretarial diploma would offer more security; Dad wanted to know (of course, Dad) — wasn't I just going to get married anyway? As I sat in the midst of this sweltering, verdant campus, tears and sweat streamed down to the collar of my once white blouse. I was certain my parents had been killed in a crash on the way home the previous night.

We were all hanging out in Ellie's room, which was big enough for two beds, although for some reason she didn't have a roommate. I envied her, but Judy said she wouldn't have it any other way and did I mind if she called me Kathy, which sounded softer and prettier than Kath. When I asked her not to, she shrugged and said, all right, everyone had a right to her individuality. Judy really was a sweet person, but I still wanted a single room. Ellie, Mary Ellen, Sally, so many names to remember.

Ellie whisked off her robe and dramatically revealed the snappy mauve and coral polka dot nightgown she had bought for Pajamarino. "Homecoming is the *best*," she explained. "My cousin met her fiancé at the Pajamarino dance."

"Well, I'm prepared." Judy winked and pulled out striped pj's with a goofy tiger's face on the front.

"Oh, I get it." Mary Ellen laughed. "The cat's pajamas! Too much!"

I missed Adele. Surely they didn't have callow events like this at Radcliffe. Why was I such a prickly bitch? Probably I was just defensive about not having a cool pair of pajamas. Wardrobe was one aspect of college life I didn't describe in my letters home. Martha would bust a gut laughing.

"Did you hear that Sally got called in for wearing pants to the library?" asked Ellie.

"What, again?" Mary Ellen shook her head. "What's wrong with her? Is she trying to prove something?"

I sat there wide-eyed, keeping my wisecracks to myself.

"Well, it's a silly rule," Judy snapped.

"What's wrong with asking people to dress decently, to wear skirts?" demanded Mary Ellen. "I mean, part of being in college is learning to be an adult."

This had never occurred to me.

"And what's more adult about wearing a skirt — particularly on a cold, rainy day — to study in the library?" Judy continued.

Go Judy, I thought.

"It has nothing to do with maturity. All to do with convention."

If I had to have a roommate, I felt grateful it was Judy. But maybe Martha had been right about college. Maybe I wasn't the type. Or maybe Adele was right in bugging me to apply for a scholarship to Radcliffe next year.

I adjusted, of course. It was in my Norwegian-Quebecois nature. My immigrant blood pulsed: adapt, accept. Not only did I attend Pajamarino but I went to parties every weekend. I knew something was wrong with me. Everything. My clothes. My references. The very way I walked — body language, Mary Ellen called it. Compared to the other girls, I felt so abrupt and gross. My posture was too tough; my movements were broad, rapid, common. Yet I persisted, thinking maybe Mary Ellen was right about learning to be a woman at college.

One weekend, at an otherwise infantile fraternity bash, I met Vernon MacLean. The following Saturday he took me to a movie, then for a long Sunday bike ride past the prim midwestern-style local homes. We visited the pens where they held the barkless dog experiments. Ver-

non, an ag econ major, informed me Davis was a national leader in research about animal husbandry and plant fertility. Before Vernon, I
hadn't known that agriculture was the largest industry in California.
Or that California was the eighth largest economy in the world.

Vernon: freckled. Gap-toothed. Lively. Convivial to my parents
when they drove up for a pricy weekend brunch with us at the famous
Nut Tree restaurant.

"The Nut Tree," joked my embarrassing father, "is it named for campus
radicals?"

"You must be thinking of Berkeley, Mr. Peterson," Vernon said with
his unfailing courtesy. "Not too many wild politicos here in the Davis
cotton fields."

"Good thing," Dad answered, awkward. "Keep your mind on studying."

Vernon smiled cordially.

He was too nice. I had known this for weeks.

"Katherine tells me you're in agriculture? That's a fine, sensible oc-
cupation."

Vernon nodded, still smiling.

Dad tried again. "My father farmed in Norway. Never went to school
at all. And Norway is a rough place to cultivate. But California is paradise. What do you plan to grow?"

"A changed economy. An end to hunger in this country."

"Excuse me?"

I studied Vernon's expression. Was he playing with Dad? Mom was
staring out the window, biting her thumbnail.

"I want to go into government. After my B.A. — to law school. Then
run for office. The state legislature first."

"First, yes, of course, first," Dad said, concentrating on cutting his
rubbery slice of Canadian bacon, which raced across his plate every
time he put his knife to it.

Mom looked to me to fill the silence.

When I couldn't, wouldn't, she tried. "And what do your people do,
Vernon?"

He looked puzzled.

"People. She means your family," I explained, spreading grape jelly
on my fourth piece of toast. I never ate this much.

"My parents are in academia."

Mom's pupils darkened. She had such wonderful, terrible, large, haunting eyes. Dad squinted nervously out the window.

"They're deans at Saint Mary's College in Moraga."

"Your mother is a dean?" asked Dad.

"Dean of students."

"Saint Mary's, dear." Mom took my arm. "That was one of the places I had hoped you would go, remember? So much closer to home."

"Yes, Mom." I nodded, gulping down the coffee. "I remember."

For months afterward, Mom asked about Vernon. Such a pleasant boy with a future ahead of him. Dad didn't ask, but he hardly ever spoke on the phone and never wrote. My answers were vague. "Oh, fine." "Fine, I guess." "Busy with his studies." Eventually, Mom stopped inquiring, without my admitting that I had grown bored with him.

I was just as happy, really, drinking pop with Judy and Ellie at the Coop, cycling into town for pizza on our dateless Saturdays. Besides, studying and my job at the dining commons kept me busy. The courses weren't hard. It was the organization of the time that confounded me, balancing lectures, sections, papers, tests, job, savoir faire. I had so much to learn about the world to become a sophisticated woman, a responsible person. The amount I didn't know was appalling.

Nancy sent pictures of homecoming at Cal State, Hayward, where she was runner-up for queen. Pretty good for a freshman. She was also active in the music club and was planning on trying out for cheerleader. I said if she could only go barefoot — with that iridescent toenail polish — she'd be a sure bet. I admired the way Nancy threw herself into six things at once. I could have taken a few lessons from her about how to be a college student. Paula sent funny postcards from UCLA. Donna didn't answer notes or phone calls.

Adele's letters seemed to mention a new boyfriend every week. She was having a good time in class, and discovering an interest in art history, of all things. She hadn't ever talked about that before. But the one time she had taken me to a contemporary exhibit in San Francisco, I'd made a philistine comment about modern canvases reminding me of monkey splatterings, so maybe she just didn't talk to me about art. What else didn't she talk to me about? Generally, Adele seemed stimulated and happy. Too bad, because I had hoped she would spurn those snobs who made fun of her accent and come home to college in California. How could she live in exile like that? How could she desert the West? Deep down I knew that I could never follow her, that I couldn't

live that far from my family. University — even a California school —
was already a big departure. Was my reluctance to move an interesting
contradiction or a failure of nerve? Well, Adele and I could really talk
this summer. We would hang out every evening. And in August, the
five of us would drive up the Sierra for another week.

Home. Home from college. My own bedroom. My old job wrapping
cotton casuals in glossy Roos Atkins boxes. Mom's mashed potatoes.
Dad's secular homilies. A Hawaiian postcard from Judy. Four weeks
until Adele and Sari and their parents returned from Europe. The summer would be half over. Every Friday I went to the movies with Paula
and Nancy, much to the irritation of Nancy's boyfriend. She insisted
she spend one night a week with the girls. It all sounded so grown up.
Grown up before our time. Word was that Donna had dropped out of
college and moved to Mendocino. We tried to track her down, but half-
heartedly, because her dropping out scared each of us in some way. If
she did, we might, too. Nancy declared she had developed a taste for
hiking. Would we have time to go to the High Country? Nancy and Paula
insisted they were still committed. Of course Adele would want to go.

"Four weeks in Europe," Dad was saying, electricity in his blue eyes.
"What will the Wards *do* for a whole month?"

"Now, Nils, what would you know? You were nineteen when you
left. And Norway is only part of Europe. The cold part. I'm sure there
are lots of galleries and museums and beaches in the civilized part.
France, for instance." She winked at me.

I lay back on the couch listening to the familiar exchange of grum-
ble and tease. Staring at the speckled white ceiling — Dad's idea of
home improvement — I ran my fingers over the tired burgundy bro-
cade upholstery of the couch.

Home, I had ached for it so much in flat, blistering Davis that I
could smell the lemon tree in our backyard. But now that I was here, I
felt like an oaf in a doll's house. Had the living room really been this
small? I missed Judy's snoring. Had the evenings always been this slow?
Of course I loved my parents and even my grim sister, Martha. But I
pined for Adele. Where the hell was she?

It was 9:45 P.M., July 16, 1966, an unusually warm night in San Francisco, and Adele and I sat next to the windows at Tweezer's Music Pub.
We had costumed each other in sparkle hairspray, miniskirts, white
lipstick, Maybelline lashes. I had picked up a few fashion tips at Davis.

Ladies' night meant free admission and one complimentary drink for each lady. Had the bouncer believed we were twenty-one? No chance. We sat giggling, checking out the cute guys.

So good to be reunited. I had never felt this close to Judy or any of the other Davis girls. Adele was smarter, funnier, more daring. (Tweezer's had been her idea.) This was not Pajamarino. Everything about Adele felt so familiar. Except the haircut — a stylish flip, though I missed the long, luxuriant curls — and her new way of saying some things. Was she changing her accent or using different words? Basically, though, this was the same old Adele. Maybe I should get with the times, too, and have my hair cut.

Haze — tobacco and marijuana. A pissy smell of beer. The high-pitched guitars of Richards, Jones. A halo of smoke around Adele's face like morning mist rising from a stand of fir. She was talking to me. Laughing. About the Arc de Triomphe at dusk. Harvard Yard under snow. Picnicking by the Charles River. Adele talked much more about Radcliffe than I did about Davis. What was there to say about a livestock college plunked in Northern California? That I was so bored I thought I might die of brain atrophy? I couldn't feel part of the place the way Adele belonged in Cambridge. No, Adele didn't *belong* in Cambridge. She was on loan. Soon she would return here permanently.

Adele was laughing again. Taking a long draft of Bud and laughing at Mick Jagger (how could she understand the words?). Laughing. Her clean, well-shaped fingernails keeping time to the music on the highly polished, round table.

On loan. She would return with her lawyer-husband, and she and I would raise our kids together.

"Dance?" He was leaning over Adele like a hatchet blade. A tall, red-haired guy with a scruffy beard.

She gave him a radiant smile. Her theatrics caused, no doubt, by the beer. How could she get out of this?

Adele was standing now, giving Red her hand. "Enchanted," she said as if she were Catherine Deneuve. And off they went, bopping to "I Can't Get No Satisfaction." Adele moaned about being a klutz, but she was a graceful, exuberant dancer. Old Red seemed to think so, too, from the way he looked at her. Leered. Well, it wouldn't last long. I hadn't been abandoned. This was why people went to a dancing club — to dance. People danced, then they sat down again. Worrying was useless. Nancy would be out there twisting away with someone *she* had asked to dance. Would Nancy be hurt we hadn't invited her? No, she knew Adele and I had a unique friendship, didn't she? Didn't we? Maybe Adele had come to dance, but I had come to be with Adele. To escape the doldrums of Alameda County in July. To see if we could sneak past the bouncer, to take a dare. All fairly immature reasons.

"Excuse me." His voice was almost inaudible. Almost.

"Yes?" Damn. Why did I respond?

He had a great face. Flushed and blue-eyed behind the glasses. And a shy way of standing off to the side, like he didn't want to be in the way in case I might rush to the bathroom to throw up. Momentarily, he seemed to forget why he was talking to me.

Then, suddenly, "Would you like to dance?"

Inadvertently, I looked out to Adele, who was being transported by Red or the music.

"Sure." I shrugged.

His dancing was, unbelievably, worse than mine. Really, this was mortifying. The whole room had become the scene of an exaggerated mating ritual. Swiveling hips and shaking breasts and bedroom eyes. As I moved stiffly to the beat, I realized these were the frigid judgments of my Calvinist father, who would have grounded me for the rest of the summer if he learned what I was doing tonight. Tom — I'd discovered his name — looked equally uncomfortable. Tense, goodwilled, and seventy-five before his time. Amusement spread across my face. Encouraged, he smiled back. My eyes sought out Adele and old Red, who seemed to be levitating from joy or booze. It might be a long night. I tried a little more shine in my step.

"Would you like a drink?"

"Sure," I said. "Let's take a break." My relief at the dancing being over was replaced with panic about elusive conversation topics. Damn Adele's effervescence.

"Charlie and your friend seem to be having a great time," Tom said, tipping the pitcher toward my glass.

"You know him? Charlie, huh?"

"Yeah, we work together — down at Don's Automotive. I slipped him two bucks to ask her to dance."

"Come again."

"I mean, I've been watching you for an hour, and I knew I would lose my dancing nerve soon. Something told me you wouldn't have accepted if she was still sitting here."

"Well." I struggled, flattered, flustered. "You're right. As you can see, I'm not much of a dancer."

"Me either. Nothing compared to Miss and Mr. *American Bandstand* out there."

We were talking about camping when Adele and Charlie joined us.

"So how are you two?" Charlie asked, taking a long drink from Tom's beer, finishing the glass.

I tried to catch Adele's eye, but she was still buzzing to the music.

We double-dated a couple of Saturdays. After our evening of *What's New, Pussycat?* at the drive-in, I knew there wouldn't be a third time.

Adele phoned the next morning. "So if that wasn't a nightmare."

"Guess you and Charlie weren't matched in Heaven."

"I'll say. The toxic dose of Old Spice was one thing. The grime under his fingernails was another. But his idea of conversation is what did me in. Baseball. Bowling. Rocky and Bullwinkle?"

I lay back on the couch, grateful that Mom was out of earshot. A solid wall was closing between Adele and me. I had actually enjoyed Tom. A lot. He was intelligent in a quiet way. He liked hiking, birds, geology. Was teaching himself guitar. And he behaved toward me as no one ever had. He insisted I never cut my long, blond hair. Said I was pretty, in a different sort of way. Original. I had found someone I could be close to — separate from my family, yet not exactly a stranger.

"Doesn't sound like your type, Del."

She laughed. "Not exactly. You and Tom put on a good show." She waited.

I waited.

"You don't really *like him,* do you?" Her voice was nervous.

"He's OK."

"Kath, I can hear between the lines. Be serious!"

"I'm too young to be serious." I laughed, anxiously. Leaning forward to the coffee table, I started filling in Mom's jigsaw puzzle of the Golden Gate Bridge.

"I mean, he's not right for you — not in any long-term, ever-after way."

"Why?" I asked, knowing I shouldn't. "Why? What do you mean?"

"Well, he doesn't even plan to go to college, does he?"

"He already has a job."

"But a career? Be serious, I mean, he's a mechanic."

"What's wrong with that?"

"You want to marry some guy who works in a garage? What would you talk about at night? Cams and mags and transmissions?"

"First, who's thinking marriage? We've only dated a couple of times. And second, he talks about a lot of interesting things. He's smart. I —"

"But dating is practice for the future. And you're not going to make your life with a mechanic?"

"My dad is a mechanic. My mother married a mechanic."

"Married!" Adele shrieked dramatically to mask her faux pas. "Married! There you go. I thought you weren't talking marriage."

"I wasn't. Oh, Del, you get things so twisted."

"Let's drop it, Kath. Let's just forget it. Who wants to fight?"

For the rest of that summer, I didn't see much of Tom. I told him I was too busy helping Martha with her new baby, Kirsten. There was a strange, new softness to Martha these days — as well as an incredible fatigue — I was honestly beginning to like her. Adele and I stayed away from Tweezer's and spent what spare time we had going to movies, catching up on the past year and, of course, planning for the Sierra trip. Three days before we were supposed to go, Nancy totaled her father's car and we spent vacation week visiting her at the hospital. I didn't see Tom again until September, when he showed up unexpectedly at my dorm.

The next June, Adele brought home her new boyfriend. She said she knew I would love Lou. She *actually said* he reminded her of me. Bright, sensitive, socially concerned, witty. He wanted to apply to divinity school and minister to people in the inner city. Great, she pictured me as some kind of burbling missionary?

Of course I was supposed to show up eagerly the first night to meet him, but I didn't want to feel outnumbered. Tom agreed to a double date. Adele suggested pizza in Berkeley, but Tom was antsy; he wanted to drive somewhere and proposed Carmel. The Yale boyfriend had always wanted to see the Monterey Peninsula, so it was agreed.

Tom waited in the car as I knocked on the Wards' front door. Mrs. Ward answered in a powder blue pants suit, the kind of outfit that made her look ten years younger than my mother.

"Why, Katherine." Mrs. Ward looked over the rims of her glasses. "So lovely to see you after all this time. How are you enjoying Sacramento State?"

"Davis, Mrs. Ward. Fine. The cows and I get along fine." Why was I such a brat? Mrs. Ward had always been a little absent-minded.

She smiled uncertainly. "Yes, well, I was hoping your young man would come in for a glass of iced tea"— she grew distracted, observing Tom's vintage Dodge Lancer, which was idling in front of the house — "before that long trip on the freeway."

"Kath!" Adele came running from the kitchen. She threw her arms around my shoulders and rocked me back and forth. "Kath! Kath! How great to see you."

A tall, dark-haired guy appeared from the corridor.

Excitedly, Adele declared, "Kath, this is Lou. Lou, Kath."

We shook hands. His fingers were long and tapered. His palms definitely clammy.

Unable to hold his glance, I stared into the living room at the black grand piano, highly polished and graced with a silver vase of fresh pink roses. Mrs. Ward talked about her Juilliard training as the best years of her life. It angered Adele that she hardly ever touched the piano now. I found it sad.

"Your father's offer of the car still stands," Mrs. Ward said merrily. I could tell she was being careful not to slur any of her words. Adele told me she had increased the tranquilizers. "It's a safe, *large* car, and I'm sure you'd all be very comfortable. I believe he filled the tank last night."

Adele watched me cautiously.

"Thanks, Mrs. Ward, but we'll be fine in Tom's Lancer. He takes good care of it, you know, he's a mechanic." I could feel his impatience. "And we should probably get going."

Tom's car rode low to the ground. I'd forgotten how poor the back springs were. After a few perfunctory attempts to engage the guys, Adele and I gossiped about Nancy's new husband, the last term at school and our families. Tom moved his powerful shoulders to the radio music. Lou seemed content to peer out the window as if he were studying California for a geography paper. Grudgingly, I had to admit he was a nice guy, kind of cute in a pale way.

By the time we got to Carmel, we were all famished. So we drove straight down Ocean Avenue to the beach and laid out the picnic blanket.

"You'll have to visit us in Europe next year," Lou said expansively.

I looked puzzled. Adele and I should have spent some time alone first. What other headlines loomed? Did they have twins in the picnic basket?

We sank into tense silence.

Tom looked from me to Adele. "OK, let's run this by one more time. You're both going to Europe?"

My fists clenched at my sides. Adele had promised that her next trip would be with me, that we would go hiking in Switzerland, in an area a lot like the Sierra.

"I got accepted at Edinburgh!" Adele did her best to be celebratory. "Remember I wrote you I was applying for junior year abroad?"

"Sort of," I said, hearing my father's suspicious reserve. She must have known about this acceptance for some time.

"Anyway, I got in. And Lou won a fellowship at Heidelberg. So we'll both be in Europe next year." She took a gulp of air.

"Nice." I nodded with my upper body as if I were in an oversized rocking chair, then concentrated on cutting ham and cheese sandwiches.

"So we, well, I haven't even asked Adele about this, but I'm sure she'd agree, were thinking you might like to come over for Christmas." He smiled with genuine enthusiasm.

What was with Mr. Perfect Friendliness? I checked my anger. Maybe Adele had been keeping this surprise for our walk tomorrow. I hated that Lou knew things about her I didn't.

Lou warmed to his hospitality. "We could go cross-country skiing, attend midnight mass in some small village church." He caught the quizzical expression on Tom's face. "As a cultural experience, of course."

"I'd love to join you all," Tom said, swallowing a bite of ham and cheese, "but I'll be abroad myself next summer."

Carefully, I wiped the rim of the mayonnaise jar and returned it to the basket. Breathing deeply, I opened the mustard.

"Oh, yes?" Lou responded with painful good fellowship. "Where will you be, Tom?"

"I have a grant from the U.S. government to study delta insects in Vietnam."

I knew Adele and Lou had been on antiwar marches. I kept my eyes lowered.

Adele interceded. "What branch of the service, Tom?" She maintained an even voice.

"Army," Tom offered, reaching into the cooler for a third bottle of Olympia. "Care for one, Lou? It's not Beck's, but it's got a decent taste."

"No, no thanks," Lou said uneasily, "I've had enough."

Conversation careened downhill from one pothole to the next. Lou was eager to hike at Point Lobos. In fact, Adele said, he had been rhapsodizing about California sea otters since he got off the plane. Tom, on the other hand, was determined to play the pinball machines at the Monterey pier. Come on, I cajoled him, let's accommodate our visitor — I almost said visitors — and drive down to Point Lobos. After all, there were plenty of pinball machines in Oakland. But he was becoming more intransigent with each beer. Finally we compromised on us going to the pier, Lou and Adele taking the car down the coast and all of us meeting at the end of the afternoon.

Tom had sobered up on coffee by the time Lou and Adele returned. I offered to drive back, but Tom would have none of it. The engine developed a deafening clank and he said not to worry, this happened all the time. He raised the volume on the radio to muffle the racket, thereby making conversation impossible.

"Mrs. Robinson."

"Yellow Submarine."

"The Windmills of Your Mind."

So much for the luxurious day of catching up with Adele. Claustrophobic, I pressed against the window, brooding on the freeway ahead.

10

Adele

1965–1976 / California, Massachusetts, Edinburgh, California

KATH LEANED AGAINST our teal garage door, her old red bike sprawled on the nearby grass. With a James Dean slouch, she tolerated the dust storm of packing, waited for my family to stuff ourselves into Father's new Lincoln Continental.

"Taking a new car, only a week old, I don't know, Geoffrey," my mother had said.

"It's not a horse, Eleanor." He shook his graying head. My father was growing ever the more distinguished doctor in appearance, attitude. "There's a complete guarantee: parts and labor. They have Lincoln dealerships even in the wilds of Massachusetts. Although why Adele had to go back East when Stanford is a first-rate school . . ."

I supposed one day Father would forgive me for defecting from California. Kath, too, who had hoped we would be at Davis together. I couldn't explain my choice, really. Perhaps it was extravagant. Perhaps I was being selfish, for Sari and Mother also hated my going. But something insisted I leave. Of course I hadn't anticipated departing in a caravan. This kind of distance was why they invented airplanes, I had argued. I dreaded traveling in the family prison van across the entire country.

"Shhh," Mother had said. "A vacation will be good for Sari's condition."

Even at home we had to whisper about Sari seeing a psychiatrist. The only "outsider" I had told was Kath, and Mother would have murdered me if she knew I hadn't kept it "in the family." Kath's response was typically useful. "Well, that's nothing to worry about if it's making her happier. I mean, she needs help, so short of a visit from the baby Jesus, the shrink is probably a good idea."

The word *shrink* made me feel better. How was I going to get along without Kath's irreverence? My heart sank as I regarded this friend, who was staring at the bright blue August sky, cracking her knuckles with studied indifference. Since Kath was no letter writer, today was a real farewell. Madly I wanted to wave to my family and drive off with Kath.

I distracted myself by engaging with Mother's hysteria about maps and sandwiches and an extra coat for everyone in case it got chilly in Colorado. Since Kath had remained dry-eyed and laconic throughout the morning, I made sure to sniff back my tears before hugging her.

"Christmas isn't far off," I said. At least that's the way I remembered it.

Kath remained on the sidewalk, her legs now astride the fiery bicycle, waving until we were out of sight. I kept peering through the back window, half-expecting her to catch up with us on the highway.

The trip, itself, was forgettable, with my younger sister sleeping on the left side of the backseat for half the day and staring darkly out the window for the other half. On the right side of the rear seat, scrunched next to the window, I read. This was the regimen: French in the mornings when I was most alert and Victorian novels during the long afternoons. My Radcliffe Alumna sponsor had sounded dubious about California public schools' preparation. I didn't want to begin the year too far behind the other girls. I stacked the books — Camus, Sartre, Thackeray, Eliot — between Sari and myself, like a fence. Occasionally Mother would try to rouse Sari by pointing to a particularly pretty field or a funny billboard, but Sari fell more listless as the trip progressed.

"I knew it was a mistake to take her away from Dr. Logan so early in treatment," she said, as if Sari weren't in the car with us.

Father ignored this and most of Mother's comments. Later I had nightmares about their long silences punctuated by intense arguments about whether we should get a motel with a bath (Mother's preference) or a shower (Father's). Bath or shower. Bath or shower. Bath or shower. Bath or shower in Utah, Kansas, Pennsylvania. Through the deserts and mountains and plains, Sari continued to stare out the window as if after an answer. Certainly any answers she needed were not lurking *inside* this bickering family. I pretended my parents were a background chorus to whatever I was reading, and they fit in particularly well with *No Exit*. In Cambridge, Sari's face was streaked with shock as I waved to their departing car.

That first autumn term, I kept a calendar over my desk and marked off the days until Christmas. The semester was much longer than I expected. In high school I had been the star of the college prep class, Dr. Ward's daughter. Here I was just one of hundreds of bright girls. Most of them had attended private academies, where they developed advanced skills in walking and talking as well as in intellectual competition. Their fathers (and some of their mothers) were astrophysicists, senators, authors. In California, I was very smart. In Massachusetts, I was still very smart, but only in the context of "brilliant," which I surely wasn't. I lacked the sophistication, the style, the brains that were so interrelated and perhaps genetically determined. Halfway through October, I abandoned a poetry notebook crammed with sentimental images of my first fiery fall. By November I decided to be a critic. All my love of writing went into letters: dutiful letters to the family; amusing, descriptive letters to Nancy, Paula and Donna; angst-ridden letters to Kath. Her short, wry postcards were enough to keep me writing every week. And once a month, we splurged on a phone call.

The second year I started writing home, tentatively, about Lou. Mother was pleased that he came from a solid family — his father a history professor at Vanderbilt, his mother from old southern money. Pleased that we had been introduced properly by Lou's *older* sister. I didn't mention that we had met at an antiwar march. Kath was the only one I told about the campus peace network. Predictably, but disappointingly, she never responded with her own feelings about the war. When Lou flew to California that summer to see me, Father confided that he was a nice young fellow, emphasizing the word *young*. He was particularly cheered that Lou could play a decent game of chess.

The person I worried about most was Kath, and I felt upset when she suggested we all go down to Carmel. I had wanted the three of us to spend some quiet time together and was disappointed to find Tom still in the picture (she hadn't mentioned him in her little postcards). I hadn't told Kath I was going to marry Lou — in fact, we hadn't formally discussed it ourselves. But there were some things you knew. Well, I told myself, Kath and I had July and August ahead of us.

Strangely, we didn't see much of each other that summer after our sophomore year. We were both busy with our boyfriends. Kath had her job at Roos Atkins. Once Lou went home to Tennessee, my parents' marriage finally erupted: Mother consulting a lawyer and Father threatening to leave her penniless if she proceeded with a divorce. Was this really Dr. and Mrs. Geoffrey Ward staging a Technicolor scene? I tried to make light of it, told myself their marriage had always been rocky and this didn't affect me; I was grown up, an autonomous adult, a Radcliffe student. I kept my attention on that day in September when I could return East to Lou and school and sanity.

Sari and I escaped the smoke and fumes of family unrest one Saturday to take a walk down Piedmont Avenue to the cemetery where we used to play hide-and-seek as kids. Buoyed by Sari's unusual alertness, I wondered if she were on new meds but was reluctant to ask. When she was lucid like this, my sister was witty, urbane beyond her years.

"Maybe a divorce is best for both of them," I tried.

"Yeah." She laughed. "Might allow them to reconstruct life in friendlier places."

"I guess they'll be lonely." The cemetery grass was astonishingly green for this late in the summer; they must have spent a fortune on water.

"Well, Father's already got a girlfriend," she said matter-of-factly, "if you can call that creaky, middle-aged bag at the bank a girlfriend."

I smiled, relieved to know Sari also understood this relationship, thinking I should talk to my sister more. "Mother is still young enough, pretty enough, to find someone else."

"The trick is finding yourself." Sari laughed. "She doesn't need someone else."

I wondered if this was a veiled comment about my relationship with Lou. Defensiveness kept me silent. We were walking uphill now, toward the garnish turn-of-the-century graves. The whole cemetery was vacant except for us and the gardeners and the ghosts.

"She could even go back to her music," Sari offered.

This seemed like a long shot, but Sari had been living with her the past two years while I was far away in Massachusetts. "They shouldn't stay together if they're unhappy."

"Yeah."

"Strange that the lives of people I love are coming apart just as mine's coming together. I mean, Tom is leaving Kath for Vietnam soon."

"Nothing you can do about that."

"Well, I don't know, perhaps I shouldn't go to Edinburgh. Perhaps I should take a leave from school and stay in California with you and Mother and Kath."

Sari turned abruptly. "No!"

"Why?"

She said something. I strained to hear her over the noise of the electric lawn mower.

"It'll all work out."

Taken aback by her tenacity, I asked, "You'll be all right, going to Cal State in the fall?"

"I'm looking forward to the dorm. I'm ready for my own life. Really, Adele, there's nothing you can do. Stay where you are, where you want to be. Live and let live."

The uncertainty between my ribs inflated to panic. I didn't know what to do, how to take care of my family and Kath and Lou and myself. The setting didn't help: this cemetery was a ridiculous place for a stroll. To think we actually *played* here as children. I hadn't expected to grow more confused as I matured. Was this kind of confusion the reason Mother took all those pills? Or did she herself share some kind of hereditary mental illness with Sari? My only serenity came from thinking about being near sweet, strong, loving Lou — even if we could only be as close as Scotland and Germany. It seemed the nearer I got to Lou, the farther I had to get from everyone else. Purposefully, I led us out toward the cemetery gate.

I had dreamed the poems would come back to me in Edinburgh. Rather, the graceful, winding streets drew me into notions of Hume, Adam Smith, Dryden, Pope. I understood how Enlightenment could have dawned in this brisk, northern city. Instead of poetry, I found myself writing long, analytical essays, enjoying the philosophy lectures as much as the literature classes. I loved the amazingly ordered world of Britain past and present, and wrote enthusiastically to Lou and Kath and my parents and Sari about the Beatles and *The Prime of Miss Jean Brodie* and the sales at Jenners and the ritualized high teas at the New Caledonian.

Lonely in this elegant, stimulating but still very foreign patrial land,

I was eager for Kath's terse postcards. When she wrote that Tom was finally shipping out, I was ashamed at my relief. I prayed that he would return safely and that meanwhile Kath would meet someone better for her at Davis: the campus had some great graduate programs, a famous vet school, for instance, and Kath was terrific with animals. I kept her cards, all my correspondence, in a red basket next to my narrow bed and read through the latest mail before I fell asleep each night.

Sari wrote, ambivalently, to say Mother and Father were consulting a marriage counselor and she worried that Humpty-Dumpty reconstructed would become a monster. She herself was still lobbying to move to the dorms at Cal State. Father had withdrawn permission, saying housing fees were a wasteful expense since they lived only twenty minutes from campus. Increasingly, I wondered why Father had allowed me to leave California, and I worried about Sari. I wanted my sister free of that house.

Then there were letters from Lou, written in purplish black ink on beige vellum stationery. I could imagine him as a medieval monk illuminating manuscripts. He had that kind of meticulousness. But we had met in this world, in this century, and his epistles evinced no interest in vows of chastity. Those were the last letters I read before switching off the light. Always, I kept the most recent one under my pillow.

So difficult to believe that this strong, handsome, talented man was in my life, that he wanted me in his. He was given to a little exaggeration, but isn't that what romance is all about? *"You're half Girl Scout, half Isadora Duncan, a stunning combination of the good and the wild, of old-fashioned virtues like honesty, consideration and generosity, splashed with revolutionary principle and flair."* I couldn't live up to all that, but what an encouraging change from Adele Ward, the doctor's nice daughter, from Adele, the consummate valedictorian, Adele, the friendly, practical girl from out West. I blossomed under Lou's gaze, and the farther I got from home (Radcliffe, Edinburgh), the happier I felt. The task, I realized, wasn't to reinvent yourself so much as to discover yourself. Sari was right.

Sometimes mail from "the States," as I had learned to call it, not "America," was unpredictable. I would receive two letters from Paula or Nancy or three packages from Mother at once. I didn't worry too much when there was no word from Kath during November. By December, I began to wonder. I asked Nancy to check on her, but Nancy couldn't locate her either. Kath was still enrolled in school but didn't answer phone calls. She could get absorbed sometimes. She would surface in her own time, Nancy advised. I walked all the way around the Meadows trying to work out my feelings. Nonchalance was fine for Nancy, secure with her husband and child. But here I was in this cold, dark country, desperate for word from my closest friend.

By late December, I grew more distracted, preparing for the Switzerland trip. I barely got off presents to Kath and my family and finished my assignments before I caught the sleeper to London. The very thought of it — Adele Ward, student of the Enlightenment, darting away to visit my lover in the Alps. Lying there in the top bunk bandaged in sterile white sheets, I thought I would never fall asleep. I imagined Mary McCarthy journeying to meet Edmund Wilson, Martha Gellhorn and Ernest Hemingway, Simone de Beauvoir and Jean-Paul Sartre and, in time, the train's rocking rhythm won me over to sleep.

We decided to be sensible and not marry until after graduation. The first letter about our engagement was to Kath. Then I wrote my family. I mailed both letters the same day because Mother would be livid if someone outside the family heard before she did. How would she know with Kath living ninety miles north in Davis? You didn't take chances with Mother's radar. Kath would have to write now. I hadn't received a thank-you for the tartan hat, let alone a present for myself, and I had been excited about finding a plaid from the Shetlands, where there was so much Norse influence. I wrote Kath with trepidation and an enthusiastic invitation to be my maid of honor.

Mother wrote back immediately with enthused suggestions about flowers and dresses. Sari sent a funny congratulations card. With a short P.S. about how she had dropped out of school for the term. Father wrote an aerogram declaring the whole Ward clan had toasted Lou and me at dinner the night before. I was dubious about my parents getting along better, but truly, I couldn't imagine them divorced. Finally, in mid-February, there was a birthday card from Kath saying she was sorry she had been out of touch. No mention of Tom. She would explain everything in the summer. And she was happy I was happy.

That was it? Not "terrific . . . congratulations . . . are you scared? . . . wow! . . . are you sure? . . . I'd love to be your maid of honor." She was happy I was happy. I felt a pang, imagining the last real scene of our friendship had been that day she leaned against the garage door, waiting for my family to pile into the loathsome Lincoln. No, I was exaggerating. We would sort things out this summer. Then next summer, after graduation, after the wedding, Lou and I would be settling into a small apartment near the Pacific School of Religion, where he would do graduate work. Divinity school would protect him from the draft, and he was now thinking of an academic career in religious studies. He also talked about Yale's program but knew I preferred California. Our small apartment wouldn't be too far from Kath, who would be finished with Davis by that time and living back in the Bay Area. Soon everything would fit back together.

I stared at the coffin, wondering if Sari's fragile body were finally relaxed. Now that she had everyone's attention. Now that it was too late. Mother and Father looked expectant, as if they were waiting for our imp to pop open the box top. A very, very hot September afternoon in 1976. The day before Sari was to begin graduate work in music, Mother had remarked this morning, momentarily emerging from her fog. Sari had finally finished college and was on her way to a career. I was sweating in my black sheath, something I had originally bought for a college reception. Sari, of all people, would have appreciated my resourcefulness. The day was macabre: the heat, the birds, the cascades of nauseatingly sweet wreaths sent by friends of the family and my father's colleagues. Sari, in her own ironic way, would have laughed at the insistent cheerfulness of the afternoon, which provided her this perfect off-center exit.

Lou's solid fingers squeezed my hand, helping me surface from numb grief. What would I have done without him? No one else to talk to, really. Mother was washed away on tranks and Father was furiously obsessed with that terrible article "Doctor's Daughter Takes Life" — as if it had been his fault, as if his being a physician had had anything to do with it.

Paula and Nancy had heard about Sari's death from their families. Both wrote, apologizing that they couldn't get away from their jobs in Tucson and Los Angeles, sending love and concern. But nothing from Kath. Not a card, a note, a call. This was the end, I decided. It had been painful enough to have her ignore the wedding, but any decent friend would acknowledge the loss of my sister. I understood that part of my mourning today was for Kath. Why had I placed such naive faith in friendship? I should have spent more time with Sari than with her. After all, what bond did Kath and I share? There had been nothing between us for years now, except an occasional Christmas card when one of us got the motivation to reach out. So we had gone to school together for eight years. So we had spent three quarters of our adolescence on the telephone confiding about sex, Milton, deodorant, socialism. We had simply been friends. We didn't owe one another anything. The nature of friendship was that it passed.

Standing in the graveyard now, I thought how I should have put all those years into being a better friend to Sari. Was her body really in that coffin? Wasn't there *anything* I could do — now, then — to bring her back? Perhaps if I had been more available to her when we had been kids, she would have been happier. However, I had been too busy planning my own escape from the liquid pain in Mother's eyes and Father's brusque, dutiful parenting. What was wrong with me? Why was I so terrified? I hadn't been physically battered as a child, or sexually molested. I had been raised in middle-class, upper-middle-class comfort, with all privileges attached: music lessons, European travel, theater tickets, nice clothes. And yet as I grew up, home felt more and more dangerous and I came to see my parents' marriage as a zone of ice, the glacier moving slowly, millimeter by indiscernible millimeter, unstoppably toward my heart. I couldn't calculate the window of escape, but I realized that one day — if I did not get out, really out, far away for long periods of time — one day I would find myself fossilized in the ice as well. And so we never returned to California for graduate school. I had visited only three times in the seven years since our wedding. This year, I had been planning a Christmas trip.

As they lowered the coffin, I looked away. Once again: the comforting pressure of Lou's large hand. I was thankful for this, and yet gratitude was mixed with strange resentment — as if Lou stood between me and Sari's resurrection — and, frantically, I could not stop wondering what else I could have done for her. At least once a year I invited her to Massachusetts. I had sent pictures of the cottage in Maine, offering her the place as a retreat if she wanted solitude, also inviting her to join the family there. I clipped articles about travel, courses in different parts of the country. Sari was unfailingly congenial in her responses. She never said, "get off my back" or "leave me alone." She would send a grotesque postcard once a year, maybe even a birthday

card. Today I kept thinking about her dismissive comments the summer Mother and Father were divorcing. "Don't worry about me. Live
and let live. I'll be fine." After a while, my attention did waver. With the
dissertation, the academic market, the first job, the tenure-track appointment, the accumulating tenure dossier. This year I had written
her just three or four times. If only I had paid more attention. If only I
had been there for Sari.

Back at the house, Mother wafted through the motions beautifully —
filling people's glasses, cutting ham, making coffee. Could the guests
tell her dosage had been increased? She had always had such a charming, distracted air. Who would distinguish among the outlines of grief
and fey sensibility and chemical affect? Certainly no one would voice
any public concern. People were already tiptoeing around Father's fury
with the newspaper. No one dared acknowledge — let alone discuss —
Mother's addiction. Psychotropic drugs were a topic for discretion.
(Was this why Kath had backed away?) You kept a family confidence
unless, of course, someone were imprudent enough to kill herself.
"Sarita Ward's family could not be reached for comment."

My father chewed on his pipe, half-listening to Dr. Gorman talk
about last week's hole in one. I wondered whether Father could ever
again be reached for comment.

Gripped by need for Kath's voice, I suddenly dropped Lou's hand
(which I had forgotten I was holding) and walked to the French doors
overlooking the back garden.

"Are you OK?" He had followed me and now placed his capable
palms on my tense, aching shoulders.

Lou was a gift. Warm and loving where Father was frozen in loneliness. What fortune to have this kind, intelligent, successful, loyal husband. Yet I worried, perversely, that I didn't love the man, that our life
together, which had been so lucky, would not be happy. Perhaps I was
incapable of happiness.

"Fine, dear. Fine. I just need a break from the community support
team."

"All right." He patted my neck, backing away slightly. "I'll leave you.
But I'll be on the couch if you need me."

Blessedly, the kitchen was empty. I poured myself a lemonade and
sat at the familiar, round oak table. Our old red phone hung by the
open window, within easy reach. Lifting the receiver, I automatically
dialed Kath's number. She had to be around. Paula said she had run

into her on Telegraph last winter. She couldn't have dropped off the face of the earth.

"Hello." Kath's father. His clipped, Scandinavian accent made me feel twelve and bursting at the seams again.

I should have said, "Hello, Mr. Peterson. This is Adele, Katherine's old friend. Is she there, by any chance?" But I didn't want to be humiliated by need, didn't want her to know I was looking for her until I found her. Instead, I said, "May I speak to Katherine Peterson, please?"

"She's not here," he answered abruptly.

"Do you know where she is? Do you have another number?"

"Who is this?" He was alarmed. "Who wants to know this?"

"I'm just trying to find her current phone number," I said anxiously, unnerved out of all proportion by Mr. Peterson's irritation. He was a big man and could be violent. Another family secret betrayed.

"She is not here. She has done nothing wrong. Leave her alone. And stop calling this number." He slammed down the phone.

I sat there stunned. Mother entered the kitchen, tears filling her eyes, yet smiling widely. "It's such a lovely party, don't you think, Sari?"

"Mother," I whispered, conducting her to a seat and exchanging her wineglass for my own half-finished lemonade. "Sit right here, Mother, and have something cool to drink."

"Yes, a lovely reception." Mother sat straight in the chair, sipping lemonade. "Hmmmm. That tastes good. Really, it's rather hot for June, don't you think?"

11

Kath

I LAY on the narrow bed between the crisp, white sheets inspecting the misspelled "Catherine" on my wristband and speculating about other mistakes the hospital would make. I should be studying. Otherwise, I would never catch up. Stupid to lie here and obsess. Yes, I told myself again and again, I was doing the right thing. Slowly, inevitably, the late afternoon dragged on, punctuated by buzzers and bells and beeps. Were all hospitals so noisy? This was no place for a rest cure. Yet there was something calming about Dr. Perry telling me my "job was to go to bed." To sleep. Ultimately to mend, to be myself, just myself again. The textbooks were piled on the bedside table. An hour ago I had been determined not to waste time. However, now I allowed myself stillness. I felt safer here than I had for months, years.

I was twenty-one, and pregnant. The last part was highly unlikely because, as the gynecologist declared, the loop was almost foolproof. Ninety-five percent guaranteed. How often did you get a promise like that? As he said when he inserted it five months before, the IUD was as safe as the pill and healthier for someone like me, who was throwing up even on the lowest hormone combo. Highly unlikely to conceive on the IUD. After his first checkup, he said I couldn't possibly be pregnant. Since my period was never predictable, I opted to trust medical science. But the next month he shrugged, declaring me the exception. Well, what was he going to do? I asked, thinking of customers who came back to Dad when their cars continued to make little noises. How could he fix me? The doctor shook his head sadly. It was out of his hands. Abortion was illegal in California. Besides, he had philosophical objections. He wished me luck.

Now, from the next room, a baby began to cry. Down the hall a woman starting labor roared as if from inside a volcano. I didn't know which one of these sounds frightened me more. A fifty-dollar IUD — the cost of which meant skipping lunch all summer — a shake of his sad, graying head and that was that. Problem was, I understood his philosophy. Abortion was a sin, maybe not murder, but a sin. Still, I had to commit this sin. I couldn't produce a child. What chance was there for a kid whose mother was a student and whose father was trudging through swamps in Vietnam? Giving birth right now was not responsible behavior. No abortions at Student Health Services. No referrals. The antiseptic smells here unsettled me. Everything was artificial, like life on a spaceship: white, spare, painfully clean.

Sitting up on the bed, I reached for my history book. With pillows plumped against my back, this would be the perfect spot to study. When the nurse placed me in the room, she raised her eyebrows at the pads and books. "Thought we might bore you?" I shrugged. Clearly she didn't know the pressures of making decent grades while holding down a job. If I lost pace now, I could flunk. Already, I was far behind in history. I needed to remind myself what was real. My courses were real. My job at the library. My love for Tom. Our future together. This hospital jaunt was a temporary interruption.

Flipping through Richard Hofstadter, I thought how kids had transformed Martha's life. Martha loved Kirsten and Sam, of course, but so much for her ambition of opening a tailoring business. She complained she never sewed anymore unless it was to fix a hem or seam. No time to pore over patterns, to scheme about opening her own shop. Her life would never be the same again, although, she was quick to add, it was a very good life, a lucky life.

Somewhere I had read about pennyroyal and cohosh tea. One night after my roommate, Judy, had gone to bed, I went down to the laundry and drank and drank, three quarts of it. The only result was cramps, deep, painful, nagging cramps for five days. So bad that I stopped going to class and missed half my work shifts. The next week I tried hot baths, hogging the tub on my dorm floor for hours at a time, only to surface lobster red, with a couple of long-lasting, nasty burns on the insides of my thighs.

Judy grew more and more worried. But how could I talk to someone who attended mass every Sunday and didn't even approve of birth control pills? She knew something was dreadfully wrong. Not confiding in her made me feel angry — at once censored and guilty. There had to be an escape. This wasn't the right time to have a baby. Other animals had natural contraceptive reflexes to keep them from reproducing during times of drought and flood. It didn't make sense to bear a child now. I would find a way out. Women had been whispering directions to one another for centuries. My rational mind searched ahead. But lower in my body, I carried a grievous panic. Weeks passed as I tried one remedy after another. A library book suggested parsley. So I boiled up a foul brew and drank the stuff until nauseated. Next day I skipped two classes, then slept through my job. For a week I was seasick, eventually breaking out in a rash all over my breasts and shoulders. It was getting harder and harder to concentrate in class, and I was missing work hours.

This couldn't continue. Soon I would lose my job or fail my classes. I had managed to scrape up the current registration and residence hall fees, but there wasn't enough for next term. It would be embarrassing to quit school, and my parents would be mortified if I flunked.

Then one night after our shifts at the circulation desk, I let my story slip to Linda Chen. Linda phoned a friend who gave me the number of a doctor who performed abortions. "Performed"— they made it sound like a magic act. Fine, if I could be the escape artist. Dr. Harder could admit me to the hospital on a technicality — my mental health! — and it would all work out. Even though I was two and a half months pregnant, it would work out.

This was the twentieth century. I was a free woman. Tom and I would have our family — six children — when he returned from the war, when we could provide for them together.

Escape was foiled by Dr. Harder's pneumonia. My procedure was postponed. And by the time he recovered, it was too late for a D & C. For three days I camped at Linda's apartment, making expensive phone calls all over Northern California, filling a yellow legal pad with names, addresses, phone numbers. Even to save the life of the mother, Catholic hospitals wouldn't do salines. Other places were booked up.

Finally, on the fourth morning at Linda's apartment, Dr. Harder phoned with a referral to a colleague in Los Angeles. Overwhelmed with gratitude, I made the appointment before calculating expenses. Gradually, over the next day, costs came into focus: bus to L.A., hotel room for the first night — maybe the Y — hospital fees, operation, another hotel night afterward, bus back to Davis. Easily this could eat up $600. Five months' salary. Where was I going to find that?

Wide awake on the L.A. bus, I recalled a short story from one of Judy's *Mademoiselle*'s last year in which a girl my age got pregnant and her mother flew her off to an English hospital. Imagine. Imagine being able to tell my Catholic mother I wanted an abortion. Imagine having family money for such travel, even if Dad weren't on workmen's comp right now. Somehow I would pay the bills. Petersons were resourceful, immigrant people. Responsibility and will were coded into my genes. In the genes of this thing, this being, growing inside me, from me, through me. No, I wouldn't think about that. Someday I'd have half a dozen children and then it would be all right.

As afternoon dimmed into evening, the hospital room filled with strange lights. The saline injection happened tomorrow morning. Tomorrow night everything would start being better. Next to my bed, red buttons winked. Blue neon glowed from the offices across the street, and yellow fluorescence seeped under the door from the hallway. Noises grew louder, too, as they do at dusk in the woods. Here the sounds were infants crying and women screaming and nurses paging doctors paging nurses over the intercom. I was lucky to be in a safe, clean hospital. I was lucky to be in a double room. Would someone else come? Would they put a delivering mother in the other bed? How would I explain my condition to her? How would I get any sleep? The voices continued to nag: About sin. About natural women. About biological destiny. I kept trying to change the station on my conscience, but the tuner wouldn't move, and I listened again and again to worry, fear, guilt. By dinnertime, there were so many babies squalling I thought my head would split.

Dr. Perry appeared at the door. Immediately firing words: "Sorry about this. Most of the D & C's are quick affairs. In and out in an afternoon. But the salines take longer. No place else to put you. Don't worry, you'll be up in a couple of days, back to ordinary life."

I nodded, comforted that I had an ordinary life. Grateful to him. After all, I was fourteen weeks pregnant — that sounded better than three and a half months — and it was hard to find a doctor at all, let alone someone who'd accept installment payments. He'd given me sixteen months. What were a few shrieks in the night? I'd heard a lot of crying babies in my life. Planned to hear a lot more.

"You'll be fine after I perform the procedure," he said as he walked out the door, reading the next patient's chart. "You'll be just fine, Patsy."

I stared after Dr. Perry, tears rolling down my cheeks. It didn't matter that he got the name wrong. Who cared? It was only a procedure, a sterile, impersonal, installment plan procedure. And he was a performer.

Lying back, I closed my eyes. Alone. In and out in three days. No one except Linda, Dr. Perry and his accomplices would know. When I had recorded Linda as next of kin, the registration clerk hadn't blinked. Parental concern was the last thing I needed now. Mom and Dad thought I was on an anthropology field trip. I considered calling Paula, who had moved from the UCLA dorm to Westwood, but some part of me believed that if I didn't talk about this ordeal, I would recover faster. I'd weighed, then discarded, the idea of writing about this to Tom. He had enough to worry about. I'd tell him when he returned, sometime after the birth of our first baby. If there was anyone I wanted to talk to, it was Adele. But Adele was probably huddled in a quaint Edinburgh pub over pints of lager with new friends, telling them about her Christmas break, skiing through Switzerland with Lou. I really should have answered the last letter. Marriage. But how could I respond, with what degree of honesty? Adele was receding further and further; Radcliffe, Edinburgh, the Alps, checking every now and then to see if her anchor were still here. I had no intention of being anybody's fucking anchor.

A nurse flashed on the overhead light, filling the room with throbbing glare. She accompanied a woman with astonishingly long, curly, dark hair to the other bed.

"Katherine, this will be your roommate, Dacia."

Dacia gave me a terrified nod. I wondered if I should say, "Welcome." I recalled Judy's sign on our dorm room, my wilted parents, the excited conversation over chocolate chip cookies. How far I had come in only two years: virgin ingenue to shipwrecked whore. I knew I should at least say hello to Dacia. Instead, overcome with self-consciousness, I nodded mutely.

The nurse introduced Dacia to the toilet, the meal chart, the call button. Holding herself rigidly, Dacia listened.

Then we were alone under the whining white light.

She lay still as a corpse in the tightly sheeted bed. Her stomach didn't

look large enough to contain a baby. Again, I wondered if my roommate would be a woman about to give birth. Was I a woman about to
give death? I had heard there was a form of execution — death by
lethal injection. I closed my eyes and listened to a baby crying in the
neighboring room. Maybe they did mix birth patients with abortion
patients. Why not? We had made different choices. Each of us was a
certified gynecological procedure. Sensible to do all the womb jobs in
one place. A gross joke, but one Adele would appreciate. Dear Adele.
Damn Adele. How did I get myself into a position where the only person I could talk to was in Europe? Of course there was Tom. Six thousand miles away in the other direction.

Alone in Los Angeles these last couple of days, I'd had plenty of time
to think about Tom. I wish I missed him more. For the hundredth
time, I cursed myself for sleeping with him. But once he received the
draft notice, I lost all resolve. I listened to the casualty statistics on Wal-
ter Cronkite. I watched the men arriving home in body bags, on
stretchers, in wheelchairs. I wanted to give him a memory to take to
Vietnam, and I wanted a memory to carry me through the lonely
months of his absence. And my body was drawn to his with a desire
that burned deeper than reason or logic or sentiment. Now I remembered those great long legs on top of me. I remembered him entering
me passionately, gently. I hungered for that coming together.

"Water, Signora?" The voice startled me. "Is there water?"

"Wait a sec." I fetched a paper cup of water from the bathroom.
"There you go."

"You are here for the baby?" Dacia looked up at me.

"To have an abortion." I tried to sound unapologetic.

"Ah." Dacia sat up. She studied my face, then started sobbing.

"Me also. The abortion. If ever my parents they should find out, I
don't know what to do. But how can I have the baby? Me, with no husband." She wept and wept, unable for a moment to catch her breath.

Gingerly, I perched on the bed, taking her hand. "It's all right," I said,
"plenty of women have abortions."

"Not so many Italian women. Not in my family. Ohhhh, I am so
ashamed. What choice I have?"

Sitting on the edge of her bed, my feet dangling above the shiny
linoleum floor, I felt like a five-year-old psychiatrist.

"What choice I have? A baby. Imagine. Sewing ten hours a day. And
a baby."

"Right," I said encouragingly.

"But I plan lotsa babies someday. Lotsa. With my husband. In a family. And you?"

"Maybe." I was surprised by my reserve. Six kids. I should tell Dacia about the six kids.

"You have what kind of job?"

"I'm a student."

Dacia looked skeptical. Amused.

"College student."

"Oh." She lost interest, glancing out the window at evening lights. I followed her glance.

"I am not a loose woman," she declared. "I would like to marry. But this man not ready. You know."

"I know," I said.

"Your family not Catholic?"

"My mother, yes," I said uncomfortably, wanting to disconnect from this woman and not knowing how. Stealthily I retreated to my bed.

"But not Italian."

"French Canadian."

"Italians don't do abortion. I know this is a sin. I know God, he will punish me."

I pretended my bed was another room. Pulling covers around me, I picked up my history book. Dacia didn't notice as she continued to describe her difficult family and the priest at her church and how the women at work would find out and . . .

The blood tests provided interruption. I turned on the TV news. Da Nang. Newark. Khe San. (I was beginning to have doubts about the war: all this devastation. Maybe Adele was right; maybe Tom was wrong. But Tom didn't have a choice. He had to go. Had to believe. So did I, if I loved him.) Eugene McCarthy. Hanoi. Football salaries. Dacia continued, her voice ringing over the television, about being kicked out of her family, about burning in hell.

Excusing myself to take a walk, I found the hospital buzzing. Cheerful in a way I hadn't noticed during my morose, isolated first five hours. Each room contained two or four women sitting in beds, eating Jell-O, watching TV, knitting, chatting. I had a surreal vision of my entire dorm being transferred here: all the girls suddenly pregnant from the breakfast cereal. I paced the entire corridor twice before turning into our room. Dacia waved enthusiastically.

"Oh, I forgot something." I swiveled and walked out. Staring at the pay phone near the nurses' station, I wondered how you called Edinburgh. Dad had called Norway twice that I could remember. Once after the death of each parent. The hospital lounge was a brightly decorated, airy room.

Four women in bathrobes sat talking, while a fifth woman nursed something that resembled a skinless rabbit. Taken aback by my hostility to the newborn, I forced myself to smile as I walked into the lounge. Two women nodded to me as the one holding the baby talked about nursery furniture. I checked my watch. 8:00 P.M. I had another forty-eight hours in this bin.

"When did you deliver?" asked the freckled woman with glasses.

Deciding to let them learn what they wanted to learn, I simply answered, "I haven't."

"False labor?" asked the nursing woman kindly.

I pretended not to hear, as if I were listening to the other women's conversation. Clearly this wouldn't do. I had lost my nerve and would have to leave. I leaned against the couch for support. "No."

The freckled woman spoke to my stomach. "Then why are you here?"

"For an abortion," I said, interested that I felt no embarrassment, "for a saline injection."

"Oh." The nursing mother blinked as she looked at her baby.

The oldest woman invited me to sit. "Motherhood should be a choice," she said to me, addressing the others. "Children should be wanted."

The tension was palpable. One woman cradled her stomach. Two others looked away as if they might catch leprosy from me.

Stupidly, I stood by the pink and blue couch trying to devise a graceful good-bye.

"Then why did they put you *here?*" blurted the freckled woman timorously.

At the door now, I replied, "Where would you like them to do it — on a kitchen table?" Flushed, I walked from the cozy lounge. Adele, where are you, Adele, old friend?

Dacia was delighted to see me. I resigned myself to listening and reassuring her conscience with the occasional murmur. Lights out at 10:00 P.M. Sleep took a while.

Then, out of nowhere, in the hospital's semidarkness: "Are you scared?"

Dacia's voice? My own? Adele's?

Because I couldn't tell, I responded softly, "Yes."

They woke me at 5:00 A.M. to take blood. Then at 7:00 to serve a liquid breakfast. Since my procedure wasn't scheduled until 10:30, I took out Mr. Hofstadter and read for my makeup exam. Dacia passed time praying her rosary until she was wheeled downstairs. Once she returned, she spent hours and hours sleeping, for which I was tempted to say a prayer of thanks to the B.V.M. After my saline injection, the rest of the day became a blur of waiting, fretting, reading about American political reform and, growing bored with that, scrutinizing tattered hospital copies of *Glamour* to determine whether the girls really looked better after their makeovers. I watched a John Wayne movie and walked up and down the hallway until I got rude stares from the nurses. I avoided the lounge. Cramps came early the next morning. Contractions. And I expelled the fetus before dawn. I didn't remember being wheeled back into the room. I did remember the nurse's sympathetic face when she woke me.

"All over?" I asked groggily.

"All over," she said with Soviet robustness. "The tissue was removed hours ago. You didn't have any complications."

She was right, I thought woozily, I had never been a complicated person. A simple procedure. No more fetus. "Tissue." I was half-grateful for the anatomical diplomacy of her language. But a fury was building in my chest. And my heart constricted with grief. No more traces of Tom in my body. Overcome now, I wept for the baby we wouldn't have. Tears streamed onto the fresh sheet, bruises on a white petal.

"Happens sometimes," the nurse whispered. "Now that your body's back, it's safe to cry."

I didn't want a baby. Couldn't afford one. Didn't have time to take care of a child. Still, I felt cleft in two. Would they tell me whether it had been a girl or a boy? No. I didn't want to know. Must have been a boy. How would I cope if it had been a daughter?

The nurse went on calmly, "Let me insert this new antibiotic for the intravenous."

I noticed the plastic tubing in my arm. "What?"

"Don't worry. Salines always get antibiotics to prevent infection.

We're using an IV because we didn't want to take any chances with your heart murmur."

What had my heart murmured? Who had heard?

She fiddled with the contraption almost tenderly.

I should tell Tom. The baby, the tissue, had been half him. But it had been my body. If I didn't feel the need to tell him before, why now? Why was I experiencing all these qualms after the fact? Why couldn't I leave myself alone? Because I had made myself alone.

The nurse reached into her tray of pills. "Look at that face, flooded!" She shook her head with a kindness I resented. "Valium time, I'd say, send you right back to sleep for a while."

At first I didn't want the pill. I pictured dazed Mrs. Ward. Out the corner of my eye, I noticed Dacia perched in bed, anticipating my return. And I succumbed.

Later, much later, I felt myself rousing from sleep. No more fetus. No more strands of Tom. No more worries. Now darkness shaded the window. Dacia's dinner tray was scattered with half-empty dishes. My eyes closed again, not quickly enough.

"The lady down the hall, she said that maybe we have no more babies after this."

"What?" My voice was groggy from the drugs.

"We are sterile now? No more babies?"

Maddeningly encumbered by the IV, I leaned over with care. "Don't listen to those old wives' tales." I could hear the anger racing to my throat. "You had, we had, abortions, not sterilizations. You'll have your family. Don't worry."

"You sure?"

"As sure as I can be of anything."

Certainty had become elusive lately. I had been so much more sure — of everything — a couple of years ago, a couple of months ago. Lying on the bed now, attached to this plastic tube, I thought about how freedom came in different degrees. Maybe I'd read too much American history, for before I'd always thought of freedom as an absolute. In the land of the free, you determined your life. But it wasn't like that. You only got to choose among certain variables. Pregnancy or abortion, for instance. If I truly had choices, I'd have chosen not to be pregnant. In fact, that's what I thought I'd chosen when I got the IUD. I'd have chosen that Tom not be sent to Vietnam. It's not as if I woke up one day and said, I choose to have an abortion, like I want to take a vacation in Nova Scotia. Or even like, I want to get pregnant. As close as I could tell, I had a choice for or against my own survival. A choice I'd be compelled to make in different ways throughout my life. What do you think, Adele? Knowing I couldn't create the variables, I could only choose among them, lifted a burden. It also made life slightly less attractive and slightly more scary.

"You know, Katherine."

I noticed I was developing an irrational fondness for Dacia.

"We are young and healthy."

"Yes," I said, encouraging both of us.

She continued pensively, "I was lucky to get you as my roommate. Very lucky."

"Lucky. We *are* lucky, that's the way to see it." I lay back again, trying to locate sleep. Instead, I wondered where Tom was, how he was. I worried Dacia might be right about us being sterile. It happened sometimes. I worried about how I was going to pay for this antiseptic resort. I had the feeling my academic life had abruptly ended. I'd never keep up with the dorm, tuition and books and these damn medical bills. It was so unfair. But what was fair? Dacia working ten hours a day in a sweatshop? Lucky. Dad always told me I never appreciated how lucky I was.

12

Adele

Wednesday Morning / Mono Pass

IN A FEW HOURS, this clear, blue day would burn blistering hot. As Kath drove us east from the campground toward Tioga Pass, I fantasized about the place during winter, when snowy roads were impassable: the longer night, the whiteness, the cold. It saddened me to think this was a land I would only know in summer, that I was a temporary visitor here, another tourist with illusions, and I was shivering although the temperature was sixty going on eighty degrees. Kath had found a parking spot in the shade.

Breathing in the sequoias' sweet-sour scent, I turned away from the road, toward the shady trailhead, and pretended not to notice the glinting line of chrome vehicles to my right and left. Kath put her thumb against her forefinger, making a spyglass, creating a view that blocked everything except — I guessed — the branches at the beginning of our path.

Her approach to parking was scientific. She seemed to be calculating solar movement and tree height. This exercise brought back her maddeningly precise questions in school and the irritated glares from teachers. Later today, enjoying a comfortable ride up to Saddlebag Lake in our cool car, we would benefit from Kath's perfectionism. Glancing at the metallic blue Bronco parked in full sun, smack next to the trailhead, I felt kinship with the impetuous driver. In the heat of midday, he'd no doubt suffer a sweltering departure.

"Gorgeous morning." I aimed for a light voice to disguise or dissolve the tension from last night. How could Kath blame me for going away to college? Still blame me! I knew her well enough not to deal with this head-on, but to let the knots appear — and unravel — in time.

"Beautiful day." Kath was concentrating on our fanny pack, placing an orange at the bottom with the celery and carrots in order not to smash the bread, cheese and avocado. She tucked our ration of bitter-sweet chocolate toward the outside so it wouldn't melt against her body.

Lou had bought nonchemical sunscreen at the Harvard Coop, and now I lathered the wet, white substance over my face, neck and arms. I handed the red and blue tube to Kath, who wrinkled her nose.

"Smells like coconut and pineapple."

I laughed.

"I don't fancy myself a fruit salad."

I insisted the tube on my friend.

"Maybe I'll go natural today," Kath grumbled. "I hate covering my-self — you know, with umbrellas, shower caps, swimming goggles. Makes me feel disconnected somehow."

Fascinating remark from someone who was so accomplished at hid-ing major biographical details: her job, her love life, the last twenty years.

I said, "Better sticky cream than melanoma." I could hear Father and Lou saying this. "Better fruit salad than chemotherapy," I continued, invoking Nancy.

Kath gave in.

We attached ourselves to our frivolous life-support systems: Kath wearing the fanny pack and me carrying the canteen. Within twenty yards of the trailhead, the engine noise and exhaust fumes had van-ished. We were floating in a bright yellow meadow surrounded by mountains.

As I tiptoed across the small stream, my spirits lifted. Each day in the High Country was, in some sense, a new start, strenuous enough and lasting long enough in the late summer sun to make you forget the day before. I regretted getting so angry at Kath, but there didn't seem to be any point in fretting, for she was cheerful this morning, too, as reluc-tant as I, perhaps, to continue talking about our estrangement. What a melodramatic word. Try *interlude, intermission, break . . .*

The words afforded refreshing, temporary shadow, a grace note for the journey ahead. We were alone, in the forest. The blue Bronco dri-ver was probably miles ahead. Judging from the multiple footprints, he had along one or two of his kids.

One of my favorite childhood expeditions was taking the bus to downtown Oakland with Kath. We never did much except window-shop and drink Cokes at Newberrys, and I loved it when Kath agreed to visit her mother, who worked at Capwell's purse department. Mrs. Peterson was always delighted to see us. Of course she took care of her customers first, but when we were alone, she would show us the new stock of wallets and bags. She told us to guess what was made from pigs' leather and what from calves' leather. Was this why Kath had become a vegetarian? I loved the oily smells and the satiny soft textures. Although Mrs. Peterson was constantly busy — either working at Capwell's or cooking or cleaning at home — she always made time for us. She asked about the day at school, told us jokes, argued politics. Actually, she was the one who had interested Kath in the JFK campaign, and Kath, in turn, had enlisted me to hand out leaflets and wear election buttons to school. I had to take off the propaganda before going home because my parents were set against a Papist in the White House. But they didn't seem to worry about what I thought. Unlike Kath's mother, they didn't ask but rather assumed they knew.

Departing the woods, we discovered another sunny field, this one chorusing with the season's last, late purple lupine.

"It's fun to identify these flowers," Kath said. "You know when I was a kid, I only knew roses, daisies, azaleas. And geraniums. They smelled so bad, I figured they must really be a vegetable rather than a flower."

I grinned at the memory of tutoring Kath with my sketches of Sierra wildflowers. The lupine dipped from side to side in a faint breeze. The aroma of a few remaining wild onions lingered in the morning air.

Suddenly a doe stepped from shadows of pine and fir. Lightly, I touched Kath's arm, finding it still moist from sunscreen, for surely it was too early for sweat.

Kath nodded, smiling with closed lips as if the glare of her teeth might startle the animal. The doe slowly lifted her head, ears fanning.

I wondered why it was so thrilling to discover deer in the wild. Because they were docile creatures? Simply because they were pleasant to behold? Because such a moment of truce, no matter how brief, no matter how one-sided, brought hope for interspecies detente? As always, there was the feeling of disappointment, of misrepresentation, as the catch of our scents or the sound of our breathing caused the deer to scamper toward safety.

Kath's smile broadened at the brief communion, and her eyes held a trace of solace.

Side by side, we ambled through the wide meadow.

"Misunderstood giants, that's what we are," I joked. "Meaning no harm to deer or vole or beaver as we pad along the trail in our soft-soled shoes."

"More like the barons of death!" Kath laughed. "Paving the mountain passes, spewing car exhaust, draining water to the cities."

"Hmmm." I laughed with her, knowing Kath was right, but also recognizing her old resistance to ambiguity. Right or wrong. Black or white. Commitment to dichotomy was one of Kath's most endearing, infuriating qualities.

I changed the topic. "Oh, the smell of this dirt, mixed with pine needles. But I wish we had eucalyptus trees up here like we do in Oakland. God, in Massachusetts I miss that pungent, homelike smell. In Australia . . ."

"Australia!" Kath declared. "When were you in Australia?"

"Two years ago. I had a sabbatical and Lou had a visiting appointment at Sydney Uni." Did I sound pretentious? I could have said "temporary job" instead of "visiting appointment." I continued, "Anyway, the Australians call them 'gum trees,' but I prefer 'eucalyptus.' The word is long and complicated, like the aroma."

"Yes." Kath said the syllables slowly, as if she were beginning a haiku, "Eucalyptus tree."

The meadow ended in a fork. "Down there's the fishing lake I always promise to visit." Kath spoke wistfully. "You know, I never do. This pass always draws me *up*."

Once again we headed toward the pass. We could have gone both places, if only we had more time. I wondered if Heaven were the place with more time.

The hike felt more refreshing than the previous day's walk. As I padded along the trail ahead of Kath, I realized I was more comfortable in the lead and Kath didn't seem to mind this. I enjoyed the exhilarating strain of climbing up. Why did I prefer vistas to valleys? Mr. Blue Bronco was probably fishing down below with the kids. Just as well we didn't take that path. He and Kath wouldn't have gotten on.

One day, I resolved, I'd return here with Taylor and Simon and Lou. Did all mothers feel guilty about pleasures outside the family and then did we all resolve to share those pleasures with our kids some other time as atonement, as recompense?

Our climb grew steep in yet another woods. This sylvan coolness made me realize how hot I'd been. I turned to check on Kath, who was close behind, and noticed the circles of perspiration under the arms of her blue cotton work shirt.

Suddenly overcome with a need to talk about the boys, I noticed my resentment that she didn't ask more about them. A little defiantly, I said, "Taylor and Simon would be yards ahead of us now, scrambling up this trail like mountain goats."

"You must miss them."

"Yes. Not that I would want them to be here with us, now, but I guess I'd like to be *there,* momentarily, to see how they're doing." I inhaled sharply. Silly to start a conversation going uphill.

"I'm sure Lou's doing fine with them."

"Oh, of course." My defensiveness mounted. "I meant that I miss their spirits. I don't know, it doesn't really make sense."

"Tell me about their spirits."

"Well, Taylor is restless, aggrieved, passionate. When he's around, I always feel as if I need a break from him. But the truth is, he provides a kind of creative disruption."

"You think he'll be an artist?"

"A musician. Of the Philip Glass school — asynchronic, provocative."

Kath grinned. "Well, it's better than becoming a serial killer."

I laughed out loud.

"And Simon, what does he want to do when he grows up?" She showed no signs of losing breath.

"Architecture. He's always loved to build and design. He has a very conceptual mind. Lou thinks he'll go into medicine like my father. But he's too imaginative for that."

I waited for Kath to ask another question. When she didn't, I wondered if she were jealous of my family or if she simply didn't know what to ask. Of course, what did I know of her life, of lovers, past and present? I shouldn't be so intimidated by her reserve. Taking a long breath, I said, "You used to want kids. I remember. Six."

"Yeah."

"And then you changed your mind?"

"Kinda."

"Why?"

"I don't know," she answered irritably. "I changed my mind about a lot of things. I once wanted to play electric guitar. Now I realize I would have been hopeless at music *and* at raising kids."

That was it. End of conversation. I wanted to know how her body hadn't yearned to have children. Why was I the norm? I mean, she could as well have asked why I *wanted* to have children. If Kath were an asker of questions. Sometimes I thought that the most profound division between women wasn't ethnic or economic or national but the division between mothers and nonmothers. It had come as a gradual series of shocks to learn that not all women had the urge to reproduce or to nurture, that not all women even *liked* kids.

Concentrate on your surroundings, I told myself, and remembered that Kath had said the Indians used to take this Mono Pass route rather than Tioga Pass when they crossed the Sierra. Our canteen bumped against my denim hip as I stretched up, up the path. The dampness was rich in the smell of ripe mushroom, moss and decaying tree trunks. I loved the nurse logs, lying in the refuse of cones, needles, leaves, shit and dirt — like ancient grandmothers with seventeen tits feeding new generations of laurel and lichen.

Sophomore year of high school could have marked the end of us. We were headed in different directions even then. There I was, going steady with Kip Houseman, basketball star, senior, son of a Mills College professor, and boring Kath out of her mind about our dates. I liked to think she made friends with Donna, the super-weirdo, in self-defense. Actually, in time, I came to love Donna, too, despite and because of her aggressively beat black wardrobe and her bad bongo music. What was Kath going to do? Kip wanted to double-date with his older friends. Kath was still too much of a tomboy for that. Even after school we were separated by my piano and flute lessons and Kath's baby-sitting. When I broke up with Kip, Kath was there for me, holding my hand through long evenings of weeping and railing. And the next year we became a fivesome with Donna's friends Paula and Nancy — going to movies and cruising the strip on Saturday nights. Sometimes I worried about losing Kath in that group of smart girls, but deep down I knew — rather believed — we would always be the best of friends.

As we ascended, I concentrated on the pressure in my lower back, imagining pleasurably loose muscles at day's end. I could feel my thighs stretch, even my sturdy calves. We should stop for water soon.

"You know, when I work this hard on a hike," Kath was saying, "I sometimes imagine my family's reaction. I mean, I think about my father greasy and twisted under a Honda at the shop. His mother cutting peat in Hamer. My mother's mother herding eight kids to the public baths in Montreal. And they're all staring at me wide-eyed, wondering what the hell I'm doing. Even my friends at work admire these 'strenuous' vacations. Maybe I make this trip out of some kind of genetic attraction to labor."

Puffing hard, I marveled at Kath's ability to talk and walk, at the rush of words. She had been like that as a girl, too, taciturn and monosyllabic for days and then *whoosh,* an outpouring of reactions, ideas.

"Or whether it's the opposite," she continued, oblivious to my awe, "an obstinate subversion of the family plan."

I stopped, exhausted, in a small clearing. "Water?" Unhooking the canteen from my woven black Camp Wildriver belt, I offered her a sip.

We drank water and gobbled trail mix. Then plodded into the clearing and up the last stretch of trail.

"Mono Pass. Elevation 10,604 feet." Near the base of the rusted sign was a gray metal box.

I lifted out the small, spiral pad listing the names of other people who had made it to the pass and read aloud the comments.

"Spectacular."

"Stunning."

"Saw two rattlers on the way up."

Kath raised her eyebrows. "No way."

Oh, that familiar sense of conviction. She had always believed truth to be some objective reality. Such a strong, clear relief from Mother and Sari when I was young, yet unnerving in her own way, for how could I achieve that unshakable confidence about what was real and what was simply imagined?

I continued reciting the entries.

"Tranquillity plus."

"Magnificent."

Words seemed too feeble to convey my response to this place. Although I admired these attempts at description, I just signed my name and the date, then I handed the pad to Kath.

"I always think of Amundsen when I come here." She grinned. "Ridiculous, given how tame the walk is. Maybe the pad makes me think of his notebooks. Look, it's almost filled from this month. Sometimes when I see all these names, I marvel at the huge number of Republicans in California."

"Come again?"

"I mean, how can you vote conservative after making that hike?"
I laughed.

"No, really. Sure, there are Republicans who don't get beyond their locked compound gates. But some of them do, and a place like this has to open up your mind, your heart. You know?"

"Oh, yes, yes." I was still grinning.

Below, a small, calm lake invited us. I wanted to take a shortcut down to the water, however Kath warned that the black shale was slippery.

"I remember eating lunch here three years ago." Kath was feeling expansive, walking with hands on her hips in a very Martha-like posture. "Finding the perfect spot by the lake, yet protected from the wind. I was munching happily and heard a rustle. A moment later there was another noise. Vole, I told myself. Marmot. The noise increased. Coyote? I started to lose confidence."

Hard to focus on the tricky trail and Kath's story. Behind us something *was* prowling in the bushes. I preferred to hear this sort of tale once I was tucked in at night — perhaps via telephone in Massachusetts. Still, you had to catch Kath when she was feeling forthcoming. And this seemed to be her day.

"Beside me, I noticed fresh bear scat. I packed up. Then I heard a stirring from behind. When I turned, I expected to be pissed off at the loud, drunk guys in lederhosen I'd passed on the trail. Instead, I saw a hunched, dark figure disappear over the rim of the hill."

I scanned Kath's face for a smile. But her jaw was set, serious, and her blue eyes were fixed in the past. The present creaking in the bushes could be wind. Or quail. On the other hand, Lou had warned me this was a prime year for bears.

"Let's move on a bit, before we stop for lunch," I suggested nonchalantly.

"Sure. Down here, past this little lake, you can see Mono Pass on a clear day."

Our day was no longer clear. The mutable mountain spirit had veiled the sun behind steely clouds and I'd begun to feel chilled. Not the place for a picnic.

"Last year," she said, "I remember it was this beautiful turquoise pool. Last year. Someday that's all Mono Lake will be — a memory — if the L.A. water moguls get their way."

"Yes." I nodded, dredging up history lessons about bloated Southern Californians drinking the state dry.

"Sorry you can't see it," Kath began, then interrupted herself. "Don't know why I'm apologizing. This is your state too. I mean, you were born here, you grew up here."

"Everything is so impermanent." I leaned on a rock, stretching my leg muscles. Kath didn't stretch before and after exercise. Did this stretching brand me as some kind of health club yuppie? "If we don't melt from the holes in the ozone layer, we could easily get tipped off by a random asteroid."

"And if that doesn't happen, the sun is scheduled to burn out in a few million years."

"Then what good will our music and theater and paintings and bibliographies be? The fact is, immortality will require a backup solar system."

"So why survive?" she asked.

"Seriously?"

"Why struggle to live — particularly with integrity — when life isn't only uncertain, it's doomed? That's the ultimate choice: survival. And for what?"

"I waver about the meaning of faith," I admitted. "Sanctuary of fools; power of heroes."

Kath pulled a face. "Well, this is pretty heavy conversation on an empty stomach." Gingerly, she picked her way over the shifting rocks to a giant granite slab. "Lunch on a boulder built for two?"

I made myself almost comfortable on the large rock, wistfully thinking back to our earnest talks in high school. I didn't realize how hungry I was until I began to eat. Somewhere down in that mist was the other side — the eastern flank of the Sierra, the end of California, the Nevada border, the beginning of the rest of the world. Noises returned: a mourning dove cooing. A chipmunk scratching up a tree. Cool wind mowed up the right side of the pass. In the distance, a thunderhead split loudly.

Before I could think better of it, I was saying, "I did miss you, you know."

Kath nodded and took another bite, looking as if she were puzzling how to swerve this conversation to a better course.

"So I left"— I was leaning forward now —"but we stayed in touch for the first *two* years. I came home for Christmas. And that first summer, we wrote."

Kath stared down toward Mono Lake.

"What the hell happened when I was in Edinburgh?" I paused, speaking to my half-eaten sandwich. "In our junior year?"

She was still staring through the haze at that damn, vanished lake.

"You not only stopped writing to me. You stopped everything. You dropped out of school."

Kath clenched her teeth, to keep from screaming, perhaps, to keep from crying.

Mercilessly, I persisted. "You dropped off the face of the bloody earth!"

She turned away.

"Did it . . ." I paused, softening my voice as if trying to get Taylor to say what had really happened on the playground that day. "Did it have anything to do with Tom?"

Kath shrugged, raising her shoulders in a long breath to hold back the tears.

"No, not so much to do with Tom." She spoke slowly. "Life just got very complicated."

"Come off it, Katherine Peterson. Tell me. I feel as if I've been banging on a bolted door for twenty-three years."

Tears. I pulled my arms around her alarmingly lean, tight body. Her shoulders shook with sobs. Eventually the story unfolded: pregnancy, months of uncertainty and panic, potions and procedures that almost killed her, an appalling time in the maternity ward, the impossible struggle to pay bills and stay in school. Finally dropping out. It all came tumbling forth in a voice colored by shame and anger, shaded with accusation.

"If I had known," I tried, "if I'd only known . . ."

"So what if you *had* known?" Kath interrupted. "What could you have done from 6,000 miles away?"

"I would have come home," I answered simply, shocked Kath wouldn't have known that. I held her tighter to me.

She repeated my words numbly. "You would have come home?"

"Of course, you needed help." Now *I* was angry. "What did you think — that I would have sent you a survey to fill out about emotional responses to pregnancy and abortion?"

"I don't know," she said. "I don't know what I thought."

My stomach clenched, angry at that past distance, fearful of this current intimacy, confined by the sweetish scent of Kath's overripe deodorant.

She continued to stare down toward invisible Mono Lake. "I don't know."

13

Kath

I DIDN'T WANT TO GO to Saddlebag Lake with Adele that afternoon. I wanted to hike straight down to the Valley. Alone. Maybe drive back to Oakland by myself. But we'd agreed to revisit old haunts. Adele had looked forward particularly to Saddlebag Lake. Get on with it, I scolded myself.

A sign on the top of the small brown store read BOAT RENTALS. LUNCH COUNTER. TACKLE. GROCERIES. Firewood was on sale near the door. Inside the small shop was quiet, the swivel counter stools vacant. No one was sitting in the big wooden armchairs or poking around the shelf of used books.

Other people were too smart to risk getting stranded on a wet afternoon in this remote area. Adele perused the fishing gear section. I studied the shadowy clouds, impressed by how fast mountain weather could change. Looking around for a map of the area, I spotted a sign — WORLD MAPS: 25 CENTS. Unfolding one, I found a quaint 1950s Mercator projection of a former world.

Adele bought cherry bubble gum. Did she chew bubble gum at Wellesley? I liked the image of an urbane college professor jawing her way across campus between classes. The snack counter sold instant cocoa from those semidisgusting packets. If we made it back alive, I promised myself, I would order cocoa.

Rough wind chopped across the enormous lake, and the motorboat skipper looked about twelve. His clear blue eyes smiled beneath wisps of blond hair. Considering child labor laws, he might be sixteen. Still, no one would investigate at this altitude. Did he understand the danger of crossing a big lake in a thunderstorm? What could we do? Excuse ourselves and phone Washington? Climb in, I thought, eyeing the fragile vessel.

Our fair-haired captain handed us each a life preserver.

"A good sign." Adele winked, donning hers immediately. Absently, she stroked the front of the iridescent orange vest with her long index finger.

The motor refused to start. A reprieve? I looked back at the store, lusting after fake chocolate. On the roof, tacked or stuck to the green trim, was a red foil wind sock in the shape of a heart. The glossy crimson kite pulsed against a bleak sky.

Once more the boy tried his accelerator. Eyes shut, Adele was breathing in the fresh mountain air.

According to my mini trail guide, Saddlebag Lake was large, scenic, great for fishing. But if a thunderstorm started, we should get off right away. Warily, I watched the gathering dark clouds. My father's brother Henrik was killed by lightning on the farm in Tjome. In a sudden downpour, he ran for cover, but too late. Henrik became an elaborate family legend: brilliant farmer, devastatingly handsome, the most charming of five brothers. One thing was certain — Henrik had been my father's closest friend, and his death was why Dad left Norway. As the legend was passed down, so was the fear. Irrational, I knew; after all, lightning rarely strikes twice in the same family, but I'd never been able to overcome my panic about storm-crossed lakes.

On the third attempt, our motor caught. It sounded like a consumptive cousin of Mrs. Castillo's lawn mower. Adele smiled faintly through thin, mauve lips.

Chugging across the water, I was terrified that we'd reunited after all these years simply to die together in a thunderstorm. I had had a premonition something dreadful would happen.

"My will, all my papers, are in the top left-hand drawer of the desk." I phoned Martha the morning I left.

"You go to the mountains every summer." She was puzzled, annoyed. "And you never talk like this."

"I'm trying to be responsible," I said.

"Drama queen." She'd laughed. And then, unable to suppress her concern, "Drive carefully."

Of course I would drive carefully. I suffered from such chronic con-
scientiousness that I'd never intentionally endanger my life. Yet there
were many times when I yearned for some natural force to take it from
me, to grant reprieve from all this pressure and guilt and sadness.

Just now Baffin's death weighed heavily. I knew I should tell Adele
about it, but I couldn't bear for her to find me sentimental. Better to
stay silent awhile, to keep the memory safe. Be grateful Baffin isn't suffering, I told myself. I coveted death as much as I feared dying. Too
much of a coward for suicide, I wanted to disappear suddenly, irrevocably. This lake could be the perfect exit.

At the end of our rather short and completely uneventful voyage, the
boat bumped against a tire-padded dock. To display my courage, I let
Adele disembark first. "See you at 5:30?" our captain inquired, his voice
loud above the putt-putt-puttering engine and much too deep for a
twelve-year-old.

"Sure." I waved casually. "5:30."

Cold. Breezy. The afternoon was a different country from this morning. Adele stretched her arms wide as she ran toward the trailhead.

Adele and I moved along the trail, separate in our thoughts. We'd
survive the morning's intimacy. Adele had always had a maddening
tendency to *find out*. I would never forget her questions about Martha's
sudden wedding. Why was she getting married in dreary *January?* No
bridesmaids? Didn't I want to be a bridesmaid? Did my parents like
Martha's boyfriend? How long had they known each other anyway?
"Pregnant," I said, finally, simply, and Adele's seventeen-year-old eyes
turned sage. The Wards sent Martha an extra deep Corning Ware
casserole dish.

Looking over my shoulder at somber Saddlebag Lake, I savored the
dark side of the country's beauty. The cool, moist air was refreshing after this morning's hot, dusty hike. After Monday's arid drive from the
airport I could feel my muscles relax in a sweet, welcoming way. I enjoyed hiking in damp weather — maybe from some primal Nordic
Bog thing. The trail was easy, not nearly as breathtaking as our route to
Mono Pass.

A coyote startled us. Standing in the path. Owning the ground.
Warning intruders with her stillness.

"Ooooh." Adele caught her breath.

"What's she doing out in the middle of the day?" I demanded in
alarm. A bad sign. For her. For us.

The bedraggled, blond animal looked pathetic, a middle-aged woman suffering from peroxide overdose.

"Molting," I observed, thinking how weird it would be to watch winter wools disintegrate from your body and find cottons emerging from beneath. Embarrassing. That's how the animal looked. Abased. Momentarily, she returned our gaze, defying contempt. In her own time, she stepped into the brush. Then disappeared. Gone. Like Baffin. Gone.

Both of us held back a second in silence and in respect.

I moved first. I knew Adele liked to walk in front, but if we didn't set a brisker pace, we'd never complete the loop before our boat returned. My lungs filled with fresh air. How good to stretch and move at my own speed. I kept an ear cocked for Adele, to gauge her progress on the path.

That summer after high school, Adele and I walked here in the lead, Paula and Donna between, Nancy in the rear. "Caboose," we named Nancy when she hiked with us, when she wasn't back at the tent, reading her magazines. She remained so much more vivid in my mind than Paula or Donna. Nancy was an expansive person — in her gestures and volume and appetites. In some ways, she held a mirror up to the group — one of those three-sided department store mirrors — capturing angles from each of us. I could see my own uncertainty in Nancy, and I envied the way she flaunted her ingenuousness, like a kitschy rhinestone necklace. She wouldn't let you forget her. Years after I tried to disappear, Nancy continued to send Christmas cards filled with news of her expanding family and details about Paula and Adele and rumors about Donna. Even Adele gave up, but Nancy continued to write, and my dutiful parents always forwarded the cards. Bless her intrusive little heart. I hoped Nancy was recovering now. Maybe she was propped up against a pink satin pillow, mending from surgery and getting a pedicure from one of her daughters.

Adele was talking, suddenly, as if meditating aloud. I missed the first part.

". . . We don't do enough hiking in Maine. We might as well be in Cambridge for all our exposure to nature. So we *do* walk down to the cove every day. In truth, though, our cabin is just a slightly uncomfortable house with a nice view and no TV, a place where we pretend to get away from it all, but where really we just get together with each other."

"That's OK, isn't it?" I asked, not knowing where she was going with this, yet understanding she needed to talk.

"Oh, I love Lou and the boys. I'm grateful for them after growing up in my own crazy home, but sometimes I worry that I love the idea of a harmonious family more than I love these particular, well-behaved people."

What was I going to say to that? Unlike Adele, I wasn't interested in getting to the bottom of things. The bottom of things was inevitably mucky and often dangerous. I checked my watch. I could see the hut from here. We were making decent time. We'd be back to the dock at least fifteen minutes early. Adele didn't seem to want a response, returning to silent musing. Sunlight shifted in and out of clouds, shadowing, then brightening, the trail.

When we were young, visiting Adele's house was like entering a movie set. Everything was new and polished and poised to be appreciated. The unusable translucent china in the antique cabinet. The unwalk-on-able Persian carpet in front of the bricked-up fireplace. Even their dog was stronger on appearance than authenticity: an Afghan named Max, who betrayed his pedigree by stealing milk cartons and impregnating neighbor dogs. I never understood why Dr. and Mrs. Ward tolerated Max's libido. I couldn't fathom the Wards at all. It wasn't until Mrs. Ward's third or fourth trip to Providence Hospital that Adele explained how her mother "suffered from depression." She was as ashamed of the pill popping as I was amazed by it. Imagine taking pills to shut out life. Well, I was young. The pills explained the tight smile on Mrs. Ward's impeccably made-up face. Mrs. Ward, who was always sheathed in the latest merino outfit — I knew from my job at Roos Atkins how expensive these weaves were — who looked like a top-of-the-line mannequin, was a kind of drug addict. How sad. How hard on Adele. My father thought it was extravagant when the Wards took their trip to Europe in 1963. But I didn't judge them. I knew Mrs. Ward needed some serious cheering up. So did her daughters.

Plink, plink. Reverie disturbed, I noticed measles on my faded blue sleeves. Adele must be appalled by my wardrobe — the same work shirts and jeans I wore in college. Meanwhile, she'd been sporting a different outfit each day of our trip. These wet splotches took a few seconds to register. By then my face was soaked. Adele was calling behind me, "Kath," and pointing to the hut.

"Right," I shouted back into the sudden wind. *Sheets* of rain poured between us.

Standing in the doorway, I watched Adele plugging up the hill. She was in decent shape, moving with speed, grace, and hardly any evident exertion, enjoying herself. I grinned when my old friend rushed through the doorframe.

Adele moved too far into the hut — to a place where the roof was memory — and now she felt the soaking rain she hadn't noticed on her high-speed race to the shelter.

"Oh, my." She gulped, plopping beside me on the bench and panting for breath. Gradually she took in the windowsill, the remains of the fireplace.

"What do you imagine?" she asked. "Two men? Tins of beans and fish from Saddlebag Lake and an occasional rabbit? Would they've eaten squirrels and marmots? Did something eat them?" She scooted closer to me.

"We seem to be doing a tour of miners' huts." I shrugged self-consciously. I hated when I chatted mindlessly to cover my nervousness; still my thin voice persevered. "First Gaylor Lakes and now this."

Lightning splashed. Too close. The frame of the ancient hut shivered and our room was filled with light, as if Nancy'd arrived with her flash camera to take a last photo of Adele and me. My heart raced. Ridiculous to be afraid of a little thunder and lightning, I told myself. Still, the silver aureole shimmered around us, threatening, haunting, caressing.

"That was kind of scary." Adele wiggled tension from her shoulders.

"Yeah, I guess," I answered, ever forthcoming.

She changed the topic. "Do you think they were mining for silver here, too?" This really mattered to her.

"Think so." I admired the delicacy of Adele's face as her dark hair straggled wet around shiny cheekbones. Usually that voluminous mane distracted from everything in her face except the eyes.

Her teeth chattered.

"Here." I produced my yellow poncho. "Use this to dry your hair a bit."

"But it'll get all wet."

"It's a poncho." I laughed, strangely giddy. "Waterproof."

Adele grinned, accepting the offer.

Her wide, toothy smile brought two dimples to each cheek and slanted those deep brown eyes in an almost Asian way. Adele was the most beautiful woman I'd ever known.

"I wonder how the Indians and miners got along." She sat straighter, looking around uneasily.

I leaned back. "The government removed the Indians by the time the miners arrived."

"Something strange about this place." She frowned.

Adele's discomfort was contagious. I stood, stretched, then walked to the windowsill, watching clumps of gray cloud chase each other across the sky. Rain beat down on the trail outside. The world smelled damp and fecund. I recognized a small, happy feeling, a remotely familiar mix of well-being and excitement.

Adele was shivering.

I wandered back to the bench. "Imagine the isolation, the self-sufficiency of the miners. I mean, I don't have much sympathy for their prospecting, but it must've been a tough life."

"No, think of the adventure." She smiled.

I noticed her silver palm tree earrings swayed as she laughed, and I fought an urge to stroke the shimmering branches.

"I wish I didn't have to go back." Her eyes brightened.

My knee was almost touching hers.

"I wish I'd kept going with those botanical prints. Can you imagine living here all year long?"

"If *you* did." It slipped out. "*I'd* give it a try." My knee had found hers now.

Adele was blushing.

Our legs together, I was greedy for more. My body grew hungry and tight simultaneously.

She didn't move.

Should I shift my foot, my thigh, to touch hers? Emotions, sensations, thoughts collided. How much did Adele understand me? — had she had lesbian lovers? — what did she feel for me? I hadn't learned much about her in the last three days: the cabin in Maine; the Massachusetts autumn. We were still hiding a lot from each other. Time passed.

Please slide closer. Please. She sat still. A movement artist playing statue. My excitement curdled into embarrassed sadness.

I heard a clearing in my throat. Beginning of the end. I couldn't tolerate the suspense any longer. The humiliation. Coward, I cursed myself.

These words came from my mouth, "But wouldn't you miss your family?" My chest filled with air and loneliness.

*   *   *

Adele straightened, moving half an inch away. She kept her tone play-ful. "Oh, they could visit us."

Surrounded by damp, quiet urgency, we sat alone together ten thou-sand feet above the Pacific Ocean.

"Rain's stopped," I said. Stupidly. Irrevocably.

"How can you tell?" Adele protested.

"Listen." I touched her shoulder.

Adele inhaled sharply, standing and approaching the door un-steadily. She stuck her hand over the threshold and tried brightly, "All clear."

I consulted my watch. Just enough time to make it. "Let's go."

During the next half hour of abrupt, crisp sunlight, we both hiked with renewed energy. Faces flushed, eyes bright, we competed with each other, naming flowers.

"Indian paintbrush," said Adele. The tiny red bloom had always been her favorite.

"Yellow monkey flowers." I was proud of that one.

"Mauve fairy lanterns."

"Blue lupine. Oh, and look at the purple ones." I recalled the prox-imity of her hip and the warmth of her knee.

The meadow on either side of the trail was filled with yellow sun. Grass glistened from the remains of the suddenly departed rain.

I needed to forget what had happened in the hut just now. I'd always been in love with Adele. It had never been appropriate — still wasn't — to let these feelings develop. By the time we were ready for serious ro-mance, Adele had found Lou and I had found Tom. Then came our "separation," as she so dramatically put it. Of course I'd never forgot-ten Adele, but I'd found a shelf for her in the back of my mind. Maybe the problem was that I wasn't large enough to be anyone's partner. I was so afraid of getting lost inside Anita, of being swallowed up the way I'd been with Tom. Once I called Anita "Adele" in the middle of the night.

"Oh, no," Adele cried.

I heard her voice registering the thunder. Then I felt the drops.

Great walls of rain descended between us. No hut here. No friendly forest. Maybe *this* was the curse of the coyote.

I dug in my daypack for the poncho. Adele pulled out a neat, square, plastic package, gave it a shake and became an identical twin.

"Good thing we're not going to the same Upper East Side dinner party." She smiled goofily.

I shook my head. The storm looked bad. No use standing here waiting for miracles. "Let's hustle."

Adele nodded, singing, "We're off to see the Wizard . . ."

The wackiness in her voice brought back Sari's offbeat sense of humor. But there had been much more of a twist to Sari's behavior. Adele was always the sane one, the together one. More together than anyone else I knew.

"Lord, it's wet," Adele declared, slushing along the path. "I haven't really liked rain since I was six or seven. I always hated the way early spring in the Bay Area turned to showers in late February or March. Those frail almond and plum blossoms were sacrificed to the relentless water."

It amazed me how Adele could talk in complete paragraphs, cogent, not a word out of place. Even when she was agitated. Maybe especially when she was agitated.

Thunder banged off to the left. I clenched my teeth. The steely sky was punctured by a silver exclamation point.

Adele didn't seem to notice. "Then I came to hate the October and November storms of Massachusetts, the way they extinguished burning leaves, dashing their skeletons to the sidewalk. The weather got wetter and wetter, everything growing hopelessly gloomy until Christmas."

Her voice was high, excited, maybe still colored by our experience in the cabin. *Our* experience?

Ghostly lightning cracked high, loud above us. Tom once wrote that sniper fire reminded him of lightning, and for months afterward I believed he really wouldn't make it home from Vietnam.

Now I worried about the boat crossing in this weather. And even if *we* reached the shore in time, there might be no water taxi. There wasn't any shelter, even at the dock. How would we survive the night outside?

"We've got to keep our spirits up," Adele said, reading my mind. "How about another song?"

"What song?" I whined.

"What difference does it make?" Adele shot back.

"I don't know. Singing would make me feel like Heidi."

"So we'll lay off the Swiss Alpine lyrics. How about 'If I Had a Hammer.'"

"You're so sixties," I teased.

"There are worse epithets. How about it?"

Silence.

I surrendered. "'If I had hammer . . .'"

"Too low. 'If I had a . . .'"

We got through five Weavers' numbers before Adele tired of the contrived optimism. Our feet were soaked.

"Look, my poncho," she said. "Tiny puncture, but enough to sink me."

"We're almost there," I lied.

"We could be struck by lightning crossing the lake," she joked.

I'd never told her about Henrik.

"Then," she rattled on brightly, "we'd become a legend for the next edition of the guidebook. I've always wanted to be a legend, but this isn't quite what I had in mind."

It was hard to tell if she was losing her grip. We were both exhausted. Mono Pass and Saddlebag Lake in one day; what had I been thinking of? The distances, the altitude, the lightning, the intimacy: I couldn't remember being this worn out.

"Do you think the boat will be too full to hold us?"

"Oh, no," I reassured her. Shit, how did I know?

She was humming something. "Michael, row the boat ashore." Surely she was trying to be funny.

This wasn't my fault. Adele had insisted on pressing farther today, not me. Still, I was a more experienced hiker and knew this was a crackpot idea. I should have said so. Jesus, I should have said no to the whole damn trip. I should be back in Oakland looking for a job, finding a rest home for my father. Doing a hundred things more realistic, more urgent, than loping across the Sierra in search of a missing friendship.

Adele was laughing loudly, wildly.

Alarmed, I'd never considered she might have a breakdown in the mountains. I turned cautiously.

She waved. "Look, look."

I saw the battered red water taxi spluttering toward us.

A much older guy piloted the boat. Our previous captain must have sent his father or grandfather. Breathing a silent prayer of thanks, I realized I didn't want to die after all. At least I didn't want Adele to die. What a ninny I was. Of course they wouldn't let us languish on the other side of the lake. They knew we were here. We had registered, "two for Peterson" with the woman who sold bubble gum and maps. People didn't die from overexposure this close to civilization. I thought sadly about the Indians, the miners. Not in the 1990s anyway.

The skipper held out a mottled hand to help us onto the dipping, swaying boat. I let Adele go first. Wind hissed up from the north like breath through the gaping teeth of a giant spirit. I wondered if the coyote was tucked somewhere safe and dry. Adele embarked unsurely, then balanced on the small seat. She stared at the sopping orange life preserver before pulling it over her wet head. Water dripped down her neck. I could see some of it trickling all the way down her back. We would be fine.

14

Adele

EXHAUSTED, we drove back to the Meadows.

"Looks like the storm left here hours ago." Kath nodded at the early evening light.

I sighed. What hubris to run up Mono Pass, then around Saddlebag Lake in one day. Off and on during the last couple of days, I had become a young body lusting after this glorious, lost land of mine. Then physical realities rudely reminded me how long I'd neglected these muscles. My compassionate communion with the country came not so much from an unconsciousness of age as from a concerted attempt to deny it, to recalibrate my deal with fate. Kath, of course, was less exhausted, actually quite alert and relaxed as she drove the car toward the small park grocery store.

"Why don't you make your call while I shop?" she suggested.

"OK, if you're sure."

"Absolutely. It'll save time."

She sounded tired. I wanted to ask if she were worn out, if she had been frightened, what she was feeling in the crumbling hut, if she were angry with me. It was so hard to reach Kath, even after all this time. Perhaps especially after all this time.

I slipped into the phone booth, closing the glass door against the racket of cars crunching across the gravel lot. Now the call seemed a stupid idea. When we were groping our way through that second thundershower, all I could think of was the boys, being back with them, hearing their voices. I was singing those songs for them. On that flimsy little boat, the impulse to phone about my adventure was overwhelming. But now, well, it seemed silly, a little self-indulgent. After all, I had told Lou I would call every five days. Only three had passed, even if it felt like a year.

Kath would be finished shopping by the time our number rang through. Do it. Irritated by my own dithering, I picked up the receiver and then memory failed. No, of course, the area code was 617. The phone was ringing. Seven o'clock here. Ringing. Ten o'clock there. Late to be out with two kids. Ringing. Oh, damn, I remembered, the baseball game. Wednesday night, Lou had tickets to the doubleheader. He was a good father. And I was a demented mother who ran off to the woods, risking my life. It was all very well for Kath to tempt fate, she didn't have children.

Subdued now, the fatigue seeping into my overused muscles, I waited in the car.

"Tofu surprise," she said brightly and tossed the paper bag in the backseat.

"Pardon?" God, I was tired, and wished I were back in my Cambridge bed with a glass of wine watching some mindless TV program.

"Tofu sautéed with broccoli, carrot, zucchini, tomato, onion."

"Sounds great." I forced enthusiasm into my voice. I had no right to be angry with Kath. Saddlebag Lake had been my fault. Leaving the family was my responsibility.

Our campground was especially noisy tonight, which made me even more enthusiastic about the next day's backpacking. Still, this busyness provided a welcome, necessary distance from Kath.

Chopping the vegetables while she started the charcoal fire, I savored the simple pleasure of the sharp knife against the succulent red tomatoes and yellow zucchini. The onions were last so I could enjoy the smells of other vegetables, and they were surprisingly mild; my eyes didn't tear or sting.

Had the pressure of her knee been accidental? Had she felt aroused? I recalled the pleasures of our girlhood closeness: talking about periods, braiding and unbraiding each other's hair, shopping for sexy nylon underwear in the days before we knew cotton protected against yeast infections. Sharing secret crushes on boys. Racing each other on our bikes. Boldly skinny-dipping together that wonderful Sierra summer. Today's intimacy had been sensual, not sexual. Just because we enjoyed a closeness didn't mean we wanted to go to bed together. I was reading too much into the afternoon. I wish I hadn't moved my knee. Kath was right that I was the one drawing boundaries.

"Smells good." She stood over me and breathed in the aroma of chopped vegetables.

My shoulders automatically tensed. She moved back to tend the fire pit.

"I'll warm a little oil in the pan," she said instructively, as if we were filming a Sierra Chef TV show. "Then we'll do the onions and carrots."

"Sounds good." I was starving. "Maybe I'll set the table while you do that, and make sure we have enough water."

On the way back from the spigot, I thought of how I had been attracted to Anna Maria in grad school and then to Marilyn in my consciousness-raising group. I had never pursued either of these relationships beyond friendship. *Beyond* friendship? Was sex beyond friendship? Anyway, I believed I resisted out of fidelity to Lou. Perhaps it was more out of loyalty to Kath. Then, again, I didn't think I was cut out for the whole lesbian subculture, with their moralistic power games and intellectual constructs about patriarchal sex. The truth was, these women scared me and, on and off over the years, I had worried that Kath had become one of them.

She stared pensively into her caldron. I filled the kettle from our cumbersome water jug. Of course it was ridiculous that three days had passed without us having talked about Kath's love life. Ridiculous that I wasn't certain about her sexuality. Maybe not so ridiculous if you knew Kath. God, I resented being the one to bring things up — about *her* life as well as my own. Why was it always me?

Kath served the steaming vegetables. She sprinkled hers with soy sauce. However I wanted to enjoy the individual color and flavor of the tomatoes, broccoli, carrots and melt-in-your-mouth tofu. All around us friends and families and solo hikers were cooking and eating their dinners. The prevalent odor was grilled meat, and my mouth watered at the thought of a rare hamburger.

We each inhaled the tofu surprise, neither of us saying a word during the first serving. With the second plate, the tension between us grew. Her strong, suntanned hand gripped the fork, her eyes refused to meet mine. Evening was dimming into night.

For some reason, I asked, "When we were growing up, were you aware of the class differences?" Women's Studies 1A. I bit my lip. What a formal old fart I had become. I wanted, needed to talk, yet there were some things I couldn't talk about. Class was easier than sex, wasn't it? My question was genuine — however stuffily asked. I'd been brooding about it over the years as I became more and more aware of economic realities.

Kath peered at me across the table. "You mean, the differences among our high school friends?"

"No. Between you and me."

She looked at her plate, clearly eager to return to silent, uncomplicated eating. Differences: this was a supremely stupid way to break through them.

"How do you mean?" she said finally.

"Well, were you angry that my family had more, I don't know, more *things?*"

"No."

For some reason, I refused to tolerate another Norse impasse. "Did you *notice?*"

"Well, I guess that I noticed more how different my family was. You know, Nancy's father was a teacher. Paula's parents were librarians. Donna's dad was a lawyer. I don't know, when I was growing up, I didn't think much about *class.* It wasn't an American concept. I guess, if anything, I thought my family was weird."

"Weird?"

"Different. Failed or something." Her voice grew exasperated.

"Failed?"

"Oh, I don't know." She stood abruptly to serve the remaining food. "In terms of schooling. And interests. I mean, you all knew you *hated* classical music and I didn't even know what it *was.* The material differences, no, that wasn't what bothered me. Although you're right, they were real enough. It was more like my parents and my sister, Martha, were, I don't know, kind of hicks."

"But you were the hippest of us all."

"I had to be."

"I see, to become one of us."

"No, you don't see. To *not* be one of *them.* It was all about betrayal."

"What was about betrayal?" I was too tired to concentrate on this conversation. Why had I started it?

"Studying so earnestly. Going to college."

"Going to college!" I exclaimed before remembering how Kath equated Radcliffe with desertion. "Sweet Lord, what were you supposed to do, have a career at Capwell's in the department next to your mother's?"

"What's wrong with a job at Capwell's?" She waved her fork.

"Nothing, but —"

"And I thought you liked my mother, regarded her as this uncomplicated maternal figure . . ."

"That's not fair," I shot back.

God, this was one of those white-knuckle moments, as when Lou would ask me if I were getting my period and I was ashamed by how quickly the question came to my own mind about Kath. Of course I knew her irritation had nothing to do with menstruation and all to do with my thickness. There was something about her I did not understand, had never understood.

I listened to *Nick of Time* beating from the campsite of the aging hipsters two tents away. Normally I would have been enraged at such intrusion, but right now I was glad to have some spunky Bonnie Raitt.

Betrayal. It seemed like a strong word for going to college. But if Kath thought she had betrayed her family by leaving for Davis, it made some kind of sense that she felt I had betrayed her, our friendship, the West, at Radcliffe. A little far-fetched, but I had always had more options than Kath. Part of me needed to believe that we met and continued living on a level playing field.

Finally, I managed, "Speaking of fairness, look at all Nancy has been through." Unfair, even dishonorable to imply her suffering erased the differences between Kath and me. Still, I couldn't bear this sudden estrangement.

"Yes." Kath sighed.

It was fully night now. We would need the lantern if we were going to sit out here. The music sounded louder in the deep darkness. I didn't like the second side of the tape as much.

"We should call her when we get back from Vogelsang," she said. "I promised to wait until a couple of days after the operation."

"She was so cheerful when I talked with her," I said uneasily.

"Yeah, she's an inspiration." Kath's voice was low, almost inaudible.

"More like Our Lady of Fatima."

"What?"

"You know, the Portuguese Virgin with the secret the Pope wasn't supposed to reveal for five or six decades?"

"Hey, that's not your religion" — she balked — "it's mine."

I laughed. "I did a paper once on background iconography in portraits of Our Lady of Fatima."

"You're not serious."

"I am."

"Anyway, 'virginal' isn't a concept I associate with Nancy. And how does she remind you of Our Lady of Fatima?"

"The secret." I shrugged.

"Cancer, you mean."

I nodded in the darkness.

"Yeah" — she paused — "it's terrible, but I think of her as some kind of scapegoat, like in 'The Lottery.' One in eight. That means there are seven of us who won't get it, you know?"

"I know."

Again we fell to silence. The hipsters had retired Bonnie Raitt. The entire campground was quieter. Whispered voices. Metal food lockers neatly clanking shut against the night-scavenging bears. One by one lanterns switched off.

"Let me do the dishes," I offered.

"We'll do them together."

"No, you cooked dinner. Get ready for bed, and I'll join you as soon as this is done."

"OK," she said, reluctant, exhausted.

By the time I returned from the bathroom with clean dishes, Kath had crawled into our purple cocoon. Quietly, I stored the dishes in her car. Night noises filled the campground with squeaks and whistles. Perhaps I was the only human stirring.

Sitting at the end of the picnic table, I inspected the sky, fruitlessly, for traces of moon. I felt the same kind of fatigue and doubt and resignation I often felt in Cambridge after a dinner party. Sitting with a glass of wine in the living room alone — for Lou collapsed the minute the door was shut on the last guest — wondering how it had all worked out, whether people had had a good time, whether I had had a good time, whether it had been worth the labor; tired, satisfied, discouraged, curious. Strange, artificial analogy to a quiet evening in the fragrant High Country, but it was the only analogy I had. Acknowledging this made me sad about the life Lou and I had created, our fortunate, successful marriage. And yet it seemed too late for any other life, too late to start over, too late even to revive my friendship with Kath. The night was dark, cold and the moon still elusive. Time for bed: what was I waiting for? I was waiting for safety, for time to pass, for the forbidding emptiness to fill.

15

Adele

Thursday Morning / Glen Aulin

"FITS FINE," I said to Kath, modeling my new blue polysomething backpack in the parking lot near Tuolumne Meadows.

She grinned. "Very chic. But don't overdo the weight. You really don't need to carry the tent poles."

I looked her straight in the eye. "I can take my share. Who do you think you are—Arnold Schwarzenegger?"

"Who?" Kath was laughing.

"The Terminator."

"Oh, yeah," she said vaguely.

"Another element of popular culture my boys introduced me to. I thought you worked with kids."

She looked blank. "Different kids, I guess."

"He's married to Maria Shriver." I stood in a pool of early sun, enjoying the warmth reaching gently, deeply, down to the bones.

Kath adjusted her straps. "Maria who?"

"Shriver. As in Sargent Shriver. The 'young' Kennedy generation."

"Oh." Kath frowned. "The Terminator. The Cuban Missile Crisis. It all fits together."

We made our way, slowly at first, across Tuolumne Meadows, which had sprung back to life from yesterday's storm. We climbed past bubbling Soda Springs and ancient Parsons Lodge into a cool pine forest. It was going to be a long day. Kath looked weary. Yesterday had been a good workout for today's backpacking expedition, but it had also been harrowing. Not that Kath had been worried; so contained all the way through. Everything had been fine yesterday, and it would be fine to-day.

Butterflies winked in yellow-green grass; the dirt smelled of sun. From a nearby stable, we could hear whinnying, snorting horses. The air here was rich with manure. I liked seeing mule shit and horseshit on the trail; it gave me confidence. If a four-footed animal carrying a ner-vous tourist or bulky supplies for the High Sierra Camps could nego-tiate these trails, I probably could too.

Wordlessly we proceeded through the elegant lodgepole forest. I forced myself to keep quiet because in the last few days, I had come to see my gregariousness as a crutch to cope with stress and distract from anxiety. Chat, chat, chat. Think, think, think. Don't let the silence in. During the years that separated me from Kath's quiet friendship, I had learned the sedative power of words, cushioning myself with internal-external monologues positioned safely in past or future. Now each time conversation moved to the front of my brain, I respected Kath's solitude, saving topics for lunch, conserving breath for the six-mile journey under unwieldy backpacks.

I should have admitted to Kath that I had never backpacked—even if I had read up on it before I came. She would soon find out. However, I felt oddly confident. The altitude was more comfortable, more nat-ural now, and I was bursting with energy, as if this were our first, rather than fourth, day in the mountains. Perhaps I had finally adjusted to the time difference, the dry air. Perhaps I was far enough from my work and my family. I felt like I could go on forever in these mountains.

Up ahead, the trail was crossed by high, rushing rapids. Discreetly, Kath moved ahead of me; she stepped on one rock, then the next, and soon landed at the far side of the creek. She made it look easy.

You can do it, I told myself, it's all attitude. I understood this. After the first false step, my toe darkened by water, I jerked back to the bank, regaining balance before trying again. It would be hard enough to do this without a big pack. Confidence, woman, confidence: don't think about falling. Concentrate on naming the countries of Africa: Tanza-nia, Kenya, Uganda, Burundi, Rwanda, Namibia, Zimbabwe, Zambia. I knew I was nervous if I had named that many and was only halfway across. Nigeria, Senegal. I walked faster and thought more slowly. Al-geria. Tunisia. Morocco. By the time I reached safety, my mind was hovering between Libya and Egypt.

Blowing the residual panic lightly through my lips, I exclaimed, "Nothing to it."

Kath smiled, but not wide enough to betray either concern or congratulation. Stepping aside, she let me continue in the lead.

Soon we emerged from shade. Together, our shoulders nearly touching, we admired a glistening, almost chartreuse, meadow and beyond that, the snowy mountain range starkly carved against a cloudless sky. The river sound, near and far, was becoming a second companion on this trip. Our path through the meadow was short, direct, leading to a wide table shelf of white granite.

"We're back on the moon." I held out my hands.

Kath watched curiously. Then, "Yes, yes, the sheer granite's dazzling. We'll come out on another great slab after this next woods."

"Do you go to Glen Aulin every summer?" I asked, taken aback by an envious twinge. Envy of Kath's access to this terrain. But it *had* been my decision to leave California, as she continually reminded me.

"No." Kath uncapped the canteen, offering water. "Usually just to Tuolumne Falls down here. I have lunch and walk back to the Meadows. It's a nice hike."

I returned the canteen, surprised by my thirst, but knowing we should save water for the rest of the journey.

As we entered a woods, two old women, erect under their bulging canvas backpacks, stepped aside for us to pass. Their bodies were tanned, fit, their faces friendly, almost indulgent as we moved onto the trail.

Yes, I loved it here. California offered some unique spark, some challenge, perhaps it had to do with living on the edge, perhaps with one's gratitude for this natural glory. I had always felt enlarged by California wilderness. In Massachusetts, I had tried to bury these memories by engaging in stereotypes of California as a failed paradise where actors, surfers, computer programmers and pensioners fermented together in orange groves. In Massachusetts, I was always conscious that "this was where it had all started," more or less, and the stratified social system kept me aware of who got there before me. In California, it was just the opposite. I felt welcome, whole, decompartmentalized. In the last few days, I'd even recovered some small political optimism. I hoped the boys inherited my tie to the West.

A while later, Kath warned, "It's a little tricky up here. But the walk from the other side to Tuolumne Falls is only fifteen or twenty minutes."

"Then you're promising lunch, right?"

"Yeah, that's what I'm promising. Gnocchi in pesto sauce. Insalata mista."

"Profiteroles for dessert?"

"If that's what Madam wants."

"Yes. Profiteroles every day."

We picked our way up and around the large, rocky outcropping. Sweat poured down my temples, between my breasts; I felt as if I were releasing part of myself to this land, wriggling from a ripe cocoon.

"You OK?" she called.

"Fine," I said, glad I didn't have to elaborate, for it was hard to talk and balance at the same time.

I heard hooves. Around the bend came a team of pack mules being led by a sunburned young man in a sombrero. Automatically, Kath and I stood aside. The lean rider waved to us. I waved back, then said to Kath, "Do you get the same idea I do — that they're lowering the age for adulthood? We were never that young, right?"

"Wrong. That and younger." Kath laughed. "Remember Nancy's green mascara?"

"The ideal backcountry makeup!"

Only a little farther to the top, so I pushed myself. Higher. Higher. A bit higher. Then, as Kath promised — a stunning panorama.

"Glorious," I declared, pulling out my camera.

"No, hold on." Kath touched my hand. For a second longer than necessary.

I waited expectantly, then found myself blushing.

Kath smiled, tapping the black leather camera case three times. "Wait till you walk further this way."

As we diverged from the trail — out to a ledge overlooking the valley — the view became even more grand: Mount Conness, Ragged Peak. From below we could hear the roar of falls. Sloughing off our packs, we stretched our muscles, then stood for several minutes, absorbing the landscape. I winked at Kath, clicking my camera once to the north, once to the east and once to catch Kath against the mountains to the south. I kept the lens on my old friend with the familiar, playful eyes.

"Another hiker hiding behind the lens."

We swiveled toward the disembodied voice.

"Why not relax and enjoy the moment?"

He stood up from behind the large boulder. "No need to preserve the vista, at least until you experience it."

Angrily, Kath whispered, "Who is this asshole?" loud enough for him to hear.

I shot back, "I don't take advice from strangers."

He leaned forward—tall, thin, blond—with confident angularity under a gloppy, beige straw hat. Then strangely formal: "I'm Sandy Archer." He walked toward us, extending his hand.

"Adele Ward-Jones," I said, annoyed for being caught in the reflex of appalling courtesy. To gain some distance, I added, "This is Kath Peterson."

We stood facing each other in a reluctant triangle.

"Actually I was just kidding about the picture." He laughed nervously. "I'm a photographer myself." He patted the telephoto lens on the Nikormat hanging from his neck.

"Let's go, Adele." Kath turned.

"No, wait," he exclaimed, wholly embarrassed now. "I was going to offer to take your picture together. I mean, I always find that I have pictures of my friend and my friend has pictures of me, but there are none of us together."

"Adele," Kath strained.

"I mean, I'm sorry," he continued. "Hope my joke didn't offend. I don't know what came over me. Guess I needed some human contact after so many days alone on the trail."

"It's fine," I said, pained by my instinct to smooth things over. "Don't worry."

"How about that picture?" he asked hopefully.

"Sure." I tugged Kath closer, my arm tucked around a disgruntled scarecrow. "How about right here?"

As soon as the shutter snapped, Kath slipped on her backpack and stepped toward the trail. I knew she wondered how I could be so accommodating to this oaf who had appropriated the view she had been waiting all morning to show me.

Sandy was still talking. "What kind of camera?"

"Pentax," I said, caught between Ms. Indignation and Miss Congeniality. This automatic amiability was deeply pathological.

Now he was inspecting my daylight filter.

"At home I use a Nikon with a wide-angle lens," I explained absently. "But it was too heavy to carry on this trip." Perhaps I was going on about the camera so Kath would know I wasn't completely a technical moron.

Hands across her chest, Kath let out a long, impatient sigh. She was poised with one foot on the trail.

"Sorry to interrupt your hike," Sandy was saying to Kath. "Hope the rest of it goes without weirdos lurking behind boulders."

I laughed.

Kath nodded. "Bye then."

He waved, silently watching us walk away.

Fifty yards along, I threw up my hands. "Men! They just open the door and step over your life."

"Yeah."

"But he was a sweet sort of guy."

"Concentrate on the trail," Kath called over her shoulder. "It gets steep going down."

At this, I did, momentarily, lose my footing, but caught myself on a tree trunk before spilling to the ground.

Kath watched me right myself. "You OK?"

I got up, embarrassed. "Fine."

We continued toward the falls in silence. I found myself thinking about what made people return home. Was it biological instinct? Was there some sense of self you could only locate through the colors and aromas of childhood? Was there a particular discovery to be made within the passage of familiar seasons? But home could also mean entrapment, suffocation.

At Tuolumne Falls, the sign said, GLEN AULIN 1.7 MILES. The day's journey was more than half finished.

Although Kath had reminded me this morning about the beauty of these falls, I was startled by the gleaming rapids. We stood on the bridge for a long time listening to water roar and crash beneath us as the Tuolumne spread south down to the fertile valleys, out to the ocean.

"Down this way." Kath tugged my sleeve.

"Oh, over there, I remember." I started off the trail to the right, where the river was backed by long, wide, smooth slabs.

We arranged ourselves on the white shoulders, our backpacks against a large tree, our naked feet tingling in the cold, foaming water.

"Heaven," I declared and lay all the way back, hands over my head.

Kath moaned contentedly, then chugged the contents of the canteen. We were only an hour or so from camp and could afford to be easy with water.

"So how are you doing with the pack?" she asked, deliberately casual.

"Fine." I kneaded a muscle in my right shoulder. "In another two or three weeks, I'll be auditioning for one of those pumping iron movies."

"Seriously"— Kath touched my knee lightly —"are you OK?"

"Fine. Fine." I stared at the falls, suddenly, disproportionately irritated. "I wish you wouldn't keep behaving as if I'm an invalid." I heard the sharpness in my voice. Agitation surged unaccountably, unstoppably.

"Sorry," Kath began.

"From the beginning you've been saying things like 'Are we going too fast? Is this too heavy? Maybe we shouldn't walk all the way to the lake?' Do I look that fragile? Am I slowing you down?" I was almost shouting.

"No." She leaned forward. "I didn't —"

"What is it," I interrupted, removing my scarf and mopping the cold, dusty sweat from my cheeks, "that makes you macha woman? Because you live in California? Because you come up here every summer?"

Kath waited attentively.

I watched her watching me and felt stupid, self-indulgent, in my wounded ego.

"Oh, I'm sorry!" I shook my head. "Perhaps it's too much togetherness. I get this way with Lou sometimes, too, when he's doing nothing but being perfectly considerate."

I could tell Kath didn't appreciate the comparison to Lou. She stared down at tumbling, bubbling water. I had no idea what had taken hold of me.

"Perhaps I need to be quiet awhile," I tried again. "Do you mind if we eat lunch sans conversation?"

"No," Kath agreed with alacrity. "Two sandwiches. Hold the talking."

I laughed.

"We'll just put the fanny pack here and make our lunch."

She sliced half the tomato and spread avocado on the bread. Neatly, she cut two pieces of cheese and lay them side by side, then handed me the sandwich.

"I'm sorry." I was mortified, confused, penitent, still aggravated. "It's just that you remind me of Sari sometimes." My need to talk was as strong as the hunger for solitude a minute ago.

"Sari?" Kath asked softly.

"She was always solicitous like this, of me, of Mother, Father, everyone, actually, everyone except herself . . ." My eyes filled.

"You know, we've never really talked about Sari," Kath offered slowly. "I was camping in Canada when it happened. When you came back for the funeral. I didn't hear about it for months."

I looked away. Through the blur of my tears, white rocks on the opposite shore looked like grazing sheep. I didn't know why I had brought up Sari, what was wrong with me today.

"You must still miss her," Kath said.

"You could have sent a card." The old rage swelled.

"I didn't have your address back East."

"That would have been easy enough to locate." I studied her bewildered face. "You could have sent it in care of my parents. Or called them for the address."

"Yes." Kath hung her head. "I could have done that. Should have done that. I know. I'm sorry." She sat up straight and tried to meet my glance. "After all this time is it still appropriate to apologize?" Her voice choked.

Cry, Kath, I wanted to say. I had needed her at the funeral to weep and rage with me.

"Or maybe it's too late?"

"Oh, no." I shook my head, impressed by how deeply, after fifteen years, I still needed to hear her regret. I gulped.

"I am sorry. Have been sorry for a long while. Will you forgive me?"

Seas of time washed between us.

Overwhelmed with sadness, gratitude, relief, I realized this late apology was not too late. I spoke rapidly to stay composed. "A lot of people don't know how to handle death. You were young, we both were, and Sari five years younger."

"Do you feel like telling me about it? About what you know?"

"I don't know what I know. She was only twenty-four. So talented. And brave to be doing her music, getting her performance degree while locked up in the same house with our bitter, disappointed mother."

I stared at the falls, wanting to lie beneath them, to sleep, to forget this conversation I had stupidly started.

"Oh, I can't blame Mother. Perhaps it was my fault. If I hadn't gone East, safe from my parents' reach — almost safe — Sari would have got a lot less pressure from them."

"Pressure?" Kath had finished her sandwich and frowned at my untouched lunch.

"To be the perfect daughter — artistic, well-married, affluent, beautiful. Sari fell for all of it, perhaps in part to compensate for my failure."

"Your failure!"

"Well, I gave up art, didn't I? — as you, yourself, warned me not to do. And I moved to the other side of the country. Hard to be your parents' handmaiden from that distance. Everything fell to Sari."

Kath touched the sandwich to my lips. I took it and had a bite. Imagined the blood sugar rushing to my head. That was better.

"Sari had choices, too," she said. "She could have gone, well, with your family's money, she could have gone to *Japan*."

I set aside my lunch. "It wasn't the money. How can I expect you to get it when after years of therapy I still don't understand, really?"

"Years of therapy." Kath took a moment to absorb this.

It was hard to believe I was rattling on amid all this natural glory; I tried to reenter it, watching the sun dappling the lichen on the rock next to me, the clouds edging eastward in the midafternoon sky.

"But Sari was making up for my defection. It wasn't just Mother who wanted the family close by. Father had moved to start his tribe. Here I was returning back East — and to Massachusetts — where his great-grandfather had immigrated from Glasgow, shoveling horseshit in the street. Granted my dad's family prospered, but Father thought he outwitted the ghosts by moving to California. And I took his lineage backward."

"It's a little convoluted." Kath squinted. "I'm beginning to see why your mom took all those pills."

I nodded. "Millions of middle-class women did in the 1950s, of course. She was just another housewife with the perfect home whose 'nervous condition' interfered with her appreciation of nirvana."

I knew I sounded like an academic twit, but it helped me to put Mother's story into a larger frame. Somehow, that way, it seemed as if there might be solutions, somehow I didn't feel so guilty.

Kath looked regretfully at my sandwich.

"That's how Sari died, you know."

Kath shook her head.

"Pills."

"Your mother's pills?"

"Her own, her own doctor, her own generation, her own condition. The same pills."

"Oh, Adele!" Kath took my hand and in doing so knocked the sandwich off my pack onto the ground.

I closed my eyes and waited, anticipating the promise of days ahead of us as I hadn't in years. That was enough. For the first time in two decades I could say, "for now," because I had begun to believe that there might be some future, that there was a chance of catching up, of comprehending, of forgiving. I released Kath's hand, leaned against the warm rock and allowed tears to stream across my face.

When I sat up, I found Kath brushing off the sandwich. "You've gotta eat. As Mom would say, you have to eat a pound of dirt before you die."

"I always liked your mom. Your whole family. They were so sane."

Kath put a hand on my shoulder and gave me the sandwich.

I took a deep breath, then bit into the bread. "Hmmmm, yes, I am hungry. That was a long walk."

Kath laughed. "Country air!"

"See, practical. I know your family wasn't easy, Kath, but they were, I don't know, better endowed with common sense."

I watched her body tighten. "Better endowed, maybe, but I'm not sure how much they used it outside of issuing homey wisdom about dirt and fresh air."

I had finished the sandwich and was peeling an orange. "I don't know. Things in your family don't seem as complicated."

Her jaw clenched. "That's because you were related to the people in your family and not to those in mine."

I didn't believe this, but knew I had wandered into dangerous country. "You have a point there."

Kath sucked on the orange and nodded.

Newly infused with energy, I felt eager to get to Glen Aulin, to set up our tent so we might take a late afternoon hike to Waterwheel Falls. But Kath clearly needed to unfold. It was pleasant here, stretched out by the water with my oldest friend in the world. I had known — and loved — Kath longer than any living person except Father. Kath had been in my life since I was ten, nine years longer than Lou, nine formative years. She had been a sister — clearly closer than Sari because we were the same age. No, it was more than that. We had always gotten along, had always shared interests: gossiping about boys, Red Cross volunteering, debates over international politics, hikes in the wilderness. We had always been able to talk about anything, yet we were different enough. Tall and short. Dark and light. One from a crazy, upper-middle-class family; one from a much more down-to-earth home. Mutt and Jeff, Kath's mother used to say in that charming Québecois accent. I had once thought I would marry Kath if she had been a man. And it was Kath's presence I had missed most at my wedding. Ah, that was all over; it was decades ago. Right now I was simply thankful that we had *this* time together. And grateful that our other friends had not come to the Sierra.

Dangling my feet in the water again, I enjoyed the sharp, almost painful cold. I closed my eyes and fantasized spending the whole afternoon here.

Then I heard myself asking as suddenly as sun escapes past clouds, boldly reopening the day, "So how is your romantic life these days?" There, I was initiating the discussion again. As much as I resented this inevitability, my longing to be close and honest with Kath — as well as my now almost unbearable curiosity — won out.

"Quiet," she said.

I waited.

She watched the water rush in front of us.

"There isn't anyone?" I tried again.

"Nope."

"Since when?"

"Oh, a while. I broke off with someone two summers ago."

"What was her — his — name?"

"Anita." She looked at me directly.

"Nice name." I smiled.

"Nice woman."

"So do you feel like telling me about her?"

"Do I have a choice?" She laughed.

"Yes."

I heard about their years together in Oakland, their vacations, Anita's desire to have a baby, Kath's reluctance, Anita's new lover, the breakup, Kath's loneliness. I felt sad for Kath and even for Anita, yet relieved in some unsettling way.

Silence took over as we soaked up the sun.

The noise was slight, perhaps it was a motion rather than a noise. Whatever occurred was enough to startle me. I looked down to find a snake — a harmless garter snake, I knew the moment I saw it — winding up the rocks, and my sudden gasp was involuntary.

"What is it?" Kath sat up.

"Nothing," I said. "Only a benign reptilian visitor."

The snake coiled against a nearby rock. Benign or not, it gave me the creeps.

"Guess we're intruding." I shrugged.

"Maybe we should go," Kath said. "Especially if we want to walk to Waterwheel Falls. I don't know why I'm feeling so lazy today."

Downhill from Tuolumne Falls to Glen Aulin. I hated this kind of steep descent. I much preferred uphill, where you could feel your lungs filling and your muscles stretching. Here progress required an almost mincing gait in which the whole body poised against catastrophe, tense and therefore likely to be damaged with an abrupt slide or twist, particularly in the sleek aftermath of yesterday's storm. The unfamiliar weight of the pack added extra stress to my back, my balance. Step by careful step, the trail had been intricately constructed from white rocks with the skill of Renaissance stonemasons. I imagined working here in the rain, covered with mud, dying of chill. The sight of fresh mule shit reminded me the pack animals had made it safely.

We wouldn't be going to Glen Aulin if Nancy had come on the trip. She probably wouldn't have made it to Tuolumne Falls with her weight. And Paula would be talking nonstop along the trails. Our energetic friend was always trying something new — jazz piano these days. She inevitably had something to say. And to ask. She wasn't like some vapid, boring talkers, like Lou's mother, for instance. Paula simply liked to engage; she was constantly on. In that way, she was the opposite of Kath. I knew Kath was fond of Paula, however, I wondered if it had been Paula's patter that had sent Kath on those solitary hikes years ago. I remembered being annoyed at the ease with which Kath simply left us — left me with the rest of them. All the same, I had admired her independence. Donna was obviously being driven bonkers by Nancy's obsession with fashion magazines and makeup. I smiled, remembering Nancy's clothing monologues. What *had* happened to Donna? Kath had said something oblique about her being into street drugs, but we had gotten sidetracked. Was she homeless? Had she gotten clean and sober and taken off for India? Walnut Creek? I would ask more about Donna tonight. And maybe we would also talk more about Anita.

The Glen Aulin High Sierra Camp nested at the foot of White Cascade, which thundered into a shallow caldron.

I could hear Kath's steady tread behind me. 2:00 P.M. We had made it in decent time, so we would be able to get to Waterwheel Falls and back by dark.

"Let's have a drink here," Kath said, nodding to a small building.

It was covered in the same white canvas as the tent cabins. I was glad we were backpacking. Imagine spending fifty dollars a night to sleep dormitory style with strangers.

I followed her, realizing how thirsty I was.

"They usually have lemonade in the office here — for people in the executive suites."

"Sounds good."

We unloaded our backpacks before entering.

"Feel like I'm removing a vital organ," I said, releasing the weighty pack. "Like when I had the boys. You get used to being pregnant, to the extra space you take up in the world."

"Yes, but what a relief." Kath stretched her arms behind her back.

"Hmmm, relief, yes, mostly that."

Six or seven hikers were hanging out at the desk, waiting to buy candy bars or get directions or stabilize their pulses. Kath didn't pay much attention to them.

"Lemonade?" She steered me to the large, beige plastic dispenser.

"Yes, please."

Parched, I consumed two cups. Then I refilled my cup and drank more slowly, staring outside at the cascade.

"Maybe we could spend the afternoon in camp reading . . . or talking," Kath said.

"Well, that's one idea."

Behind us, someone was talking about Waterwheel Falls. I turned and could tell from his broad shoulders and his straw hat that this was the man from the vista. Sandy.

Kath pulled a face. "Guess we should go, if we want to find a decent campsite."

"Oh, do you mind waiting a sec?" I asked. "I'm dying for a chocolate bar."

Kath stared at the back of the guy's hat. Clearly she was itching to go. "I guess not," she answered neutrally.

I started to demur. After all, there were those five pounds I needed to lose before the conference.

"I think I'll wait for you outside," she said curtly. "To make sure the packs are safe."

16

Kath

Thursday and Friday / Glen Aulin

I WATCHED THEM WALK into the brilliant sunshine. He was a head taller than Adele and much more tanned, but they seemed to fit together like siblings reunited in a country distant from their birthplace.

"Sandy says he'll show us the best campsites." Adele was talking rapidly. "And he has directions to Waterwheel Falls."

I nodded. It would've sounded pompous to remind Adele, to tell Sandy, how often I had camped here. Pulling on my backpack, I adjusted the shoulder straps, disappointed at how sore I felt. What was wrong? Why did Adele have so much more energy?

Sandy smiled at me, congenial, distracted. He turned to Adele, who was comfortably slipping on her heavy pack. "The ground is great this time of year. Lots of pine needles, soft. Dry though. Lovely smell."

I knew we were in trouble. Only your sensitive, liberated guys said "lovely."

"You come to the Sierra often?" Adele asked.

I listened, impressed by her capacity for socializing. Of course she didn't care about this guy, she was just being polite. She'd ask a few more questions, that's what you did with men — ask them questions until they were on a roll and then they floated along a stream of self-revelation.

"How many days are you here?"

Had I been boring Adele? Maybe I hadn't been forthcoming enough. Of course I needed her to understand my life. I was a dyke. But I didn't want to have to tell her. Partially out of some weird Norwegian reserve. Partially because I resented how my life had to be explained while hers could just be assumed.

"Crazy really." He was chatting in what I guessed was a Michigan accent. Maybe Illinois — one of those squeezed together midwestern voices. "Being an environmental lobbyist keeps me in a small office with one window forty-nine weeks a year. Or on airplanes between here — I mean San Francisco — and D.C. It's not what I expected. I should have joined the Park Service, where I'd actually get some fresh air."

Adele laughed.

I dropped back several steps to inspect a stand of mountain hemlock. Maybe I was being defensive, resisting Adele's curiosity about my life. Mom claimed it was like pulling teeth to get me to talk. But what more would Adele want to know about work, about Anita? Should I tell Adele this generous, vivacious woman had it all figured out — successful practice, good relationship with her parents, admirable community activism? The baby was the next stage in a model life. Should I tell her I wound up feeling part of Anita's whole, well-loved, yes, but also scared of suffocation? Already with Adele I was totally exposed, my conversational reserves depleted. Maybe Adele did need to talk with someone more stimulating.

"This way," he was saying. "I'm afraid I took the best site — next to the river here." He pointed to his neat navy blue nylon pup tent and backpack hung expertly out of bear range. The ground around his campsite was swept so clean I wondered if he did cocaine.

"But there's a nice spot back there." He indicated a clearing ten feet away.

"And my favorite place is down the trail a bit," I found myself adding. "I usually stop there. Shall we, Adele?" I hated my proprietary tone. And I loathed people who were more camperly than thou.

"Oh, right," he said, gingerly. Disappointed but still cheerful, he persisted, "Maybe I'll see you as I walk down to the Falls."

"Right." Adele smiled. She observed carefully.

Setting up the tent calmed me. Conjuring the tent. Nothing one minute. Then, presto: a small lavender dome with room for two sleeping bags and most of the contents of our backpacks.

"Now for the bear rope," I said. "Help me hoist it up between these two trees."

After securing the rope, we practiced raising our packs into the tree-tops, then watched them sway next to each other like two old women battling their way along a windy sidewalk.

Sitting on a log, Adele surveyed our campsite. "Cozy. Home sweet home." She was so much happier today. Buoyant.

"How about a little trail mix?" I offered, sitting down beside her on the small log, our hips almost touching.

"You know, you have such a California complexion," she said.

"What do you mean?"

"Well, vivid. No matter how much time most Easterners spend out-side, we never achieve the vitality of California complexions. My color is always so temporary."

We heard the sound at the same time. Slosh. Slosh. Like a slow bear with a nasal condition.

Sandy Archer appeared before us, canteen slopping against his thigh, his straw hat askew to the left. Around his neck was a different camera.

"Thought this is where you'd settle. Pretty good site. A close second to the one by the river."

I felt like he'd walked into my bedroom.

Adele stood, opening her hands hospitably. "We don't have much to offer. Some trail mix?"

I stared at her, realizing this welcome was something she couldn't help: a dinner party hostess syndrome inherited from her mother. Still, I was pissed. With her. With him. With the way the two of them be-haved together.

"No thanks." Sandy smiled. "I can't hang out if I'm going to Water-wheel Falls and back before dinner. Just stopped by to show off my other camera. Sounds like the one you have at home." He peeled a leather case from the sleek black instrument.

"Pretty nifty collection for someone who complains about people 'hiding behind the lens.'" I walked over to the tree and tightened the bear rope.

"Well." He grinned. "I brought it by way of apology. I mean, to show I was kidding back there. I'm sorry. As a ploy for meeting you, it *was* fairly obnoxious."

I checked the other side of the rope.

Adele stood next to him now, holding the camera. "Pretty good range," she said approvingly.

As the two talked photography, I wondered why I was surprised by Adele's expertise about lenses. She'd always been good at art.

Sandy noticed my silence. "Better get going."

I managed a pleasant farewell nod.

"And I was wondering if you — both — would like to join me." He was still talking. "I'd say it's four hours max there and back. You'd return in plenty of time for supper."

Adele turned to me.

I did my best to look noncommittal. Surely between the two of us we'd come up with a line to brush him off.

We both spoke at once.

"It's been a long day."

"That sounds great."

We turned to each other and asked in unison, "What do you think?"

I shrugged.

Adele stared at the ground. "Well, maybe you're right. We kind of overdid it yesterday."

Sandy shuffled anxiously. "No problem. A friendly, casual invitation."

"No." I took a deep breath. I was being petty. Adele had been raving about that Smithsonian article on Waterwheel Falls since I picked her up at the airport. "We can each do what we want here. I'm wiped out, so I'd rather stay in camp and read. But, Adele, you're all revved up, you should go."

Adele stood very still.

I continued, "You and Sandy. You'll make it back by 6:30. In plenty of time for dinner."

Adele betrayed a small smile, pleasure at being released or amusement at my tone, I don't know. Jesus, I felt I was sending her off on a first date, giving them a curfew.

Clearly she was torn. "Maybe I should rest too."

Sandy shifted his feet and fingered the braided rainbow camera strap.

I squatted to collect a couple of sticks for kindling. "Listen, you want to see the Falls. Go ahead. I'll make supper."

"No," Adele protested. "It's my turn."

"Don't worry," I said agreeably. My pride insisted she go now. I wasn't possessive. Wasn't threatened by this gangly guy. I could use some quiet time for myself.

"No, really," she said.

"You can do the dishes."

"All right, if you're sure you'll feel secure here without me to protect you from the bears."

"I'll dial 911 if there's any trouble." I bent down for a few more sticks. Sandy laughed.

Adele waved.

They were off.

I putzed around the campsite, gathering wood, moving a small boulder in front of a log for a makeshift table. The perfect place to spend a solitary afternoon reading, thinking, writing in my journal. But I was overcome with fatigue. Yes, maybe this was why I'd lost my cool about Sandy. Really he was harmless enough. It was nice to have a photo of Adele and me on top of the dome. He was just a little lonely and didn't know how to meet people. I was completely overreacting. What was wrong? I'd lost the meditative attitude with which I usually traveled these mountains. I always appreciated quiet afternoons like this after a long hike, to reflect on the day, the year.

Each year the land reminded me about balance. Here, for a short time, I felt part of nature and refrained from judging myself in that panicky, urban way. I remembered that our task is to continue. To contribute to each other's continuing. To thrive insofar as we don't obstruct others' continuing. Each year walking through the wilderness I also felt, in a small way, like the land was a companion. And I couldn't get enough of it.

But today I wasn't only too tired to go to the Falls, I couldn't stay awake to think, to read. I found myself surrendering, crawling into the tent and settling in for a nap. Closing my eyes, I breathed in and out the fragrant aroma of mint. Behind my lids, I saw red fir, white fir. . . . I thought of Baffin, missing her, musing that Adele hadn't ever met my long-lived cat. . . . Jeffrey pine, lodgepole pine, sugar pine . . .

The thunder woke me. Bolting upright, I lifted a tent flap. Clear blue sky. Thunder, it had sounded like thunder. A roar of some kind. Fear ringed my solar plexus. Adele. I'd been having a dream about her. There were bells. She was wearing a red scarf. Some dream. I felt so wiped out. Couldn't reassemble the pieces. Did I have the flu? I shook my head, sat up and leaned back on my elbows.

Pulling out my journal, I thought it was about time to write something. After a minute or two, I was surprised by what poured forth.

"For some reason, Tom's been hovering this week, maybe because being with Adele reminds me I have a past, a past that isn't closed the way I pretend. Even when Tom is old or dead (drinking, living on the streets, he could be dead now), he'll always be part of me and I don't understand how people who have been one can separate. Can completely detach themselves in time and space. Does this capacity mean humans really are completely autonomous? Does it mean we develop shells around ourselves between relationships? And can those shells be melted or cracked?"

I was writing down what I couldn't tell Adele yet. Funny, over the years, I often imagined my journal as a letter to Adele. The Adele of my memory, my fantasy. A different Adele from the one I was hiking with? Definitely a less demanding one. An Adele I felt safer with.

"For sure, Tom had grown some kind of shell — more a thin, oozing scab — by the time he came back from Vietnam. The first few weeks, his mood swings were mostly up — at our bodies being inside and beside one another again, at long, fragrant walks in Tilden Park, at hanging out with his old buddies from the garage. But as the months passed, a wild, raging dissatisfaction developed with what he called his 'dead-end job,' the 'asshole president' and me. He slept fitfully, waking with screams and night sweats. Only a six-pack would put him in a good mood. And by the time he smashed his hand at work, I *had* expected some kind of accident. We did our best, joking that the disability money was a scholarship. A chance, maybe, to go back to school. But he spent it on booze. His nerves got thinner and thinner. I tried to find him help. Then I was the enemy and he started knocking me around. It wasn't his fault. He couldn't control himself. I could be rigid, overly rational, demanding. I wondered how much was my fault. So I stayed. Maybe I was afraid that if I lost him, if I left him the way Adele had left me, there'd never be anyone to love again.

"I stayed with him until he brought home the gun. And then I had to get out. San Francisco wasn't far — but it was far enough and big enough if you laid low. Within twelve months I had metamorphosed from college coed to fugitive. For years I lived in terror he would find me. Eventually rumors drifted back about him being in one detox center, then another, then on the street. I knew he had become harmless, except to himself. And that he had started a gradual, if relentless, disintegration.

"I guess I'm a real fool to admit it's only been in the last couple of years that I noticed Dad's violence to Mom. OK, it was less dramatic than Tom's. Maybe in its slow way of building, more terrifying. But obviously Dad didn't start knocking Mom around just since he became senile. Now he was less self-conscious about his temper. And Mom had fewer resources to hide the bruises and bumps and broken bones. Sad, humiliating to think of her as a battery victim. My own mother.

"Then, does this mean I was programmed, like Anita'd say, to grow up and mate with a brute? Was it genes? Environment? Bad luck? There had to be some route out. I was grateful I left before Tom did more harm to himself or to me. Before we had kids. The silence, the covert escape, had been crucial then. As crucial as avoiding silence now.

"These were the lessons I learned while Adele was getting her Ph.D. I didn't know how to talk to her about them. Didn't know if she'd want to talk with me. Time passed. When I got back from Canada and heard of Sari's death, I was a coward and let yet more time pass. Time was my drug. If it didn't erase problems, at least it dimmed anxiety. Now, on this trip, I've realized time is a temporary sedative. Adele's still on my mind, in my bloodstream, so's Tom. You can't be cured of the people in your heart. They simply relocate to another part of your body, only to appear under stimulus. Tom will always be with me. This awareness brings comfort, shame, terror, resignation and a painful, old desire for intimacy."

Enough. I stuffed the journal under my sleeping bag, still feeling oddly drugged. Maybe Adele was right about chocolate. Maybe I needed a serious jolt of sugar. Or a shower. I would splurge and buy myself a shower at the Glen Aulin High Sierra Camp. I never did this kind of thing when I was alone. Was Adele turning me soft? Civilizing me? Well, a shower would make me smell fresher, lift my mood and altogether make me a better companion.

I could hear the laughter, Adele's high-pitched peal. His deeper rumble. I concentrated on the chili — although there wasn't much to think about, just stirring and making sure the fire didn't get too hot.

"Mmmm. Smells good."

His voice. I didn't look up. The shower hadn't improved my mood enough.

"Perfect timing." Adele's light, ringing voice. "You really do have supper on the table!"

I rose, overcome with happiness at seeing Adele. "It does smell pretty good."

Sandy played nervously with his lens cap, as if waiting to be dismissed. What was with this guy?

"Good hike?" I asked with grudging civility. "Perfect weather for it." There, that was better. He was just a guy, a harmless guy.

"Great!" declared Adele. "I'll tell you about it over dinner. But first, I need to conjure myself a ladies' room."

She darted into the brush, leaving us to make small talk.

"Well," he said finally, "I better get back and start my meal."

"Sorry we've only got enough for two," I said, not exactly lying because I had dumped the excess chili in case Adele was overcome with a severe case of hospitality. So much for the remorse about my coldness. I hoped I'd kept enough food for Adele and me. I was famished now, after the shower, with the sunset approaching.

"No problem." Sandy beamed at my cordial overture, filling me with guilt.

Adele appeared, listening with a smile.

"I brought too much grub myself and don't want to carry it down, at least on my back." He massaged his trim stomach. Then that shy, eager look in his eyes. "In fact, I have extra hot chocolate if you two care to come over for a nightcap."

I could feel Adele waiting. I smiled back in a way I hope reminded her how I put a hex on one of her high school boyfriends and how the poor guy fractured his elbow before the homecoming game.

"Thanks," Adele said, "but I'm pretty wiped out. Think I'll crash early. I don't usually get this much exercise in one day."

"So be it." He tipped his hat. "*Bon appétit.*" After a few steps, he turned to Adele. "Sweet dreams."

"Vice versa," she called.

I kept busy stirring the chili. The damn stuff had started to stick while we were chatting.

Adele watched Sandy tramp out of sight.

"Brrr." She shook her shoulders. "Guess I'm catching the evening chill. We've been walking so fast, so as not to be late for the feast, that I didn't even notice." She ducked inside the tent for her sweatshirt.

"Hey." Her most lighthearted voice. "Dinner smells terrific. Remember I'm doing tomorrow night."

"Yeah." I nodded, pulling out the plates.

Adele placed her arm over my tight shoulder. "You doing OK?"

"Fine." I felt myself soften. I stood there letting Adele hold on to me, stiffening against my own desire for closeness, telling myself that it would be all right, that by the end of the week we would find comfortable proximity. "How was the hike?"

Stepping apart, I inhaled the spicy scent of beans. Adele closed her eyes to savor the smell and blew on her first hot spoonful.

"I prefer Le Conte Falls to Waterwheel Falls, myself," I said. "Less spectacular, but I don't know, prettier somehow."

"More discreet," murmured Adele. "I know what you mean."

"But Waterwheel *is* steep, exciting," I halfway conceded, "particularly in the early season."

"That's what Sandy said." Adele took another tentative bite of the rich chili.

"You liked him?" I attempted lightheartedness.

"Sure, he was a real kick. He knew all the trees by name."

"I guess that's what 'ecologists' do."

"You say *ecologist* as if you're saying *proctologist*." She laughed.

I smirked.

"But the strangest coincidence."

"Oh, yeah?" I was gobbling the chili while it still steamed. I should have used more pepper, but Adele seemed to like it.

"Yes, he went to grad school at Yale. At the same time Lou did. We even had a couple of mutual friends: Morton Carter, who's doing environmental law in New York and who used to give the greatest charades parties with his roommates —"

"I was never very good at charades," I said.

"And Marjorie Rogers — this funny woman in linguistics. And, oh, yeah, Pokie Eagelson, who quit poli sci and became a lobbyist in Washington. You know, I thought Sandy looked familiar. We decided we must have met each other."

"That hat of his — it looks like it's left over from charades." I knew I should try to control the hostility.

"What?"

"Oh, nothing."

We fell silent.

I couldn't resist. "Doesn't sound like you had much time to enjoy the scenery."

"What do you mean?" Adele held her voice even.

"I mean with both of you singing 'Boola Boola' all the way to Waterwheel Falls and back."

"Boola Boola!" Adele chuckled. "How do you know that?"

"I'm not illiterate, you know. I mean, a lot of people went to Yale, even the president." I was annoyed about losing my cool. Adele looked hurt now. I stared at the remains of the fainthearted chili.

She held back the tears in her eyes and ate every last bean.

Remorseful and angry, I finished the meal in silence.

Morning was cold, but dry. Normally I would have suggested we stop at the High Sierra Camp for coffee, but I didn't want to run into old Ivy League. I felt too ashamed of yesterday's jealousy.

We packed quickly, efficiently. I concentrated on the familiar routine.

Once we had loaded the packs, I reached out to her. "Good sleep?"

"Like a log." Adele sounded cheerful. Forgiving. Mature.

I let her take the lead as we set off. Ascending for a good distance now. Up the stone steps toward Tuolumne Falls. I told myself to grow up. So what if Adele had a nice walk to Waterwheel Falls? So what if she enjoyed swapping Yale stories with him? The simple explanation was that I felt envious of part of Adele's life I didn't share. And whose fault was it that I didn't finish college. That I couldn't get up the nerve to go back now?

"Reminds me of climbing the pyramids in Mexico," Adele said.

"Oh, yeah?"

"Yeah, Lou is such a masochist, he made us climb all the way to the top of Teotihuacán."

"That's near Mexico City, isn't it?"

"Yes. Have you been?"

"No, but I've been hoping to get to Chichén Itzá someday. And Uxmal."

"The Yucatán?" Adele asked, breathless, but reluctant to let down her side of the conversation.

"Yeah. Someday."

I would apologize to Adele at lunch. My jealousy of Sandy was childish. I really didn't know what had gotten into me.

Tuolumne Falls looked even more refreshing today after our long climb. Maybe the two of us could talk here. Reflexively, we both headed over the bridge, for the spot where we had eaten lunch yesterday. The temperature had gained twenty degrees since morning. I pulled off my sweatshirt and lay down on the warm granite slab with my eyes closed, listening to water cascading over the rocks.

Adele sat with her knees against her chest, inhaling the fresh California air. "You know, it's interesting how often joy is poised against sadness . . ." She trailed off.

A couple of minutes later she continued pensively. "How my pleasure at being here is balanced on my plan to leave. To leave the Sierra in three days and to leave the state in eight days. Still, I am appreciating the time here, this sky, these scents, these noises. Yes, I am here. Now. With you."

I could feel my cheeks burn and was glad Adele was staring out at the water. I closed my eyes, soaking up the sun.

Abruptly, she began to dig into the pack for lunch.

"Hey, let me help with that." I blinked widely and pulled myself up to my elbows.

"No way," as my sons would say. "You concocted the chili last night."

"Concocted?" I blushed deeply. "You know, after we went to bed I remembered that episode at Cafe Luisa years ago. How you couldn't take the chili peppers." Anita would say my recipe was passive aggressive. But honestly, I'd just forgotten.

Adele grinned. "Let's say my stomach has become less provincial over the years."

I patted her shoulder. "Listen, there's something I want to say —"

"No, first, I need to apologize."

"— to apologize." I said at the same time.

We broke into giggles.

I recovered first. "No, I was petty about your hike. After all, I was too tired to go to Waterwheel Falls. Why shouldn't you have gone?"

"No," she said, still laughing. "*Mea culpa.* I broke feminist law number one. Don't let a man stand between you and your sister."

I shrugged to hide my gratification and stared out at the bridge, built in two segments to allow a tree to grow in the middle. Beneath the wooden slats water splurted, gurgled and roared into the cascading river.

"I mean, we're having a fine time on our own. I should've spent the afternoon reading. I shouldn't have left you alone in camp."

"I was absolutely fine." Surprised that I was still irritated, I tried to keep my voice neutral. "Perfectly safe."

"Of course you were safe. It's a question of camaraderie, of honoring our time together."

I stared at the rapids again, eyes stinging.

"Anyway"— Adele handed me lunch —"he won't be part of our scene anymore. He was headed out to May Lake this morning. Opposite direction."

"From the looks of his campsite, he cleared out early."

Adele said nothing.

"You like him, don't you?" I asked.

She nibbled a stray bit of cheese.

I took a sharp breath. "At least *he* seemed smitten with you."

"Yeah." Adele reddened. "It's hard to admit, but I *was* flattered. You know, he's bright, successful"— she paused —"a mature man you could talk ideas with and not just careers."

"Troubles with Lou?"

"No, not troubles exactly. I mean, we don't fight. He loves me. He's a good, attentive father . . ." She looked away.

"Is there something else?" I asked gently.

"Oh, well, he did have an affair a year ago. But I don't think that will happen again. Given the example of my own father, of course, you never know. But Lou is terrified of — almost phobic about — AIDS. So I believe he's faithful — in the sense that he doesn't have a lover."

"But in another sense?"

"Well, yes, you know how in some cultures the middle-aged man's mistress moves into the domestic scene? Well, I feel that's happened."

"A mistress?" I wasn't following. Or had Adele gone off the deep end?

"Well, his academic reputation has become like a mistress. Something that's seamlessly accommodated in the marriage. I swear he has an almost sexual rush when he's invited to give a paper or contribute an article. He gets up at 7:00 on Saturday morning and goes to his desk. I haven't had to take my diaphragm out of the box for months."

"That sounds tough." What else could I say?

"And the truth is, I have a mistress hovering around the house too."

"Pardon?" My heart pumped rapidly.

"I was offered a job," she began with hesitation.

I nodded for her to continue.

"At Berkeley." She watched me closely. "And, it's, well, very tempting."

"I'm sure every relationship goes through changes," I heard myself saying. How did I know this? All I could think of was having Adele back home.

Her eyes were quizzical.

"I mean, what are you thinking about doing?"

"Doing?" Adele threw her head back. "Most people, well, many people, would die to be in my position: healthy kids, stable husband — yes, I know I overdo the gratitude sometimes, but he is stable — secure job, career satisfaction."

"That sounds like a sociological profile, not a personal appraisal. Isn't the point life satisfaction?"

"Who has that — really?"

"The question is — do you?"

"Oh, I don't know. I wish I hadn't met that silly Sandy. I mean, all these niggling discontents don't add up to much worth worrying about. He made me feel that I was a little, I don't know, a little . . ."

"Lonely?"

Adele nodded tightly, sucking in her lips.

I scooted closer and put my arms around her. She sniffed, inhaled deeply, began to sob.

"Lonely," she managed. "Ridiculous when I have so many people in my life, when I'm so lucky."

I held my friend until she quieted down.

The walk back to Tuolumne was much easier than yesterday's hike. The afternoon was drier, our packs lighter. My body relaxed. Maybe I was *finally* acclimating to the mountains. It was fun to share this place again.

I wished I knew how to advise Adele about Lou. But it was hard to sound objective, let alone *be* objective, since Lou and I had never gotten along. I'd tried to like him all those years ago but didn't have the strength of character to carry it off. You were supposed to be happy when your best friend found "Mr. Right." And he was, by most standards, a great catch — smart, nice looking, decent sense of humor. But there was, well, something lacking — in the kindness category for instance. Nancy and I had gossiped for an hour after the engagement party. He was a crashing bore.

Old Lou had everything figured out. He had transcended the values of his southern aristocrat parents: "Of course we have to progress from the position of someone like my father, who would say . . ." However, he was simply the next predictable generation of semienlightened gentleman. Nancy and I had known, under our nervous snickers, that we were losing Adele to this man and his well-ordered life on the other coast. I think we knew this long before Adele did. Why? Perhaps because Adele had always been the most idealistic of us — believing that all her options remained alive. She regarded life as a string of possibilities while I faced it as a series of consecutive sentences.

To be candid, I'd never forgive Lou for stealing my dearest friend. Rather, for holding the door open to her. Surely I had to admit that Adele had left willingly. What gave me any claim on her? Maybe, in fact, she was trying to escape me. Maybe my intensity had driven Adele away. For years I let myself twist this particular knife in my gut. But clearly Adele's leaving had to do with something larger and deeper.

Our afternoon ascent to the Meadows was gradual, easy, a pleasurable tug on the muscles. Soon we'd come up Curry Stables Trail. I could smell the sweet horseshit from here. Adele didn't seem to be having trouble balancing her way across the creeks this afternoon. And I had found my mountain legs — yesterday's fatigue vanished — once more at home in the High Country.

17

Adele

Friday / Tuolumne Meadows

BLUE SKY. Bright blue. Olive green shrubs. Gray outcroppings crunching down to white slabs. Beached dolphins. Bleached dolphins. I felt so light, suspended in well-being. Kath also seemed to be finding the walk easier today. High Country summer was joyous wakefulness and the rest of the year just hibernation. Perhaps, I thought, I should give up my vainglorious intellectuality and look for a job in the Sierra waiting on tables. Simon and Taylor would be a lot healthier here than cooped up in Cambridge. I could get an early shift doing breakfasts and lunches at some café and have every afternoon to climb mountains with the boys after school.

Kath paused on the trail, handing me the open water bottle.

Greedily I drank. "Thanks." I rested my hand on her forearm.

She took a long breath, then drew away slightly. "I think we should indulge tonight and have dinner at the lodge. We could get showers first. It's been a long couple of days. We deserve a treat. And we could call Nancy from the lodge phone."

I concealed my disappointment. Perhaps Kath was more tired. But I'd been looking forward to cooking my mushroom-veggie stroganoff for her tonight. It had always been a hit with Lou and the boys and was easy enough to make over a campfire. I could get all the ingredients at the park store. Tonight was the only time left, for we weren't going to backpack burgundy, sour cream and onions up to Vogelsang tomorrow, and after that we were headed down to Palo Alto. I hoped Kath would agree; I wanted to do something for her.

I tried a lighthearted voice: "Yes, let's call Nancy. And take the showers — even though half my tan will wash off. But I feel like cooking, it's my turn."

"You really want to?"

I nodded, surprised by how much I needed to fix Kath a meal.

"Fine." She sounded doubtful. "It's not every day someone is begging to cook for me."

"This would give me great pleasure," I said definitively as I strapped on the water bottle.

The late afternoon sun lit up the Meadows during this last leg of our trip. "If only we could camp *here,* on this wide, fragrant lap of land beneath the stars."

"But hikers have eroded it so much as is," Kath responded in her irritating, earnest way. "Can you imagine what'd happen if people pounded in tent stakes and made campfires . . ."

"Hold on, John Muir!" I reached out to massage Kath's rigid neck. "It's just a whim. A notion. I promise to be an ecologically appropriate camping partner."

Kath grinned self-consciously.

I stirred stroganoff, enjoying the scents and evening sounds: jays squawking, squirrels yipping, leaves rustling. We had been lucky to get this secluded campsite and lucky the person registered next to us hadn't shown. The evening light softened the edges of distant mountains, the companionable trees and Kath's serious profile as she sat at the picnic table, book open, eyes straight ahead, in a trance.

Sensing my attention, she looked up. "So what's in this mess?"

"Guess."

"Cloves?" She sniffed.

"No, you'll never figure it out." I stirred.

"Cinnamon?"

"Cinnamon!"

"Well, you said I'd never figure it out."

I laughed, attending to the scrape, scrape, scrape of my wooden spoon through the softening vegetables. From the dense woods behind us came an argumentative caw, caw. I closed my eyes and wondered if this were perfect happiness.

Then, "Oh, no!"

"Are you OK?" Kath turned.

"Fine"— I shook my head —"but you know what we forgot to do after the showers?"

"Jesus. You're right. Nancy."

"As soon as we get back from Vogelsang, we'll call her, before we do anything else."

"Right," Kath agreed, staring at me as if about to say something else. Instead, she returned to her trance.

"Remember that song Nancy wrote when we were here?" I asked.

"About the lumberjack with plaid socks."

"And the two left thumbs." I laughed.

"Yeah, that part was gross." She shook her head, grinning.

"A lot about Nancy was gross."

Kath waited.

"I mean, she wasn't afraid to be outrageous. The best most of us monotonously good girls could manage was silly, but Nancy had that admirable, perverse streak."

"Yeah"— Kath rocked back and forth —"like when she tried out for cheerleader in that nun's outfit. I mean, she knew people would be offended. But it was *so* funny. I still laugh about it."

Filled with seriousness, sadness for Nancy, I said, "With that kind of panache and humor, I wonder why she didn't do better."

"Do better?" Kath asked.

"Well, you know, she had those three broken marriages and the drinking and the weight."

Kath shook her head. "And lots of good times in between. I don't know, Nancy wasn't the kind of person to take a straight path. I mean, she wasn't going anywhere. She was simply being. And enjoying it a lot."

"You think it's my bourgeois construction that she could have had a more fulfilling life."

"Whatever." Kath sounded annoyed.

"No, really."

"Of course, the breakdown and the alcoholism and the cancer haven't been any fun, but —"

"But what?" I demanded, feeling stupid and desperately wanting a happier interpretation.

"But who's to say she hasn't lived more intensely in a *positive* way too? I mean, she has a great capacity for love — writing to us all these years, continuing to reach out. She has four devoted daughters. She has an original, wild sense of humor. She's always lived more largely than anyone I know."

"You think she's had a happy life?" I asked, still puzzled, still wanting to make it OK.

"I didn't say that. Who has a happy life?"

I turned back to the stroganoff.

Kath resumed reading.

"Voilà," I declared. "You can turn around now."

Kath swiveled to find two plastic cups of red wine next to plates of steaming vegetarian stroganoff.

I fidgeted. "Only a cup of wine for the recipe. We might as well have a toast. Wouldn't want to waste the rest of the bottle."

"No, we wouldn't want to do that." Kath raised her glass. "Here's to conversation."

"Here's to loving friendship." I floated in the fragrance of drink and dinner, conscious of a happy flush rising in my cheeks. Perhaps what I needed all these years wasn't a lover but a good friend.

"You know in the dark like this — under the lantern light, starlight, you look like you did in high school," I blurted, "all the wrinkles disappear and —"

"Wrinkles? Me, wrinkles?"

I laughed, then lifted a fork of stroganoff to my mouth. It was too hot, and I blew on the steaming food. "How much do you think we *have* changed since those days? They say people basically stay the same — or become more like themselves."

Kath snorted. "I've never trusted 'they.'" She swallowed the hot food with a long drink of burgundy. "You think we haven't changed?"

"You think we have?"

"In some ways. I hope so," she answered cautiously, then concentrated on her dinner. "Say, this is terrific."

I shook my fork at her. "Evading the topic is something you've always excelled at."

"See." Kath grinned. "Another longstanding talent. But really, this *is* a great meal. And *you've* never been good at accepting compliments."

"Thank you." I bowed my head. "I'll work on that. Always room for improvement."

"That's the only thing that keeps me going."

"So, how have you *improved* with age?" I persisted. One of the things I loved about being with Kath was our unapologetically sincere conversations. During the last couple of days I'd been delighted to discover I hadn't lost the knack. Nostalgic for our idealistic girlhoods, regretful about the subsequent years of cool, smooth, small talk, I asked, "Really, tell me how you've changed."

Kath took another drink. "Well, I hope I'm a hell of a lot less naive about the world. I know about pregnancy tests, about abortions, about post-traumatic stress syndrome, about drugs, AIDS, Alzheimer's, death, survival."

I envied Kath's certainty. "How has that *changed* you?"

She frowned.

"Aside from wisdom accumulating. How has your *behavior* changed?"

"I don't know. You were always one for those cosmic conclusions."

"Come on."

"Well, I used to believe that if you leaned on a problem — just kept your shoulder against an obstacle — it would move. Now, maybe I've developed a little finesse. If the idea is to get beyond the boulder, I think about walking around it. Or over it. For a long time that was compromise."

"If it's not compromise, what is it?"

"Humility." An immediate answer.

I tapped the fork against my tin plate. "But —"

"Eat, Adele, eat. It's delicious and it's getting cold. Or maybe you really do subsist on words and ideas."

In our silence, in the dark, the night sounds amplified: roar from the highway; wind in overhead branches; clatters from the woods. Bear? No, I felt utterly remote from menace. Our night sky grew brighter with stars and satellites and planets while here below the atmosphere was murky from too many campfires.

My plate was empty. "So how does this humility work for you now? The other day you said you were laid off, that you could probably get a secure job if you went back to school, but you refuse to apply."

Kath shifted uneasily. Perhaps she was still hungry. I should have cooked more.

"Ego," I tried.

"I'm too ancient to sit in a classroom with eighteen-year-olds."

"Awww. There are plenty of returning students, particularly women."

"And I have all this family shit to deal with. Finding a retirement home for my parents. Martha's daughter needs spine surgery, and I really should be around for that. Besides, I'd have to get a loan for tuition and find a part-time job to eat. And my family would flip out if I went back to school at forty-four. They thought college was weird enough when I was eighteen."

"They did? Everyone was going to college."

"Not everybody. I keep telling you. Gloria Delgado didn't. Not Steve Dixon. Or Sammy Woods or Wilson Holmes. All those guys went to Vietnam. And Wilson didn't come back."

"I was really sorry about Wilson. I liked him. But, Kath, we're talking about you and you're changing the story."

"I'm *not*. That's what you can't see. These people *are* my story. In some ways I was a lot closer to them. I mean more similar to them — than I was to you."

I winced. "Class. Yes, well, of course, I know. We've talked about that. But you were *smart*, Kath. And interested in ideas."

"I passed. Passed as a college preppie, but I didn't belong in your club."

This stung as it was meant to; however, I wasn't going to let her divert me. "You have a right to finish college."

"And a right not to."

I was being rash; this evening I couldn't hold back. "What are you afraid of?"

"Oh, don't be stupid." She turned away.

Unable to conceal my frustration, I said slowly, "It's as if you've been in a holding pattern all these years."

"In comparison to what?" She flared. "Your life? I could ask you what you've been running away from!"

I nodded.

"But it's also possible to see our lives apart from one another, to use separate gauges. OK? Try — I exist apart from you and you apart from me."

Her cold matter-of-factness was scary.

Overhead a helicopter whirred.

"Late for that," Kath observed. "Must be some kind of emergency."

"Emergency?" A chill blew down my neck. "Oh, I guess like twisted ankles. Heart attacks. That sort of thing."

"Yeah, they've got a hospital in the Valley. But it would be a pretty bumpy ride down there."

"Count your lucky stars, as Mother would say."

"Which are those?" Kath looked up.

"As I said before, one way you haven't changed is that you've always been brilliant at shifting the subject, when the subject is you."

"Wrong. I have changed," she insisted. "I'm much *better* at it."

"Improvement, yes, I see." I laughed, happy to shelve this particular disagreement. I split the rest of the burgundy between us.

"There's Scorpio," declared Kath.

"Where?" I asked.

"See, there." Kath pulled out her flashlight and traced the long tail in the sky.

I nodded. "I do see. You know, I've never been able to find that before. The enormity of it makes me feel so small. Of course everyone says that, still, do you feel that, too?"

"No," Kath said. "I guess I don't. When I look at the sky hanging there, the Milky Way blurring in and out of the closer, brighter stars, I guess I don't think of myself in proportion to them, so much as in relation to them. I don't mean I'm a star, but part of the universe."

"But they're so huge, sending all that light from miles, years, away."

She looked at me blankly.

I couldn't tell how I was being unclear. "Like the mountains; doesn't the hugeness of Half Dome or Mount Dana make you feel small?"

"No," she mused, "no. Maybe I don't feel all that large to begin with."

I stared hard at the sky.

"There's Sagittarius."

"Yes." I pointed the flashlight. "Hey, you're pretty good at this stuff."

"I've got a telescope at home. Not that you can see much in Oakland, with all the city lights. But sometimes."

I laughed. "A telescope. You do amaze me."

Kath made a long face. "You've always said that."

I swirled the dregs of wine in my glass, smirking.

"So tell me more about this job at Berkeley," she said abruptly. "Would it be good for you? For your career? Would you like it?"

As Kath asked these questions, I shivered again at how little we knew about each other's worlds.

"Sure, it's a stimulating place. I'd love to work with graduate students. The program at Berkeley would give me more research flexibility. It'd be great to be back in the Bay Area."

"But . . ."

"But, my father —"

"Right. Your father. I get it."

"And Lou."

"Couldn't he find something at Berkeley? Or San Francisco State?"

I gave a short laugh. "I don't think he would consider State. But actually, there's a good possibility for him at Stanford if this particular guy retires soon."

"So?"

"So, he's happy where he is. And anything after Harvard — except *perhaps* Heaven — is a step down."

"I see."

"Besides," I said.

"Besides?"

"Besides, I'm not so sure I want him to come."

Kath waited.

"At least not the first year. I mean, we could use some space apart. Plenty of couples commute."

"Across the country?"

"Across the Atlantic!"

"Well." Kath hesitated.

"What I do worry about is the boys. But they keep saying they want to spend more time in the Wild West. It might be good for them. Shake them out of that East Coast provincialism."

"Sounds like you have it all worked out," Kath said. "What are the big doubts?"

"Father, really. He does loom large."

"Adele," she spluttered, then modulated her voice. "I know your dad has been difficult in the past. But I have a hard time believing someone who's been around the world, around several worlds, can be so intimidated by an old man."

I shrugged.

"You're a mother. A big professor. You've published — what? — two books."

"Three," I answered, instantly embarrassed by my pride. Or was it my attachment to precision?

"Three books. Two kids. Great job. You're just remembering who he was to you as a little girl. He's a ghost, Adele."

"No!" I swallowed the remaining wine in one gulp, wishing I had bought two bottles. "No, Kath," I said deliberately. "Sari and Mother are the ghosts. Sari and Mother are the dead ones. Father and I are left dueling."

I thought about the gathering after Mother's funeral. The same scene as when Sari died: everyone collected in the house for subdued conversation and airbrushed memories. Everyone a little older: grayer, stouter Father leaning more heavily against the mantel, but standing in the same place, talking to the same people; Lou, model husband, assisting in the kitchen. This time the boys were there, being reverently appreciated as if their existence were some compensation for Mother's death.

"Can't you refuse to fight? The duel isn't obligatory."

"It's pre-obligation. Instinct."

"Oh, right."

"What do you know about it?" I glared into the speckled night. "You think that just because we have some money all our difficulties are abstract. Listen, Kath — my mother and sister are *dead.* For all our problems, there was some hope of reconciliation while they were alive. Some hope."

Kath reached across the weather-warped wooden table for my hand.

I felt the warm, rough texture of her fingers. My shoulders relaxed and I was on the verge of tears, in danger of melting altogether.

"I don't know what got into me." Her voice swelled with regret, embarrassment. "I don't butt into other people's lives. You don't need an outsider telling you what's what."

"You're not an outsider." I gripped Kath's hand.

"I mean, I'm not a relative." She shifted back on the bench. "I'm not —"

I interrupted, whispering ferociously, "You're not an *outsider.*"

"I'm not related by blood or anything." She blushed.

"Oh, I think there's quite enough blood spilled between us."

She pulled back her hand. "Is that good or bad?" She looked at me directly.

"Both good and bad." I held her gaze. "And the stains are indelible, so in that way, we're related, marked for life."

She nodded. I detected a slight smile.

Suddenly my mouth was filled with a metallic taste: too much wine, sour cream, pasta. "This is going to sound ridiculous, but I absolutely must brush my teeth."

"Hey," Kath laughed, "I bow to absolutes of *any* kind."

As I pulled out my toothbrush, I could hear Kath busily collecting the plates. We both needed a break.

"Look. In the sky." Her voice startled me. "Shooting star."

"Oh, damn." I finished putting away the toothpaste and brush. "Missed it. Let's sit down and wait for another one."

"Think I'll take care of these first," Kath said, still clearing the table.

"No, we'll do those together later."

"Unfair. You did the cooking. I do the washing."

"Just sit with me and watch the shooting stars," I pleaded. "We can argue afterward."

Kath accepted a place on the bench and looked up at the moonless night.

As we waited for the sky to explode, I felt the warmth from her body — three inches away.

"Peppermint toothpaste," she broke the spell.

"There's the Big Dipper," I declared.

"And the G.E. satellite!" We laughed.

I searched for spaces between the stars. Night in the wilderness could be the most lonesome, most intimate of times.

Quietly, Kath unwrapped the Toblerone we had been saving for dessert. Her movements were slow, stealthy, as if she didn't want to disturb her fellow concertgoers. But it was her very deliberateness that made the foil crackle like lightning. She broke me off a piece of the dark chocolate. We sat, letting the bittersweetness melt on our tongues. Suddenly a shooting star streamed light diagonally across the sky.

I nudged Kath with my elbow.

She laughed. "I saw it. Yes!"

Scooting closer, I felt our hips touch.

"Another!" Kath declared.

I could scarcely breathe. To distract myself from Kath's warm softness, I took another piece of chocolate, which tasted as dark and mysterious as the night between the stars.

18

Kath

1965 / May Lake

SLOWLY, through soft rain, we were climbing the trail to May Lake. Of course it would shower the day we cajoled Nancy into an uphill hike. Still, she didn't seem very bothered by the rain or the ascent. She and Paula chatted nonstop at the tail end of our parade. Ahead of them, behind me, were Adele and Donna studying trees: red fir, silver pine, hemlock.

Grayness had seized the sky like an occupying army. Maybe yesterday's blue had been imaginary. Or a blessing we no longer deserved. Wetness weighted fragile tufts of grass down to the ground. Beside our trail, bright green moss on a log. Rocks glistened with moisture. I'd promised myself not to think about the fact that we had only two more days left before we scattered to different colleges. After all, we'd agreed to return here together next summer. And we were a pretty reliable crew.

I liked the protected feeling of these giant shoulders all around us. So often in the Bay Area I was aware there was nowhere to go but out to sea. Now I understood these peaks were California, too. A safer, more welcoming California. Somehow — despite the bears and snakes and coyotes — these were mountains you could lean on, aspire to. They were a kind of spine oozing nourishment — the fertilizing snowmelt — to the rest of the state. Not recognizing the Sierra as California was like disinheriting your ancestors. In fact, in a strange way, I felt I'd finally located home after living in this state for seventeen years.

I walked faster, out of range from Nancy and Paula's buzz. I wondered where they *found* all these words. What a different experience you had if you set aside the talk and thinking and simply *observed*. The sandy trail had turned to a pleasant, sticky mud. The rain was subsiding now, gradually, like sighs of laughter. I listened for silence between drops. Even Nancy and Paula had grown quiet. And then the soft pit, spit, dregs of shower, like waves after an earthquake.

The trail widened onto some slick, granite slabs.

Out of a stand of lodgepole pines appeared a tall, dark woman carrying a pink flowered umbrella.

"Where is it, the Snow Flat?"

Uncomprehending, I stared at this vibrant apparition of cosmopolitan fashion.

Adele to the rescue. "Can we help you?"

At that point, the husband walked toward us, brushing off his spotless white slacks and shirt. His crown was a beige safari hat.

"*Buon giorno.*"

Nancy and Paula had caught up. Nancy looked truly interested for the first time since our hike began.

"Snow Flat," the woman persisted.

"The trailhead?"

"*Si.*"

"Down there. Just follow the path."

"The path, *si!*" The signora happily nodded her umbrella.

Her husband grinned at us and headed downhill. "*Grazie,*" he called.

"You're welcome," I said.

"*Prego!*" shouted Paula. Something she learned from her Italian pen pal.

Noticing the rain had ceased, the woman collapsed the umbrella and catching up with him, hit her husband on the shoulder. "I told you so. I told you so!" she declared in ringing, accented English like someone accustomed to audiences.

We stood, tittering together for a moment, then regrouped in our original formation. I lost sight of Nancy and Paula on the steep slope but knew they would catch up. What great views of Cathedral Peak, Mount Clark and Half Dome.

Nancy was ready for lunch the moment we reached the shore of gloriously clean May Lake. The gray had lifted from the sky, and the whole world seemed blue again. We spread our raingear on a quiet part of the shore away from tents and anglers. Paula distributed peanut butter sandwiches she'd made that morning. I hated peanut butter, the way it stuck to my teeth and landed like a rock in my stomach, but this trip was teaching me flexibility. Teaching me that if I didn't develop some pliancy soon, I'd turn into a crank by the time I was thirty. A sunny spray of buttercups made me think how these flowers had different designs in order to attract bees, beetles, flies, hummingbirds.

Nancy sat, cross-legged, telling some silly joke, a smile of unqualified delight radiating from her pretty face. I suppose this is what Mom called "joie de vivre." Whatever it was, Nancy won us all over with her infectious carnality. This passion was why we forgave the lateness, the hecticness, the sloppiness. She was, in some grand, inexplicable way, a source of light.

"When I see older people, you know, in their fifties, carrying books out of the library, I wonder why they bother," Nancy declared.

Had I heard her right?

"What do you mean?" Adele leaned forward in that long, graceful way. She selected an apple and polished it on her jeans.

"I mean, I guess, I see reading as kind of utilitarian — reading to catch up on something, to learn, to develop a skill."

"And?" Donna asked with the amused disbelief with which she often faced Nancy.

"And, I mean, what's the point when you're that old? It's all determined by then, anyway."

"What?" Even Paula had lost her patience. She started gathering the lunch litter in a bag and shoved it into her pack.

"Life." Nancy shrugged. She handed around her mother's homemade trail mix.

"Tolstoy didn't publish some of his best stuff until he was almost sixty." Adele entered the game.

"What kind of writer will you be, Adele?" Paula asked. "Novelist? Poet?"

Silence.

"She's going to be an artist!" I declared, immediately embarrassed by my vehemence. In a more neutral, informative tone, I said, "Botanical prints. Watercolor landscapes."

Adele smiled. "Oh, maybe that — as it fits into raising kids. What I'd like most," she said, a glimmer of discovery in her eyes, "is to have a happy family."

"And you, Kath, what about you?"

This inquisitiveness was not my favorite part of Nancy's personality. How could I admit I couldn't imagine living to fifty? I knew something horrible would happen long before then, and I didn't want to be around to suffer the consequences. But Adele and I had made a pact to raise our kids together, so I said, "Fifty, guess I'll be a grandmother by then." And to gain some ironic distance from that fate, "With a gray bun at the back of my head, leaning on a cane."

"Hardly." Adele laughed. "The girl with the highest IQ in school shriveling into the old woman in the shoe! Fifty is young."

"Young?" Nancy demanded.

"Really, Kath?" Paula asked. "The highest — even higher than Bob Thornton?"

I glared at Adele. She had promised not to tell.

My best friend glanced down to the lake.

"Do you think you'll be yourself in, let's see, fifty is thirty-three years from now?" Nancy asked, leaning back against a tree.

"Come again?" said Donna, stupefied.

"I mean, are you always the same person? Or do you become someone else when you get older?"

"That's ridiculous," I said.

"Yes," Adele spoke. "Of course you become someone else."

"No," I declared fiercely. "Of course you're the same person. You grow, you develop, you learn. But you're the same."

"Fascinating." Donna pursed her lips in her sardonic, world-weary way.

"What?" Nancy asked, eager not to miss anything.

"The Bobbsey Twins over here, arguing with each other."

"It's just a disagreement," explained Nancy, who hated bad feelings. She was a nice person — loving, inclusive, peacemaking — too nice for her own good.

"We better get going," said Paula, "if we plan to hike back, fix dinner and still have a decent walk in the Meadows tonight."

She and Nancy led the way down.

In the sunlight, this was a different path. Wildflowers had sprung back to life. Silver pines gleamed. Squirrels chased one another over the slopes — their feathery tails undulating in mountain grasses. Behind us, I heard a woodpecker tap, tap, tapping, and some other, unrecognizable, bird singing. The High Country had transformed from a pale, heavy rainworld to a festival of light.

At the trailhead, the parking lot was filled with the vehicles of other day hikers. As I unlocked the car door, an older woman called us over.

"Excuse me." Her voice was urgent, nervous.

"Yes?" I walked toward her. The others were unloading packs and canteens in the trunk.

She was a hefty person, with a row of painful-looking pimples along her graying temple. "Have you been on the May Lake Trail?"

"Yes."

"Well, have you seen a man wearing jeans, a purple sweater and a Giants baseball cap?"

By then, the others had gathered around.

"No."

"No," we all agreed.

Her mouth puckered. Silently she peered at the trail through her windshield.

"Has he been gone long?" Adele asked.

"Eight hours." She sniffed.

I looked at Adele.

"He's my husband." She shook her head helplessly. "He left at 7:30 this morning."

"He'll be back." Nancy smiled kindly. "People lose track of time on these beautiful trails. There's so much distraction."

"Yeah," she whispered, still staring ahead through the front window.

"No, don't worry," Nancy said. "I'm sure it'll be fine."

19

Adele

1965 / Mount Hoffmann

THE EVENING WAS WARM; at least there was that. Morning cloudiness had completely disappeared, so it would be a clear night at the summit. Wildflowers bloomed on the steep bank: fairy lantern and mariposa lily. I wondered if the scent of these delicate blossoms was as subtle as their size.

Kath tramped three yards ahead on the Mount Hoffmann Trail — keeping the rhythm, the faith, for both of us. From here, with the sleeping bag tied to her back, she looked like a displaced Bedouin. I didn't know how she could climb this fast. My goosedown sleeping bag was strapped securely but made me feel clumsy, unsure of bodily perimeters and gravity. The bag of food also slowed my pace. Sweat dripped down from my temples and under my arms. Kath, however, showed no stress. In fact she could be a deodorant spokesman as she trudged dry, fresh, vivacious, ever upward. Would I spend my entire life trying to catch up with her? She would reach the top with or without me.

It was a stupid idea from the start, but when you got Kath angry, nothing could be done. And she was furious with Nancy's arrogant new boyfriend. Leave it to Nancy to find romance in the High Sierra. This premed Occidental College junior was as clearly smitten with our urban miss as he was provoked by Kath. First, they had a blazing fight about whether sequoias always fell uphill. Kath said yes. He argued no. We looked it up and, of course, Kath was right. Then he bragged about climbing all the major peaks — Clouds Rest, El Capitan, Half Dome — telling us it was a "guy thing" to climb mountains and a "girl thing" to bird-watch in the meadows. Nancy agreed with alacrity, but Kath, well, one word led to another, and soon she was planning her solitary hike up here. All afternoon I waited for her to come to her senses, and when she didn't, I insisted on going too. The others would stay below and we would flash lights down to them.

Up, upward we climbed, panting in the thinner air, and I could see from Kath's brisk step there would be no pausing for a while. She breathed pride rather than oxygen. I enjoyed the feeling of soft earth and pine needles beneath my feet, wondering how I would acclimate to the pavement when we returned to Oakland the next night. *If* we returned. No, Kath and I would be safe. The sky had that pleasant softening, "used" quality that comes before dusk, when the eye has finally made peace with the brilliance of mountain blueness.

Out of the wooded area ahead, we heard voices. A mother and father loudly urging their son to walk faster. "You want to make it out of here before dark?" asked the mother.

The dust-streaked boy — who seemed seven or eight and on his last legs — answered simply, "I'm tired."

"Easier on the way down," his father cajoled. "And there's a Fudgsicle waiting for you in the meadow."

"I don't want a Fudgsicle."

"Listen, Mike," said the woman, "sunset is soon. We have to get down before dark. You don't want us left alone on the mountain, do you, pal?"

At that point, they saw us. "Hi," the man said quietly.

Kath waved and moved on.

I nodded.

"You know it's another mile up," the mother warned doubtfully, parentally. "And it's getting dark."

"We're camping overnight at the summit."

They glared in exasperation, as if we were betraying adulthood.

With renewed energy, I savored the adventurousness of my friend. When I had to write about inspirations for my college application, I mentioned Helen Keller, Sojourner Truth, Mahatma Gandhi. More deeply, of course, I had been affected by Kath: stimulated, urged, pushed — sometimes over the edge. I knew she was mad at me for going to Radcliffe, but in a way, it was her doing because she taught me to look ahead, beyond, straight into the future, and I found the door open. I saw that if I didn't go through it now, it might swing back and I'd never get out.

"Hey, Del, look at this!"

I glanced up from what felt like a ninety-degree ascent and saw her standing on a sheer precipice.

Be careful, I prayed silently, for saying it aloud would only provoke her more. That was the trouble with inspirations, caution wasn't one of their governing principles. Catching up with her, I stood farther back on the trail, getting most of the vista.

"Yes, spectacular," I agreed, as the sun descended in the west, the direction we would all take tomorrow.

Kath caught the — cowardly? pragmatic? — hesitation in my voice and turned. Grinning, she looked up at the summit. "Not far."

"No, not far." I struck on ahead, determined to show her I could make it.

Up, up I climbed. As we approached the top, I was filled with new spirit, as if being *pulled* higher. Perhaps I had simply lost my senses in the thin air, but nothing could stop me, us.

Alone, together, at the top, we had glorious views. Astonishing how different the land appeared in the east and in the west, proving that the primal rising of this mountain segregated the habitat ages ago. We had about half an hour of vision in the pinkening evening and set to arranging our sleeping bags.

"First star tonight." Kath sat up, her legs bound together in the bag like an aerial mermaid.

"Tell me your wish," I said.

"No, you lose it that way."

"Ridiculous superstition!" I pestered.

"So's wishing."

"Come on."

"I might lose it if I tell."

"I'll tell you mine."

A pause.

"OK," Kath said, "you first."

"I wished that we all live to our fiftieth birthdays and that we start by making it down tomorrow."

"Scared?" she asked with tender responsibility.

"A little," I conceded, "but we'll be OK, together."

"Yes," she answered, almost wistfully, "together."

"And you, what did you wish?"

She peered into the dimming light, suddenly a nearsighted ancient. Kath had always had one of those enduring faces — with strong bones — that could look five one minute and seventy-five the next. This was one aspect of her miraculous reliability. I would always recognize Kath.

"I wished that we return to the High Country next year."

"Oh," I said, disappointed that she'd wasted her wish. We'd already agreed to come. "Yes, I wish that, too."

More stars. Planets. A slice of moon.

"Ready?" she inquired.

"Aye, aye, Captain."

She stood, switched on her flashlight, moving it up and down. Up and down. I sat there, taking in the strength and grace of her movements: up and down, up and down. My friend, my best friend, confidante, companion, provocateur, partner in madness, pal. Up and down.

"Well." She glanced at me. Yes, the plan had been for her to start first and then for me to join in with the smaller flashlight — so the girls could be sure it was really us.

Up, down. Up, down. I searched the valley below as my arm rose and fell to Kath's rhythm.

"Look," she declared.

"Yes, yes, there they are." The first mate sighting land. "There, yes, there."

Nancy, Paula and Donna responded with prearranged signals. On, off. On, off. On, off. Three times. Then twice. Then once. On, off.

Kath and I stood together, two stars in the firmament, blinking, winking, together.

20

Kath

Saturday and Sunday / Tuolumne Meadows to Vogelsang

OUR WATER GRUMBLED to a boil. Slowly, I poured it through the beige coffee filter to our cups. This morning was cool and crisp, a perfect mountain beginning.

Adele was also meditative over breakfast. Maybe less meditative than sleepy. It had taken her hours to drift off last night. When she crawled into the tent, she said softly, "Kath." I should have responded, but this new closeness was no fun. Emotional currents were bad enough, but physical intimacy was unbearable. Had Adele been aroused last night as we snuggled together stargazing and sucking on chocolate? I didn't know which would be worse — if she was or wasn't feeling the same attraction. She'd probably disappear for the rest of our lives at the end of the week. Last night I imagined Adele spoke my name in a dream. I liked the idea of Adele dreaming about me. For the most part, I liked the idea.

I extended a steaming cup of black coffee. Her eyes were grateful, her hands cold. "Thanks."

"Don't mention it," I said emphatically. She looked dreadful.

"Did you sleep well?" she asked.

"Not really," I confessed.

"Hi, there!" A lively greeting from behind us. I didn't turn.

"Thought I'd find you two here."

That familiar voice. Automatically, I inched away from Adele. At least she managed to remain silent, stifling the automatic, polite welcome.

"Adele?" Approaching, he was less confident. "Kath?"

"Adele and Kath, right?"

He was still wearing that idiotic straw hat.

"Right." Adele's voice was formal, as if she were grading a multiple-choice test.

I sighed.

Then, still teacherly, Adele asked, "Weren't you going to May Lake, Sandy?"

"I was." He swayed from one foot to the other. "I was. Then I got to thinking how crowded May Lake is with day-trippers. You know, because of easy access from the road."

She nodded.

"And I remembered those great wildflowers up at Vogelsang. Even in August. Decided you ladies had a better plan. I lucked out and got a spot here when someone canceled." He pointed to the other side of the campground. His voice was gaining confidence, volume.

I told myself he was not an intruder. Just a lonely, bumbling, well-meaning guy.

He was still talking. "I decided to walk around to see if I could find you."

Pulling back my arms, I stretched away some of the tension. Maybe I should be grateful for his interruption. Suddenly the most amazing thing came out of my mouth. "Hey, we're being rude. How about some coffee?"

Adele stared at me in disbelief.

"No thanks, really. I came by to see if you'd like to hike up together."

My eyes widened. I recalled Donna's hoarse, sardonic laughter.

Nervously, he continued, "But I don't want to intrude. I mean . . ."

I lost it, threw up my hands and began organizing my pack.

"You're not intruding," Adele declared.

Would this female reflex exaggerate or diminish with menopause? Menopause — one of the hundred topics I still wanted to raise with Adele. Did she have night sweats yet? Was she going to do estrogen replacement? I had heard something about a natural remedy of rubbing yams on your skin. I kept myself busy thinking about female hormones while they chatted.

He glanced at his watch. "Whoa, I didn't notice how late it was. I haven't decamped yet."

She looked from his anxious eyes to my tired, rigid jaw and back again. "Well, why don't you let us talk about the hike while you pack up? Meanwhile, I have to get some water and I think the faucet is on the way back to your site."

When she returned, her irritation seemed gone. She scooped yogurt from the carton into a bowl. Eventually, she said, "I told him no. Explained you and I had a lot of talking to do."

I waited.

"I felt terrible saying no. He was just trying to be friendly. He's actually very interested in your work and he's a volunteer Big Brother. I think you'd like him."

Jesus, she didn't get it, still. It would have been easier to spit than speak.

Adele stammered, lost. "B b b but I said no."

She had said this three times.

"Maybe . . ." I began.

"Yes?" Adele took a long drink of cold coffee.

I hated her tone.

"Maybe," I repeated to get back on track. "Maybe you *should* go off with him." There. Freed.

"Oh, he wanted to hike with *both* of us." Her alarm rose. "He's such a nice guy, I'm sure you'd like him."

"Well, I'm *not* so sure about that." I glared, ready now for a fight, poised to tell the truth.

She looked exhausted, baffled.

My voice took on weight. "I don't care if he's Nelson Mandela. Look, Adele, we've been together six days now. Any two people can use a break after six days. Don't you think?"

"Actually, I hadn't thought about it." Critically, she inspected the uneaten yogurt.

Damn her polished denial. I had to do all the work, break down all the walls. Well, I wasn't going to spell it out for her. Instead, "So why don't you and Sandy have a nice chat on the trail? I'll chill out."

Yolanda was always telling me to chill out. The thought of that kid's "attitude lessons" almost made me smile. Of course I'd been useful to Yolanda, but I was sure I'd learned more from her. Chill out, I tried to conjure Yolanda's mischievous expression.

Still no response from Adele.

"Meet you up there, OK?" I said.

"No, Sandy wouldn't like that." Her fine hands rested on the weather-splintered table.

"Sandy!" I shouted. This was almost comical.

"*I* don't like it!" she declared.

I watched her carefully, gratified by the anger.

"I came thousands of miles to spend time with my oldest friend and now she's saying she can't stand me for more than six days."

At least she was putting herself on some kind of line. I didn't know if I should be angry at Sandy or grateful. I did know I needed a rest. "Who's saying I can't stand you?"

She stared, uncomprehending.

She could probably use a break from me, too. "Put it down to cantankerousness, Adele. I want some time *alone*. We'll only be separated for five, six hours. You'll have a good hike with Sandy."

"Shit, Kath . . ."

I was half sorry she stopped there.

I left first, almost racing down to the Lyell Fork Bridge. Such a glorious morning, so clear and dry. Obviously the storm rumors we'd heard at the lodge were wrong. Standing on the bridge, I watched water swirl over the submerged rocks. Black, white, gray, silver rocks. The river was the steadiest of companions. Rushing along of its own accord, but not rushing me. The best of hiking partners, a reassuring but not intrusive presence. Ever there for refreshment, for a splash, a dangle of the feet. The trail followed the water. The water accompanied the trail. You could always go back to the source. Unlike human companions, the river gave you a clear, objective sense of where you had been and where you were going. This water watching calmed me. Released me from Adele. My expectations of Adele. My stupidity about Adele. It was good to get an early start like this. I'd hardly seen anyone on the trail so far. Sometimes I did wonder if I was a crank. I liked individual people. I was politically aware, engaged. I simply *failed* in social groups. Unintentionally, inevitably, I left hurt feelings.

Martha, for instance, could never figure out my reluctance about holidays. Christmas *or* Thanksgiving, I'd said often enough, but my sister still expected me at both. How could I tell her I hated holidays? I always finished them feeling breathless, my muscles aching from unasked questions, from the hundred and one defensive maneuvers to avoid bruising feelings, being hurt, revealing too much. The only way to survive a family holiday was to leave early and jog five miles in the hills near my apartment. If I didn't do something like this, I'd lose all sense of self for the next week and be the baby sister, the one who had it easy, the girl who went to college, the too-serious daughter who never got married.

Sometimes I thought Martha's envy of my carefree singleness outdistanced any real concern about my missing satisfaction and security. Martha had a tough life, cutting hair, raising two difficult kids — Kirsten with scoliosis and Sam hyperkinetic. She fretted a lot about Bob's job at San Quentin. I suspected Bob beat Martha, but maybe I had beatings on the brain after finding out about Dad and Mom. Anyway, Martha had told me for years it wasn't natural for a woman to be so long without a man. As she put it, everyone has urges. Now she was reduced to sending Ann Landers's columns about middle-aged romance. I was more touched than annoyed when the last envelope arrived, also containing an article about how to use condoms without losing the glow of the moment.

What was I doing, wasting solitude obsessing about my family? Well, it *was* less painful than obsessing about Adele.

Climbing upward in a darkened wood, I knew this was a different world from Lyell Fork, with its expansive meadows and mountain-jagged skyline. Often I felt safer in the dark. At least not so overwhelmed by color and sound. These forests provided such rich tranquillity. I suppose some people could have the opposite reaction.

Pausing for water, I noticed I'd taken the canteen we were sharing. Surely Adele would remember there was another bottle in the car. No matter. Sandy — or whatever she was calling him now, San — would be happy to share his canteen. I hooked the bottle on my belt and continued. Later, I'd take longer rests, but right now, I wanted to make sure they didn't catch up with me. All I needed was Sandy's well-meaning observations about inner-city youth. I was being a bitch about this poor guy. He was a decent sort — gentle, concerned — just carried away with his enthusiasm for Adele. Tree roots zigzagged across the trail, making the climb easier in the muddy bits.

Sandy's enthusiasm wasn't so different from my own for Adele, initially developed in the fifth grade. Bold, bright, she shone against the rows of dull, good girls in our class. Adele dared me to play hooky that first week, and soon we were fast friends. Always nudging each other a step further. Once we enrolled in the advanced class, the dares took different shapes: to learn Latin, to memorize ballads, to read the Marquis de Sade. Neither of us understood how these feats were more reckless for someone from my family. They seemed audacious enough to Dr. Ward, who took bemused pride in his daughter's bizarre decathalon scholarship. My parents grew uneasy about all this studying but knew I could be in worse sorts of trouble.

Adele and I spent more and more time together — in the library, at the museum, in the shopping mall. Mom thought Adele was a nice girl from a good home and hoped some of that breeding might rub off on her contrary younger child. Martha called Adele "that fancy girl." Once when I was fifteen and Martha seventeen, she advised me, "You can hang out with that fancy girl all you like, but someday you'll learn that family is what counts. They're the people you owe and the ones you pay back." I blamed such talk on the Catholic Youth Group to which Martha belonged that year. Of course I loved my parents and my older sister.

Often I wondered if Mom ever regretted starting this family in the first place. In the first place, how do you locate the first place? Wasn't our family simply an extension of Mom's own family? Marriage was a much safer transition than the tuberculosis which killed three of her brothers and sisters. I never had any trouble understanding why little Sylvie from the Montreal tenements was drawn to the cool, capable, handsome Nils, emmisary of a better, more rational, more comfortable world. And I also understood why they stayed together. But how sad we'd never talked about problems with Dad, at least not until recently, not until the blows had been too severe to conceal. Now all she could say was "He doesn't know his own strength. Accidents happen."

Here, at the edge of the forest, I finished the steepest climbing. The high meadows were next, strewn with boulders. At Rafferty Creek, I splashed my face, took off my windbreaker and rearranged the pack. It was safe to pause now. I had made fine time. They'd never catch up until I'd camped at Vogelsang. Maybe I'd be lucky enough to see a bear like last year. I still remembered the affronted face of the huge cinnamon creature before she rambled into the brush.

The ideal campsite: shaded and five feet from Emeric Creek. Tent almost assembled, I realized Adele was carrying the stakes. Teamwork, I reminded myself, requires other people. The flapping tent looked like a morose umbrella missing spokes after a windstorm. I shook my head. It would really be something if Adele forgot the stakes. Still, we'd manage. It would almost be funny. OK, OK, I knew I was taking Sandy too seriously. Sure, he was an asshole for intruding. On the other hand, he was a polite asshole, and I was really pissed off that Adele got so distracted by him. It was silly to be threatened.

I pulled out *Yosemite Indians* and leaned against my sleeping bag roll. A postcard of Mount Hoffmann dropped from the uncracked pages. One we had bought at the lodge last night, a get well card for Nancy. As I opened the book, I realized that I'd been ashamed to read much in front of Adele. Would she have found my taste too elementary? Not scholarly enough? What else were we hiding from each other?

Anita always said I should open up more. My fault, of course, for getting involved with a shrink, but I was hurt when she insisted I was closer to my cat than to most humans. Anita and I had five good years together. I learned a lot about people from her. And she claimed to be grateful for my mellow practicality. It wasn't a bad relationship. Not the flaming passion of youth. I loved her, though. And I suppose we would still be together if she hadn't wanted a family. Was I unnatural because I didn't want to be a mother, even a co-mother? Anita said I had too many boundary issues. But once you've been inside the whale, you watch your step. Sometimes I wondered if I made the right decision. I missed my smart, funny Anita. When I visited her and her new lover, Lisa, and their son, Anthony, I felt both sad and relieved.

Shifting to the other side of the tent, I faced the creek and tried to get into the book. Jesus, I'd been abrupt with Adele. Well, this separation wasn't a big deal. Part of a morning and an afternoon. I turned the page. Would Adele see me, hidden from the trail like this? Yes, of course, she'd recognize our tent. Everything was going to be fine. I turned the second page. Time passed. Hours. Pleasantly, quickly, the sunny day ripened into afternoon.

"Hi there." Adele's face was sunburned or flushed.

"Hi." Too abrupt. Relax, I told myself, temper is only a reflex. "How was the hike?" There, that sounded more friendly.

"Great!" Adele exclaimed.

"Where's Sandy?"

"Oh, he went off to find his homestead."

"I see."

"We saw bouquets of Sierra daisies. Brilliant sky. Perfect weather."

"Yeah, great day." My voice eased, lightened. "Couldn't finish the job without your help." I grinned at the pathetic tent.

"Bet you thought I'd forget the stakes." She looked uncertain.

"Never occurred to me." I realized how much I had missed Adele and unnerved by this admission, I stupidly called her my "trusty companion."

"Oh, yeah," Adele laughed, sloughing off her pack. "End of suspense." She held out the stakes. Her face grew serious. "Peace offering?"

I felt tears welling up. "Peace." I accepted the stakes.

Adele wrapped her arms around me. "Oh, I *am* glad. It would be terrible to climb to 10,300 feet and find I had lost you."

"Terrible," I agreed.

After dinner, we took off for Vogelsang Pass, another 600 feet up and promising splendid views of High Country mountains and lakes. Just past Vogelsang Lodge, a marmot performed for a gray-haired man and woman. Farther along, another marmot peered skeptically from behind a tree. The trail was still fairly wet from recent rains. We crossed the roaring creek balancing on a long log. In a more turfy section, tree roots rose in the trail like veins in a hand.

Adele was panting.

I slowed down.

"It's worth it," I called over my shoulder. "Wait until you see the sunset over the mountains."

She nodded. "No problem. I'll make it."

On the way, I pointed out Fletcher Peak, Mount Conness, Clouds Rest and Half Dome.

"Wonderful," said Adele.

"But the view from the pass is the most beautiful."

She frowned wearily.

"No, really, it's only 600 feet above camp. Not much farther at all."

"I'm with you."

At the pass, marked by dainty, durable whitebark pines, I greeted Mount Clark, Mount Florence, Mount Maclure, Mount Lyell. The Indian names were probably more musical; I'd look them up in the book tomorrow. Rosy expectation suffused the evening sky.

"This is the best time." My shoulders relaxed as they hadn't in days. "Moments before sunset."

"Why? How do you feel?" she asked.

"I don't know, a kind of deliverance from the day, a peace, a melancholy."

Adele moved closer and rested a hand on my shoulder. "Really? Melancholy?"

"What do *you* feel?"

"Pleasure in sharing this with you. Not so much melancholy." She was thoughtful. "The opposite, I guess, a kind of excitement."

As sun dropped down the mountains, our voices seemed to get louder.

"Shhh," I said, nodding at the deep red smearing across the horizon. The two of us stood there watching as the sky turned bloody. Then pink. Yellowish. Coral.

"Gorgeous," she whispered. "Red sky at night. That means it's going to be a fine day tomorrow."

"Hope so."

"Well, we better start down." Once more I studied the splattered sky, as if trying to acquire it for my permanent collection. "We want to be back at camp before dark."

"Right," Adele said.

"So what's on our agenda tomorrow?" I asked.

"Sandy recommended Hanging Basket Lake."

"Beautiful place," I answered. "I was thinking of something more tame, like walking around Ireland Lake. We don't want to wipe ourselves out hiking if we're going down to Tuolumne tomorrow and driving back to the Bay Area."

"Sad this is our last night."

"Where's Sandy headed tomorrow?" It slipped out, but I had to know if he was going to Hanging Basket too.

"Vogelsang Peak, I think he said."

I persisted, "Were you sorry to leave him?"

She shrugged. "He offered to show me around the East Bay trails if I take that Berkeley job."

"Hmmm." Was I satisfied now?

Turning back toward camp together, we each passed gingerly over a slab of slippery granite. One after the other, we traversed the log across the creek. Adele searched for marmots, but they had disappeared. I switched on the flashlight. We were wordless, listening to the night noises, until we reached our tent.

At this altitude the air was noticeably thinner and the ground colder. Together in the tent we lay, attending dreams, motionless and busy as corpses merging with the earth.

Sleep eluded me. I meditated on the green pebbles glistening on the banks of Rafferty Creek, on the gray-blue seams in the boulders out-side our tent, the silky mud on the trail to Vogelsang Pass. But I was so distracted by Adele's current silence that I longed for the tranquil se-curity of my usual Sierra solitude. I was guilty and embarrassed by my anger. This might as well be downtown Oakland on Monday morning for all the spiritual transcendence I was experiencing.

Gradually the sleeping bag warmed up. I could tell from Adele's shallow breathing that she was having a hard time too. If we could zip the bags together, we'd be much warmer. Good thing they were unzip-pably different brands.

"Kath?"

"Yeah?"

"I'm glad you suggested a break."

"Oh, yes?" Careful, I told myself, we were on the edge of truce, be generous.

"I'm sorry I pouted. It was a good idea, really."

"You must have got to know Sandy pretty well." I couldn't help my-self.

"Yes, I guess so," she began. Then, "What do you mean? What's wrong?"

I hated her innocence. Her dimness. It couldn't be dimness. Adele had always been the bright one. Finally, I said, "Nothing's wrong. On the contrary. It sounds as if Earth is on course and you've found your cosmic twin."

Adele propped herself up, peering through the dark. "What are you talking about?"

"That grace note about Berkeley. So is he going to drive to Stanford after your conference? Or maybe you're skipping the conference alto-gether." I couldn't believe this was all coming out. What horror, what release.

"Oh." Adele expelled a long sigh. "No. You've got it all wrong."

I should have backed off. I knew this. Instead, "You must know him pretty well to reveal the 'big secret.' I thought the Berkeley job was con-fidential. I mean, what're you aiming for — trading Berkeley and Sandy for Wellesley and Lou for a trial year?"

"Kath!" Adele moaned. "You're being ludicrously unfair."

"Frankly, I don't know what you're waiting for. You liked our recess so much today, you could take a nocturnal break with him as well. It's his tent you should be lying in!"

She lay still in her sleeping bag, her body turned away from me. I shouldn't have said it. Mom told me I'd inherited all Dad's temper. She was right. Adele was right. I was wrong. Soon, too soon, I'd feel the remorse. But right now I'd enjoy the sweet anger. And I'd wait for Adele to contradict me.

Crawling from the tent the next morning, I prepared my reconciliation speech. I would jokingly congratulate Adele for being the first one up. I would thank her for the coffee, which I would like to inject straight into my aorta. I wouldn't directly refer to last night's conversation unless Adele brought it up. Then I would apologize for my tone. I had a right to be angry, but not nasty.

Mist still hung low over the lake. I was disappointed by the gray sky because I had hoped for sun to light the path back to Tuolumne Meadows. Inhale the soft, quiet day. The silence. Something drew my attention to the bear rope. A note was pinned to my pack.

Dear Kath,
  Sorry not to check this with you. Couldn't sleep much. So I got up early and am heading to Hanging Basket Lake. Will be back by noon, no problem, for our hike down. Needed some time alone.
  Love, Adele

"OK," I said to the vacant day. I wouldn't worry. Of course I shouldn't have barked at her last night. Of course I'd apologize when she came back at noon. But this wasn't such a bad thing. We could use a little more separation.

I turned to breakfast making, remembering this was my last full day in the High Sierra until next summer. A tentative sun was breaking through the clouds. In the bush, an anonymous, small animal rummaged. The creek gurgled and popped as it flowed by. This fragile morning, dark clouds hovered in the west. I savored the pleasure of being alone in the abundant, desolate, scarred, perfect, unforgiving, mountain absolution. Nearby, a cluster of tiny mariposa lilies gleamed under a thin stream of sunlight.

21

Adele

Sunday / Vogelsang Area

I KEPT MY HANDS WARM in my pockets as I walked between Upper Fletcher and Townsley Lakes. The morning was soft, moist. In the distance, a bell struck, the metallic noise vibrating abrasively through high, thin air. Not a bell; of course, that wasn't possible. More briskly, I continued along the trail, inhaling the morning, breathing clarity. The increase in altitude between here and Tuolumne Meadows made me lightheaded. Almost a two-thousand-foot ascent, according to the map. From my left came a high-pitched pipping, but I couldn't locate the source. This path was soft — not marshy like last night's walk to Vogelsang Pass — more reminiscent of the spongy land around Gaylor Lakes. Two California jays flitted before me, washing the air a rapid blue.

Then the sky faded and the world was draped in vagueness. On the way to Hanging Basket Lake, I made a couple of wrong turns but maintained confidence. I did not need Kath as a compass. Was I more annoyed with Kath for jumping to conclusions about Sandy and me or with myself for enjoying Sandy's company so much? Why, after my declaration of sisterly solidarity, did I continue to flirt with him?

How blissful to be alone after this intense week. Thrilling. It was also a little scary out here by myself after a sleepless night. Finally I spotted — yes, checking the landscape against my topographical map, there it was — the ascent to Hanging Basket Lake. It looked like a ninety-degree climb. Who knew if there was a lake at the top? Don't be a wimp, I heard Simon's voice. Cautiously, I proceeded toward the bouldery wall.

"Are you sure you want to do this?" I imagined Kath asking in that infuriating, solicitous way.

"Sure," I would say. "But if you don't want to . . ."

"Oh, no," Kath would declare.

I climbed farther, cherishing last night's red sky, anticipating a brighter day any moment now. Twenty yards from the "trail," I checked again. "Are you sure?"

"Absolutely," Kath would say, "that is, if *you* are."

Thus I continued, Kath beside me, as I crawled up the mottled escarpment toward the unseen lake. Any second I could unleash an avalanche of rocks. Because of my stupidity, I'd be killed or maimed. Would I rather be dead or spend the rest of my life as a vegetable? Mother Cauliflower, née Adele. Slowly, gradually, I pushed upward from one rock to another. Glistening with sweat, I climbed as much with my arms as with my legs.

"Hickory, dickory, dock, the mouse ran up the clock." I remembered Taylor's favorite nursery rhyme from so long ago. What responsible parent would scale Annapurna alone?

"Our Father, who art in heaven . . ." Enough of that. One rock. After another. There was a clear — if not always horizontal — path upward, onward. Others had gone before me.

"Let me introduce this year's winner of the Pulitzer Prize for criticism."

"Ooops." My left foot slipped. I grabbed a branch. Never a wise idea, wood could snap, especially if it were aging wood, dried of sap. Stupid. Stupid to strike out alone. Even if I had no choice. Yes, I needed to be alone today, I needed to think, needed not to think. I wanted to prove to myself that I could make it — whatever *it* was — on my own.

"Middle-Aged Professor Killed in Minor Ascent." Once more Father would be publicly mortified by a daughter's death.

As sun emerged from behind scrambled clouds, the warmth restored my confidence. There, the foot held. I righted myself. Now on to the next flab of granite. Flab? What had happened to my romance with the lunar landscape?

I was getting hungry and wished I had packed more than a rubbery cheese sandwich and an apple. One more boulder, I told myself.

Again.

One more boulder.

Again.

One more boulder.

And yes, here I was. Standing by a pretty little lake bordered by three walls of granite. I sat down for a couple of breaths. I'd made it.

Perfect picnic spot, but now I'd lost my appetite. I missed Kath terribly. I was cold, depleted after that wretched night. A mild wind blew in from the northwest. Eat. I should eat. As I looked down to unhook my fanny pack, I noticed some bear scat. No, Tonto, relax. No bear was stupid enough to make this climb.

Bear? Mountain goat? Giraffe? How would I know the difference? I didn't have the most elementary information for this trip, had leaned on Kath the entire week. Just as I leaned on Lou. I didn't know how much of this was dependent, exploitative, and how much was natural. Deep down, I understood you were journeying alone. In the end, it was you and the universe. You couldn't count on anyone, ultimately. Sari and Mother had taught me that. You had to get along, get through, by yourself. I envied Kath's head start, her self-containment, her long practice of solitude.

Miraculously, my sandwich was intact. I bit into the dying bread and savory cheese. Then I saw a drop of water on my knee. Red sky at night. Another drop on my boot. Quickly, I unfurled the poncho. The rain came more steadily. Just a shower. I tucked as much of myself as possible under the poncho. God, it was cold, how would I make it down these already slippery boulders *in the rain?* A shower, surely just a shower.

Food was reaching my bloodstream, and the altitude seemed less celestial. On the other side of the dainty blue lake, between water and granite, was a stand of deep purple lupine. A fairy sort of place, the kind of Heaven I envisioned as a child. I remembered going to Lake Merritt with Kath when we were in the sixth grade. Such an expedition, taking the bus to downtown Oakland, walking around the water, buying popcorn to feed the ducks. Lake Merritt might as well have been Lake Como, so vast and sophisticated it had seemed then. I supposed it was one of our first adventures, the two of us, in the large world, together.

Sun slithered out once more, and warm benevolence soaked through my jeans. I stretched out on a flat rock. How tired I was. What was going on with Sandy? He was a nice enough guy, but the last thing I needed in my life right now was another man. Pulling myself forward, I shook my shoulders. The old mind was wandering and I wasn't sure I was following it. All the women had left me. But Kath had come back, Kath was at camp, waiting for my return, waiting again, Penelope, still waiting. I had left Kath. The soft sun soothed, lulled. I shouldn't fall asleep. What if a bear ambled by? Silly fear, no one had spotted a grizzly up here for decades, and black bears didn't eat humans unless they were desperate. In mid-August, bears weren't starving; they still had plenty of bugs and fish. I rolled on one side. The sun soothed my stiff left shoulder and lower back.

Sandy continued to return, unbidden, to my mind. Yesterday's hike had been a delight. I had stopped worrying about Kath by the time we completed a mile of the trail along lower Rafferty Creek. The day passed so swiftly as the two of us retrieved the names of people who might have been mutual friends at college. I was startled by our parallels. Both of us had grown up in California, gone East for school, married, had a couple of kids. But Sandy had returned West ten years before, when his marriage broke up.

"How often do you see the kids?" I asked tentatively.

"Three or four times a year," he said. "More if I get a trip back to New York for work. We always manage at Christmas, spring break, the summer."

"That's good," I said encouragingly.

"Could be worse." He nodded. "Not enough time, though."

I found myself liking this man, his accessibility, his willingness to be uncertain, unlike Lou, who had all the answers. I also appreciated the fact that Sandy didn't talk nonstop, the way many men my age did. Young guys probably did, too, but I hadn't noticed this much when I was young — perhaps because I didn't have as much to say in those days. Sandy was a sensitive, bright guy. Good company. It was wise of Kath to suggest this break. Why had I panicked?

"Water?" He stopped and unhooked his canteen.

"After you." I remembered now that Kath hadn't taken the only canteen, that we had another in the trunk behind the cooler.

He had a long gulp and handed me the water. Running my fingers over the round, leather-covered vessel, I asked, "This has stories behind it?"

He smiled. "Bought it in the old market in Mombasa. Twenty years ago. When Lila and I were on our way to work in Mozambique."

"You lived in Africa?"

"A couple of years. Fighting neocolonialism as information officers for Frelimo. In Maputo." He raised his eyebrows. "Soon enough Samora decided we were neocolonialists ourselves."

I drank thirstily.

"He was right. So we came home with some wisdom about politics and geography and a few souvenirs like this canteen."

"You've had quite a life." With reluctance, I handed back the worn, yellowish brown canteen.

"You sound sad!" He laughed. "I trust it's not over yet. I hope I'm only about halfway through."

I was thinking about the safety of my choices. If Kath thought I had abandoned her, it was only because Kath didn't understand I was following a predictable route home, to a home that wasn't a place so much as a pattern. Self-delusion all the years I thought I had escaped — for I hadn't done anything except return to Father's native land on the other coast and reproduce two boys as my parents had had two girls. Mirror images were, of course, not oppositions at all, but the most precise and engaged reflections.

The trail meandered farther from the creek now, upward into a forest of lodgepole pines.

"This is where the trail gets steep," he called over his shoulder. "You OK with that?"

"Sure," I said.

We walked silently for a while.

"So tell me your dreams," he said, climbing steadily, confidently, uphill.

"What a time to ask!" I stalled. "Let me catch my breath." How long had it been since Lou had asked me about my dreams — or since I had asked him?

I don't mean to pry," he added.

"No, I like that you ask questions," I said. "I wish this one weren't so hard." Sun had vanished into cloud, and the forest, crowded with shadows, suddenly turned cold.

"Maybe more precise questions would help." He seemed to have reached yet a new level of good-naturedness. "Where do you want to go? Who do you want to meet? What are you looking for?"

"Well, I feel I'm at the cusp of my career. I mean, there are journals where I'd like to publish, conferences I'd like to attend." I turned to his expectant face. "But somehow this doesn't seem to be what you're asking."

"No?" he said.

"What are you, a shrink?" I laughed, remembering his interest in Jungian art.

"Just a curious friend."

"Well, 'friend,' there's this job at Berkeley I'm thinking about." There, I said it again — first to Kath, now to Sandy — and each time it felt more exciting, more possible. But I was still scared.

"Berkeley" — his tone revealed nothing — "who wouldn't prefer Berkeley to the frozen reaches of Massachusetts?"

"Lou for one."

"Who?"

"My husband, Lou."

"Well, you could always try it for a year — take a leave, right? — and maybe he'd see the light."

"Perhaps."

"How long have you been married?"

"Twenty years."

"Maybe you need a rest stop." He pulled the hat down farther on his forehead. "Sometimes I think if Lila and I had taken a break, we wouldn't have split up. A little separation can be good for two people."

I laughed. "So I've been told."

"I like to be amusing" — he shrugged — "as a human service."

"I'm sorry, it's just that . . ."

"No need to explain." He laughed. "Beatrix Potter said, 'Never apologize, never explain.'"

"You really are something." I grinned. "I like you, Sandy Archer." This was out of my mouth before I thought about it.

We stood in a wide meadow, with views of Mount Dana and Mount Gibbs.

"Stunning view, eh?" I said hurriedly, to cover my embarrassment. He looked at me. "Lovely."

I woke to a gray sky. 4:00 P.M. This was terrible. Perhaps I had knocked my watch against something. I couldn't have slept all this time after lunch. Horrified, I saw the second hand tick, tick along. There was nothing wrong with the shockproof, waterproof Eddie Bauer watch Lou had given me for Christmas. I could do one of those John Cameron Swayze commercials: from high on a rock in the Sierra Nevada, woman climber testifies to product reliability. I fastened the fanny pack, took a sip from the canteen and told myself not to hurry. I always got confused when I hurried. Kath would be furious. It would take us three and a half hours to hike to the Meadows, and that wasn't counting the time it would take me to get back to camp. Shit, rain again. I slid. Damn, tiny pains snapped at my ankle. Slower, I told myself, take it easy. My arm pulsed sharply where I had used it to break the fall.

Climbing down was tricky, and I had to concentrate. There was so much stress on my thigh muscles, on my nerves. The ankle was just tender, not sprained or broken. In younger days, I rarely thought about falling and now I was always conscious of the possibility, because I knew so many more people who had fallen, because I was that much more brittle, because I had learned to worry more. Concentrate, I instructed myself: one step after the other. I would be all right even on these slippery boulders. Wind rose and rain came down harder. I wouldn't want to wreck an ankle and show up at the conference wearing an Ace bandage, hobbling on a crutch. Concentrate. Rain continued intermittently.

Absolutely terrified, I reassured myself by thinking of the hardest things in my life, like facing Mother and Father after Sari's death. Then smaller terrors like introducing Kath to Lou, doing my Ph.D. comps, having my first baby, having my second baby, learning to drive. This actually was quite a short climb. If I'd made it up, I could make it down, I would be fine. Not worth dying here; they had already named the peaks and lakes. What was left to commemorate me — probably not even a tiny wildflower that bloomed in alternate Julys.

That's it, think about flowers. I did miss those botanical sketches and wished I had had the courage to continue drawing. The academy processed your mind the way Kraft processed cheese, removing the impurities and idiosyncrasies and originality. If I returned to California, I *would* take up sketching again. And now to cheer myself, I recalled the favorite blooms: mountain heather, dwarf bilberry, Lemmon's paintbrush, alpine aster. I loved alpine aster, with its yellow center radiating into delicate purple petals.

At the shore of Lake Townsley, I found a grayness thicker than the blanket that haunted me all the way down from Hanging Basket Lake. Shivering, disconsolate, I set out in the direction of camp. The day seemed eternal, yet I knew night would come: an abrupt, dangerous precipice; I had to get back to camp before dark. Kath must be frantic. Exhausted, cold, I found will leading the way.

An hour passed. Another thirty minutes. Definitely, I was lost. L-o-s-t. Sheltered by a high outcropping, I gobbled a handful of trail mix. Almost choking on the chewy, salty, sweet stuff, I slowed down by taking first a raisin, then a pumpkin seed, then a cashew — Sari always liked cashews — then a walnut, then a Spanish peanut. This did no good; I was still speeding. The Donner Party and their disastrous shortcut loomed large. Still, I had food, water. It wasn't all that cold, just wet and foggy. I simply needed to keep my wits, and the wisest thing would be to stay in one place until the mist cleared, but standing still had never been my talent, and it was too late now.

Suddenly, thank God, it came to me that I had taken the wrong turn a mile back. Filled with relief, I retraced my steps, found the trailhead and set off, finally, in the direction of camp.

I hurried, knowing Kath would be furious with me when I arrived. Because I was racing along the trail, I overlooked a root, slightly raised, but enough to catch my boot and topple me. Kath would probably draw attention to the hidden strength of these fabled root systems. Damn, why hadn't I seen it? Cautiously, I lifted myself to a sitting position: upper body OK. With exaggerated slowness, I stood, grateful to discover nothing was broken, although my right knee ached. Well, I could handle this, just decrease the pace a bit. I forced myself to calm down, to eat another handful of nuts and raisins and take a sip of water.

Sun flitted in and out of clouds, roiling murky white sky and streaking the trail with dark patches. I wished I had brought along the Harris sweater. Still, the worst that would happen was that I'd arrive at the conference with sniffles. This well-traveled path revealed fresh boot tracks. Yes, it must be the right route. Yet as I walked, I grew less certain and I found myself searching for signs on the ground, the way after a long winter I would stare at the maple tree outside my study for the promise of tiny green leaves.

Walk carefully, I heard Kath advising in that infuriatingly correct way of hers, so as not to aggravate your knees. During the past few days it had become frighteningly clear how central Kath was in my heart. I should never have left. What would have happened if we had gone to Davis together? Perhaps I could have helped her through the abortion . . . walking cross-country now, I simply followed the sun; you don't need a compass when the sun signals west and east . . . perhaps Sari would have been able to talk with me . . . yes, I was on the right track now, I was almost sure . . . perhaps I could have helped Mother break away from Father before her life got completely waterlogged . . . really this was going fine . . . why had I been so anal these last six days about sticking to trails? . . . perhaps everyone would have been better off if I had stayed in California. No, not everyone. Leaving had meant saving my own skin, my own semblance of sanity. So as much as I regretted losing the West, I couldn't have done it differently. OK, it hadn't worked out all that well, but my real grandiosity was in believing I could orchestrate a perfect life.

My body yearned for Simon and Taylor — to touch their faces, to hold them close. Until I had given birth I hadn't realized that motherhood was such a lifetime physical bond, not just me to them, but them to me. Being a mother had widened my circle of compassion metaphorically, literally. There was incomparable pleasure in comforting them with my body, aiding them, locating my own strong tenderness, and such poignancy in seeing them grow up. At this moment, I wanted nothing so much as to walk into their room and watch their sleeping faces.

My knee was throbbing intensely now. I forced myself to look at the time: 6:30. Jesus, I must be walking the wrong way. Even if I could retrace my steps, it would be dark by the time I reached the turnoff.

Then, abruptly: a trail appeared to the left. Probably smarter to keep traveling in this direction, going somewhere. But I'd have to watch the knee. To distract myself and maintain courage, to scare away animals, I began to sing, "Let there be peace on earth and let it begin with me . . ." I didn't want to end up as a midnight snack for Mama Bear and her cubs.

"This little light of mine . . ."

Sky was dimming. A wind came up. I studied branches scattered on the trail as if they were some sort of magical calligraphy. But their messages were indecipherable. Pulling my hat farther down over my ears, I plodded on.

"You are my sunshine, my only sunshine . . ." I hummed, having just about exhausted my voice and my repertoire. I thought of Poor Tom walking Gloucester across the heath. How much was masquerade? How much was the opposite, a sort of discovery of himself in that costume? How much sense was I making? Not much. I was still alive, but was I still awake? I shouldn't be awake, I knew. I would need my strength to find camp when light returned tomorrow. Tomorrow I would go home, back to California, find Kath in camp. Poor Kath must be worried sick, poor Kath.

This site — nestled against a broad boulder, under a canopy of trees — was as good as any. I spread my poncho on the ground and scrunched up to conserve heat. Sure, this would be fine. I couldn't continue walking in my dazed state. I felt grateful that exhaustion forced the decision, grateful that in the end, body ruled mind and my eyes closed under heavy lids.

Tick. Tick. Not my watch. A rattler? If only I had a flashlight. I was surprised how much I could see in the dark, cones or rods? Biology had never been my subject. With the cloud cover, I could make out a fair amount. The noise ceased. A rattler poised to strike? Breathe in . . . out . . . in . . . out. One minute. Fifteen minutes, half an hour later, I understood it wasn't a rattler's sound. Perhaps a hungry cougar. Apparently, cougars had been feeding on mountain sheep being reintroduced by the Park Service. A wounded cougar, stumbling across a long-awaited dinner. Breakfast. Tomorrow couldn't be that far away.

I wasn't as afraid of death as I was afraid of being torn limb from limb. Terrified of suffering. I wouldn't mind going down in a swift plane crash or with a sudden heart attack. But I would never take my own life. I had witnessed what suicide did to a family and I wasn't going to bequeath that guilt to Simon or Taylor or . . . Lou.

"Adele."

I swiveled, startled, but there was no one, nothing, just my imagination.

Huddling down, I rubbed my hands together. Often enough in the past ten years I had found myself wishing for death, hoping my car might crash, a truck might hit me in a crosswalk. But now, I realized, I did not want to die *here*. I wanted to be back in camp with Kath. During the last week, for all its ups and downs, I had begun to understand I needed to return to California. Something about the smell of the dirt, the yellowish green of the leaves, the quality of the air, was recalling me, reclaiming me. As much as I was Simon's and Taylor's mother, Lou's wife, my students' teacher, my friends' friend, I was also Adele, and this place was part of Adele; I was part of it. My body reminded me that I had never felt completely comfortable in that bluish green of Massachusetts or Maine or the Adirondacks. I thought of the leafy arcade between our cottage and the highway in Maine, where each year the branches would reach toward each other, high above the dirt road, lovers' fingers lusting for touch. I thought about the golden viceroys imitating monarch butterflies and about the forget-me-nots scattered in the pastures. Beautiful. Delicate. Elegant all of it, yet lacking the vitality of California. Somehow not quite real.

I shifted against the rock, letting in a pocket of cold air.

"Adele."

No, I wouldn't be fooled again. I concentrated on physical reality, blowing at my hands. God, I feel stiff. What time was it? Too dark to see my watch. Too tired to judge reasonably. Perhaps I had been here an hour; perhaps three. The color of the sky remained constant — a sheet behind which stars and planets shifted. Would I live differently, if I had it to do all over again? No, life wasn't beginnings and endings; it wasn't this *or* this, but rather this *then* this. It was continuing.

Well, if I could track the swings between my dazed, pseudo-insights, I'd be fine. I would become a scout at the back of my own brain. God, Kath must be panic-stricken. Perfect, Adele. I'd struck out on my own for solitude, for meditative time, to prove to myself and Kath that I was competent in the woods. And look what I'd accomplished — enormous trouble for both of us. How had I got so blessedly off track yesterday? Today? Whenever.

Another noise in the woods now. No, my imagination again. A large, amorphous fear hunkered over me, bigger than a terror of harm or death, for harm and death are circumscribed by time. How would Simon and Taylor cope if I died here? Would their entire lives be haunted by the image of a mother frozen on the mountain? Yes, it was the fear of something eternal, the kind of fear you risk when you reproduce, forever after, all you do has resonance for your children and their children. Death by stupidity was not the legacy I wanted to leave.

Birds, did I hear birds? The sky grew paler. My body had let go. Birds were an omen of daylight, or a warning, not worth thinking about it, I was safer this way, putting off fewer pheromones of fear. Damn reactions were shot. Daniel Boone kilt him a bar when he was only three. No, that was Davy Crockett. By the time they were forty-four, they were probably both dead, their celluloid futures ensured. Father had a rattlesnake key chain that Mother made him keep in a drawer. Disgusting, disturbing — I couldn't remember Mother's exact response. Cold. Rain? Mist.

"Oh, hello." My words this time, a warm, friendly greeting.

The huge black bear wore a necklace of pine cones and bells. Gently, she moved, almost daintily, waving a long red silk scarf from her left side. For seconds I was transfixed, feeling no danger. Then common sense kicked in and I calculated possibilities of escape. She was too close for me to simply back away. Thirty feet. Fifteen feet. Ten feet. Closer, closer, she seemed to dance, the scarf flowing, the bells jingling. Had I summoned her? This was what happened when you flirted with death.

Back against the boulder I scooted, far back. Standing abruptly might alarm her, incite her. Noise worked sometimes, banging a pot — or stunning them on the nose. I slapped my hand against the side of the water bottle. She cocked her head.

Carefully, I lifted the canteen and aimed for that dark, wet snout, but the water bottle went flying over her huge shoulder. I heard it hit the brush, a soft, impotent landing. She turned away, interested in the pathetic bouncing. Gingerly, I inched up to a standing position. Perhaps I could slip away while her head was turned. Something, a shift in the wind, a sixth sense, made her turn back toward me. I was struck to find a sad curiosity, rather than menace, in her face. As she turned her head this way and that, the silver bells dinged faintly through the thick air.

"Adele."

I could smell her now, and I was amazed how long it had taken me to notice this fierce stench. She stepped closer. I held my ground. What was I doing, being seduced by this enormous predator? Scream, I warned myself. But again her huge, sorrowful eyes held me. Scream. I thought of Taylor and Simon. But I continued to watch her, caught in a strange courtship. Shout, I heard Kath say. I opened my mouth and nothing came out.

Nothing.

Nothing.

I swallowed oceans of cold mountain air. And tried again.

"Adele."

My voice.

22

Kath

WHAT LUXURY to spend a whole morning reading by gloriously quiet Lake Helen. I stretched out over a body-sized piece of granite and savored this perfect time to finish the book I'd been carting around for six days. A few sprinkles. Then sunshine and gentle breezes. Translucent green leaves bobbed in nearby branches. I hoped Adele was having a good hike.

Guiltily, I enjoyed this time to myself. OK, so I had driven her away with petulant jealousy. I would apologize, would try to reform. Meanwhile, I'd bask in this familiar solitude. Being alone was a necessary part of my regular tune-up. Sometimes I got lonely or frightened — at night or during a slippery climb on a rainy day — but getting through always gave me a buzz. And there were so many other moments when I felt miraculously unencumbered. Like this morning.

The local Indians had been both more free and less free. Looking down at my vintage leather hiking boots, heavy wool socks, well-worn Levi's, faded blue work shirt, I wondered what it would have been like to work the way native women did, in moccasins, a buckskin skirt and no top. What a rigorous existence. And surely their huge burden baskets weighed more than my backpack.

Across the lake, a father and son were fishing. Trout, they had told me before assuming their mute stations on the secluded far side. Last summer they had caught four trout here. The High Country was filled with brook trout, rainbow trout, cutthroat trout, golden trout. Frankly,

I thought they'd do better if they fished the white-water rapids, but they looked content staring into the placid lake.

Something flitted across my line of vision — like when my watch crystal reflected a streetlamp at night. Moth or butterfly. My reflex was too slow for a good view. Streetlamp: damn urban reference points. I usually shook them within two or three days, and I'd been on this trip almost a week. Maybe my head was still in the city because of Adele. No, I couldn't really blame her. After all, I'd been distracted about my parents, my job, this decision about going back to school.

Shit. I'd completely lost the disciplines that could shape a mountain visit. Normally I'd hike two or three miles longer at a stretch. I'd stop less. Eat lunch faster, read a chapter each night and morning and during the day meditate on what I'd read. The routine created a wholeness, became an accomplishment. I always brought a mystery and something about Indians plus a book about wildfowers or birds or mammals. Last year I studied Miwok basketry and geology. This year's funky reprint of Galen Clark's 1902 *Indians of Yosemite* was as interesting for what it revealed about the great white naturalist as for what he said about "the aboriginal people." But just now I found myself caught by a description of the legendary Tis sa' ack, whose "dark hair cut straight across her forehead and fell down at the sides."

Overhead the birds became insistent. Filled with strange sadness, I understood that although I felt intimate with this land, I'd never know any of the animals, really, individually. Maybe that's why urban people adopted pets — as a deposit on some kind of interspecies harmony. Jesus, I missed Baffin and knew I'd miss her all the more when I returned to the apartment this week. I felt familiar here, yet alone, the way I felt *almost* at home in San Francisco. There I knew the streets and buildings but not the people. I could tell when someone looked out of his neighborhood — as a beaver would, lumbering through meadow grasses — but I didn't have many friends in San Francisco.

Tis sa' ack was a dramatic figure, drinking all the water in Mirror Lake and being exiled to Half Dome and causing chaos among the Ah-wah-nee-chees. I often thought that Adele with her bangs and raven hair looked Indian. Smiling, I remembered the time I asked Dr. Ward if there was any native heritage in their family. Alarmed, he stared at me for several seconds. "Pure Scots." He slowly recovered his dignity.

Acorn mush. Roots. Lupine splashed with manzanita cider. Sorrel. Wild caraway. Their diet sounded delicious. That is, if I could have skipped the deer and fish. Had any of the Yosemites been vegetarian? I found myself getting hungry and was surprised to see it was after one o'clock. I'd left Adele a note saying I'd be at Lake Helen. Maybe it'd blown away? Was Adele taking offense at being summoned? Had she been waylaid by Sandy and more of his photographic questions? Reluctantly, I stretched and headed back to camp.

My stomach knotted as I saw my note flapping against the backpack. No trace of visitors. I knew now — as I had tried not to know — that Adele was with Sandy. Damned if I was going to fetch her. I pulled out a piece of bread, broke off some cheese and made myself almost comfortable on a log. The canteen was nowhere in sight.

Still . . . I could understand how Adele would weary of my playing Ranger Kate. In fact, I *had* been obnoxious in the way I'd been sharing these mountains — as if I owned them. Rather than was rediscovering them with an old friend. What the hell was wrong with me? I had been so controlling this week, the crone set in her ways.

"Hi there. You have a good morning?"

Sandy strolled energetically along the trail. What on earth did Adele see in this guy?

"Adele back yet?"

"Haven't you seen her?" Relief. Then fear. If Adele was on her own all this time, she could be lost, could have fallen . . .

"No." Sandy looked alarmed. "Has she been gone long?"

"Oh, don't worry. She'll be right back," I explained to both of us. "She's kind of an absentminded professor at times. Probably off reciting her paper to herself."

"That Stanford conference sounds pretty high-powered," Sandy offered, with irritating congeniality.

Had Adele told him her whole damn life story? Shit, why couldn't he just disappear? Maybe if I implored Tis sa' ack . . .

"Yes, I'm sure she's fine," he was saying absently, although he didn't look at all sure. "She's a very competent lady."

"Right." I nodded curtly. Implying, I can't take anymore. Please leave before I start throwing rocks.

He got the message. "See you later." Raising a palm, he ambled off to his tent.

Rattled, I sat back on the log and started at sky. He was a decent guy. The only *really* outrageous thing he had done was to interrupt us on the Glen Aulin Trail. Since then, I'd been at least as rude to him. I'd been dreadful, but my feelings for Adele ran so high.

He was right that she'd be fine. I remembered her in high school campaigning door to door for the Fair Housing Bill. Despite her parents' objections. Despite threats from Thomas Winslow and his junior KKK thugs. I thought of Adele traveling across country and negotiating her way with the snooty private school girls. In those days, we were both fueled by a beautiful anger, raging against unfairness in the world, racism, colonialism, poverty. What had happened to that lovely fury? These days I groped after it, as if after a lifeline. But I was more conscious of fear than anger, fear of menopause, cancer, senility. Death. My own, other people's deaths. This fear ate all the air and pride in my chest, diminishing me as surely as age shrank the spine.

Of course Adele would be fine. I sat up and stretched my tight neck from side to side. After all she had been an environmentalist before the word was invented. Conservationist we called it in those days. She owned a whole library of John Muir books before we graduated from high school. Such egotism to believe I was the only one who knew what I was doing. After all, I was an unemployed dropout while Adele was an international success. She would be fine. Adele was, as Sandy said, "a very competent lady."

I yanked our packs down from the trees. We'd leave as soon as Adele returned. If she was too tired to walk down to Tuolumne Meadows today, we'd have to beg the ranger for an extension on the camping permit. Of course she was fine, probably just distracted by the landscape. Maybe storing up images and longings to sustain her in Massachusetts.

As I leaned back against the firm pack, my mind grasped for distraction. Slow down, I told myself. I focused on breathing in the sun-ripened greenery. Pay attention.

The photograph showed an Indian in a long skirt, her hair shorn to widows' length, carrying a load of wood on her back. This woman looked tired, competent, stoic. The caption read, "As in all Indian tribes, the women do most of the work."

Adele could use this picture in one of her feminist studies classes. I thought of how we had crammed together for the SAT during our senior year, sitting side by side in the library, sharing Good & Plenties and trying to stump each other with algebra questions. I allowed myself to feel how much I had missed Adele in the years between then and now. But this suffering posture was exaggerated, really, because other people had sustained so much more grief. Carter's wife died in a train crash. Adele lost both Sari and her mother.

I, myself, was lucky my parents remained alive. Dad's mind was gone in some ways. But in others, he was still here. As long as life continued, so did the possibility of forgiveness. I guess I'd always been a puzzle if not a disappointment to Mom. Martha had spent at least forty years trying to shake me up and reshape me. And Dad simply wanted a son. One daughter was enough. He didn't quite know what to do with two. So if these people really drove me nuts like this, why didn't I go, as Adele did, far away where they couldn't touch me? It had something to do with place. This California was as much mine as theirs. And it had something to do with loyalty. That made sense. What didn't make sense was that that same loyalty kept me from finishing my degree. Deep down, I knew that graduating from college was immigrating to another country.

Enough self-consciousness. The best things about Clark's book were the legends, like the one about how the mountain peak El Capitan emerged from a boulder. Two small boys slept on the boulder while the earth pushed granite toward the sky, stranding the children at 3,300 feet. Despite all rescue attempts — by the great leaping grizzly and the broad-jumping mountain lion — the kids were unreachable. Until the modest measuring worm inched its way to the top and recovered the children.

The first drops of rain registered on my head. Looking up, I found a huge dark cloud migrating from the northwest. We would never make it down to the Meadows in the rain at this hour. Drops struck the tree stump where we set the lantern last night. Gene Krupa, Ricky Ricardo, Ringo Starr . . . I wasn't very good on drummers' names. Had Adele taken her poncho? I combed through my friend's backpack anxiously. Yes, it was gone. Fine. She'd be fine. Adele knew how to take care of herself. But in case something was wrong, I decided to go to the High Sierra Camp and report her missing. Oh, Del. What have you done now? What have I done? Please come back. Safely. Soon. Now.

Night felt dark, cold, and our tent was cavernous without her. During the first phone call, the ranger hadn't seemed particularly worried. Hanging Basket Lake was close, he said. Adele had gone off with food, water, a poncho and a topographical map. Regular Girl Scout preparation. But her bulky green sweater was still here. The real danger was hypothermia. It surprised a lot of people in summer camping. And Adele, so long back East, wouldn't be used to these altitudes, where it got frigid at night. Hypothermia produced lack of judgment. She could be wandering off a cliff right now — or lying exposed in some deceptively cushy mountain meadow.

I lifted the flap, searching the uncommunicative, overcast sky. Just as the sun and moon disappeared, so did my moral and emotional signposts. I had to have faith that they were still there. The earth was still revolving on its axis and the stars would reappear. Even invisible, they were doing their jobs.

The ranger had even been a little flip: maybe she was meditating on wildflowers? I tried to believe him, remembering Adele's wonderful botanical sketches. But at the back of my mind was Sari's death. Adele's preoccupation with the Berkeley job. Our fight the night before.

Now I flopped on my stomach, resisting sleep as much as I desired it. Cursing my repressed, private personality, which held back the kind of information that would have gotten his goddamned ass moving sooner. I had spent the afternoon walking back and forth between our campsite and the phone at Vogelsang Camp, debating whether to tell him about this history of suicide in Adele's family, about the other pressures that could distract her if not drive her over the brink.

At first the ranger didn't even want to extend the camping permit. Then, he relented. And about 4:00 P.M., when the mist was soupy thick, he agreed to send out a search party. Helpless, I remained in camp, pacing, praying, staring at a tree branch bending in the windy rain. Of course it made sense for me to wait here, but waiting was not my strong suit. While my body held vigil, my mind raced across country. Scouting for Adele, chasing away dangers. Singing madly into the wind. Hours after dark, the soggy searchers returned, saying they had found nothing, not a scarf, a scrap of litter. Not a body. The reassuring ranger said to remember she had food, water, a map. The rain had ceased. Because of the cloud cover, it wouldn't freeze tonight.

Well, I didn't know about that. It was certainly too cold for *me* to fall asleep. I cursed my temper again. Why had I clung to my silly rivalry? So what if Sandy helped ease her way back to California? At least she'd be in the Bay Area. She'd be home again. And he wasn't a bad guy. He was only a guy.

If I'd been more tuned in, I would have known Baffin was sick, maybe taken her to the vet that morning instead of flying off to the jogging trail. And if I'd been more sensible, I would have noticed Mom's bruises before she was taken to the hospital, would have found a way to explain Dad's behavior to Martha without sounding like a know-it-all professional. If I'd been more generous, Anita wouldn't have left.

Adele was smart. She'd be OK. She'd conserve the food and water and find shelter. She'd be safe as long as she didn't run into a cougar or trip in the mist. Or throw herself off a mountain. But, Jesus, it must be cold out there. I listened to the wind — maybe an airplane — attending closely to the howling night. All around me the sounds were wistful. Melancholy. Scary.

My tent exploded with splinters of yellow and orange light. Sunset. Sunrise. Flashlight. My eyes and mouth blinked open. Relieved, I saw Adele crawling through the flaps. My shoulders relaxed back into the sleeping bag, back into the pine needles, back into the mountain floor. Then I heard the noise behind her. Wet, heavy, aspirated, harsh, like a snow shovel scraping the sidewalk. A dark form followed her.

"Adele!" I warned, but she took no notice.

"Adele." If she could only make it into the tent, she'd be safe, I thought foggily. No, that was ridiculous. The creature would simply eat both of us here. The only hope was to get outside, on our feet. Here we were trapped in the plastic ribs and nylon skin. Reaching for my pocketknife, I knew the best escape was out back. I could pull Adele through, leaving the bear dazed with poles and stakes and ribbons of tent around her head. We could run for shelter at the High Sierra Camp while the animal wrestled her way through the polyester and poles. I had it all figured out.

"Adele," I yelled. How could she be so oblivious?

"Adele."

"Adele," she said strangely.

I woke at the sound of her name. Alone again.

My first groggy thought was, What if Adele is hit by a shooting star? I looked at the semi-iridescent dial on my watch — 3:00 A.M. — pleased, horrified that I had fallen asleep. Two and a half more hours until dawn. Ready to take off at the first light, I would find Adele myself.

23

Kath

Monday / Vogelsang

I WOKE to a milky daylight. Too early to call the ranger, so I forced myself to stay in the cold, clammy sleeping bag. I hadn't been able to get warm all night. 6:00 A.M. Birds insisted the day forward. Eyes closed, I knew it was impossible to rest.

Crawling into the marbled gray morning, I guessed there was a fifty-fifty chance of rain. Damn. I forced myself to eat an orange. Sugar shot straight to my aching muscles. Was Adele waking up now? Cold and fuzzy, but I hoped fairly dry under the poncho. Behind me, one jay screeched to two others in a whitebark pine. Then together the birds bleated loudly, saxophones pulsing toward a cloudy ceiling.

God, I felt terrible: ghostly hollow, body ambulating without heart as I collected trash, extinguished the fire, unbuttoned my flannel over-shirt. Limbs and carcass moved while spirit was tethered high in one of these pines, watching for Adele's return. Better reconnect body and soul before phoning the ranger or they'd cart me off to a loony bin.

On my way to the phone, I had to pass Sandy's site. He was up, eating an apple.

"Any word?" he called out, apprehensive about Adele, yet cautious, keeping a respectful distance.

I thought of Carter telling me I had intimidated him for the first two months in the office. I still didn't get it — how could these huge men be frightened of a small, taciturn female? Well, whatever worked, I guessed, and it saved me learning karate.

"Not yet." My voice was friendly. I needed his help. Someone had to stay in camp in case Adele wandered back. This had gone too far to rely on feeble notes. The ranger was much more likely to agree to my going off in search of her if he knew "another friend" was waiting behind.

Sandy consented to stay. He shrugged off his satisfaction at being enlisted by saying he needed to repair a couple of holes in his tent anyway. And he had a lot of reading to do.

All the way to Hanging Basket Lake it drizzled. The ranger thought I was overwrought to insist on looking in the same place he had checked yesterday. But he held his peace when I promised to return by noon. I kept my eyes wide open as I walked past Upper Fletcher and Townsley Lakes, pained by the thought of our carefree swim here two days ago.

It was a fair hike to the lake, a real act of faith to scramble up these boulders, for who knew if there was anything at the top? I remembered the water: teacup-sized compared with many of the lakes up here, but worth the hike for its isolation. If I hadn't competed with Sandy for eloquence about this place, Adele and I would be in the car this very minute driving back to Palo Alto.

As I feared, Hanging Basket Lake — about half a mile in circumference — was deserted. Still, I called loudly, "Adele. Adele." My voice echoed back, "Adele. Adele," in desolation. How alone I was. How alone Adele was; somewhere out there, somewhere by herself. Exhausted, I rested on a rock. Bending down, I wept into the unforgiving ground.

I walked cross-country to Vogelsang Lake, instead of catching the easy trail back to camp. Maybe Adele decided to return this way. Damn her charming unpredictability. And her deathly fear of boredom. Is that why she "took up" (as Mom would say) with Sandy? Was I that tedious?

I recalled the slumber party at Paula's house where we listened to the score of *West Side Story.* I remembered Adele singing each part with humor, flair, trying to organize the five of us into some kind of harmony. I had sat back watching Paula and Adele and Nancy in their gigantic pink rollers and Donna wearing the headgear that held her orthodontic retainer in place. Her face smeared with skin-tone Clearasil. We were all trapped in wholesome adolescence. If there was a way out, Adele would lead us.

This walk back down to Vogelsang Lake was easy enough, although Adele hated descents. Anyone could have slipped in yesterday's muck.

Closely, I inspected each side of the trail as I walked along. "Adele. Adele," I shouted. "Adele. Adele," I demanded. Above, a helicopter drowned out my voice, a loud zipper frantically opening the morning sky.

Vogelsang Lake was a lusciously large body of water compared with Hanging Basket. Concentrating on the still, greeny surface, I tried to absorb some tranquillity. No use. My mind dashed back and forth: Where could Adele be, what could I do? How had I caused this catastrophe with my sullen pride? I walked the entire circumference. There was nothing to do now except head back to camp.

No news, the ranger's office reported. I promised to wait. And there I sat in my tent, pretending to read. I put the last piece of cheese and bread out of my mind although I was surprisingly hungry. I knew Adele would be starving by the time she arrived. Yes, of course she would arrive. Of course everything would be fine.

As if on cue, Sandy ambled by with a hard-boiled egg and an apple.

"Thought you might be running low on food," he offered.

"No, I'm fine." I sat straighter, appearing alert, well-fed.

"Go ahead." He squatted beside me, a gossiper in a Nanjing marketplace. "I bought extra," he insisted.

I smiled, accepting the food. "Have a seat."

He sat and nervously traced a twig over the sand and pine needles.

Famished, I cracked the shell and ate as slowly as I could. I knew the egg would be more filling if I concentrated on the experience of eating it.

"No luck?" he asked cautiously, his urgency undisguisable.

I could tell what Adele saw in this guy.

"Not yet." I shook my head.

"Ranger's still looking, though?" he asked optimistically.

"Oh, yes."

"Mind if I look this afternoon?" he tried again.

My neck flared red. In his presence, my feeling coursed so deep, I lost all equilibrium. Of course he should go. I had promised to remain in camp. No point in us both staying here. Us both. I hated how Sandy had gotten enmeshed in our vacation. But this was no time to be jealous. The more people looking for Adele the better. I shuddered at the image of lanky Gulliver rescuing the distressed damsel. Jesus, that would be perfect. Immediately ashamed, I nodded. "Sure," I said, "that would be great. Thanks."

I watched him head for the trail, strong, purposeful and energetic. In comparison, I was overcome with fatigue, as if I had eaten a huge meal. Maybe the sleeplessness was catching up. Still, I tried to read. I guessed some part of me believed that my staying awake kept Del alive. A candle in the window. Picking up the Clark book, I was distressed that I had almost finished it. I set my poncho on the ground, leaned against a tree and stretched out my weary legs.

Several minutes — maybe an hour — later I was awakened by a ground squirrel rapturously inspecting my apple core.

I closed my eyes again.

From deep within my sleep, I heard a familiar voice — Sandy? — booming above me. Summoning my newly acquired tolerance, I pried open my lids. Against the sun's glare, I made out a ranger's hat. The man's white teeth gleamed.

I sat up, clutching knees to my chest.

"Your friend was more conscious than you."

"You found her?" I jumped to my feet.

Grabbing each of the ranger's arms, I shook him, demanding, "She's OK?"

"Yup," the man said.

I noticed now that he was younger than I. Paternal, nonetheless. "The chopper picked her up walking. She was fine, but lost between Gallison Lake and Parsons Peak. They're keeping her under observation down at Tuolumne Meadows."

"Observation?" I was alarmed. "Was she hurt?"

"No, standard in a case like this. They check for bruises, breaks, shock."

I was jamming my book and poncho into the backpack. "Oh, thank you. Thank you. I better get going." The pack fit as snugly as a pair of wings.

We both stared at Adele's pack. My face fell.

"That's all right," he said with rangerly benevolence. "We can send it down with the mules tomorrow. You go on now."

"Thanks." I waved good-bye.

"My pleasure," he declared, heading off briskly like the Lone Ranger.

I had gone 500 yards when I remembered Sandy. He said he'd be back by 4:00 P.M. It was 3:30. I knew it would be best to wait and go down together. Then again, he might be late. If I was a nice person I would wait. However, I decided I was more a smart person than a nice person. A note pinned to his backpack would do. I knelt down to write, "Adele safe. Thanks, Kath."

I didn't have to say where she was. He could find out from the ranger. This was enough.

The sky had cleared to a deep blue, and there was a light breeze. My body reached the pass before my mind, and suddenly I noticed the other hikers, hot and dusty, coming in the opposite direction. It had taken four hours to climb up here, but I could make it down in three. The descent was about 1,700 feet. Unlike Adele, I was an easy downhill hiker. The sun shone amiably on the white boulders.

Adele was safe. Anxieties were dissolving. Adele was alive. Unhurt. Waiting at the end of the trail. I entered a shady area of whitebark pine. What delicious, fresh, sour scents. No longer did I feel tired from last night's vigil. Or sore from our week of climbing. Adele was alive. Adele was well. Adele was back.

Basking in this renewal of heart, I considered how much I had surrendered these last few years. The attrition of my spirit had been gradual, yet undeniable. It was crazy, absolutely nuts, to limp from one soft-money job to the next. If I was going to get anything secure before I went on Social Security, I'd have to finish school. It was either this or win the lottery, or as Dad would have said (in his alert, sardonic days), an apparition from St. Peter with a combination to the Vatican coffers. My whole life, I'd focused on trying to do the right thing, not knowing how different that was from doing the successful thing. The disjunction made no sense, but there it was. And before I died, I had to learn to compromise. In this case: a cosmetic college degree. Right now the other people in my agency — my former agency — were the *real* people. The permanent appointments got real raises, real health benefits, paid vacations. Of course they were underpaid, too, and therefore more conscious of what they didn't have than what they did have.

Martha would laugh at my returning to school. She had thought college was pretentious enough twenty-five years ago. And she had had ample time for I-told-you-sos. No, she would laugh her head off. Going to San Francisco State for a social work degree when I had all these years of experience. What could they teach me that I didn't know? But I had argued back to her now, experience without credentials was worthless. Don't be so abstract, Martha said. You need power to change things, I retorted. Power, Martha laughed, power. Who do you think you are, Jerry Brown?

On some level, I knew Martha was afraid of losing me. My family was an extension of myself. I was trapped by their expectations. If I left, it was my fault. There was no easy escape. Only a coming to terms. Only another flawed treaty.

The trail by Rafferty Creek was cooler today in the late afternoon air. Water rushed and gurgled beside the path. It was 5:30 now. Had the ranger told Adele I was coming? Mammoth Peak gleamed white in the distance and Mount Dana vibrated redness. I took a full breath of fresh High Country air.

In 1962, Adele sent me a postcard of the Space Needle from the Seattle World's Fair. In tiny, precise handwriting, she described the science center, the food circus, the international exhibits, the monorail. Seattle, Martha had sniffed, who would want to go to Seattle? It's always raining. I remembered Adele teaching me the twist when we were freshmen in high school and how, the next year, in the middle of a Chubby Checker song at Homecoming, I noticed I was stealing her boyfriend. The romance didn't last more than two weeks, but Adele refused to speak to me for a month. I expected her outrage. I enjoyed it.

Now the trail was turning steep again. I climbed down, through the forest of lodgepole pine. Finally, when I reached the footbridge over the Tuolumne River, I calculated I'd see Adele in less than half an hour. It was a mile to the ranger station from here. Would Adele be shaky, scared, angry, relieved to see me? Disappointed not to see Sandy? Ready to go back to the city? The ranger had said she was OK. He had meant physically. Just how close did Adele get to Sari's edge? Of course she was different from her mother and sister, but that was, in part, a carefully constructed difference. As if she were creating an alternative personality on the other side of the continent. Safe. Durable. Stunning how adaptable Adele was. Still, she kept Ward in her name. She would always be haunted by her mother's life and Sari's death.

I was almost there now, sensing the lower altitude. I felt more grounded. Conscious of traffic fumes and noise, I hurried toward Adele.

The woman behind the desk looked up expectantly. "Hello."

"Hi." My voice was shaking. "Hi. I'm here to see a friend."

The woman frowned.

"A patient."

"I'm sorry," she said carefully. "We have no one here at this time, although we've had several in the last few hours. What's the name? I can probably tell you which hospital —"

"Hospital." I gasped. "But the ranger said she was fine." I was frantic. "No broken bones."

The woman raised a patient, practiced eyebrow.

"Adele," I said finally, reluctant to sacrifice her name for this dour authority. "Adele Ward. Jones."

"Oh, yes." Her face relaxed. "Adele, yes, lively gal. She's fine. In fact, gone now."

"Gone?" I exclaimed.

"We tried to keep her but only managed to get her to rest a couple of hours. She insisted she had a friend coming down from Vogelsang to meet her. And we managed to find them a tent cabin — a miracle at the last minute — at Tuolumne."

"A friend?" I leaned against the wall, suddenly aware of my backpack's weight.

"Yes." Her patience was wearing thin. "We sent word through to the ranger. Several messages."

"And the friend's name was?" I hesitated. The little room was hot, stuffy. I wiped sweat from my nose with the back of my hand.

"Kathleen, I think." She looked puzzled. "Kathy? Is that you? Didn't you get the message?"

"I got the message." I nodded, approaching the door. "Thanks." I grinned foolishly.

"Well, your friend seems OK," she called after me. "But I'd keep a watch on her. Don't let her overdo it. She promised to check back with us before she left the park tomorrow."

"I'll make sure she does."

Buoyantly, I walked toward Tuolumne Lodge Campground, looking forward to seeing Adele as I hadn't in years, maybe since our first summer in college. Certainly I hadn't looked forward to that painful twenty-fifth high school bash. I'd dreaded it for months. And I'd been terrified about this week's journey, had cursed Michael Bagley for dragging me to the reunion. But this afternoon, I was eager to find Adele, to see how she was, to know how she passed the night, to tell her of my own fears and the search.

Light wind swept low across the ground, stirring the grass. There was at least another hour of sunlight, but the squirrels and voles and quail scurried around as if the curtain was about to fall. These neatly ordered white canvas tents with their concrete floors weren't my idea of camping. Who cared? Inside one of the tent cabins, complete with potbellied stove, firewood, towels and metal cots, was Adele.

Number 46 was in the back row, by the woods. My breath came in short, nervous huffs as I rapped on the green wooden doorframe.

Adele appeared. Intact. Healthy. Tired. Wearing an oversized black T-shirt and borrowed pants that her long legs had translated into pedal pushers. Still freshly showered, she looked like a TV soap commercial.

I felt hot, filthy, a hobo intruder. Stinking of sweat and dust, my hair hung down in strings.

We exchanged cautious stares, two prodigal sisters taking the other in. We stood there, relieved, and in our reprieve, experiencing the true terror of the last two days. At the same time, we broke down crying.

She drew me inside the cool, dark tent. "Oh, Kath. I love you. I was so scared. I'm sorry. You must have been frantic." She hugged me.

"All of the above." I beamed at my friend. "Scared. Sorry. Frantic." I was looking into a mirror, into the future, into a clear, bottomless lake.

24

Adele

Tuesday / Tuolumne Area

WE SLEPT VERY LATE that morning. The comforting beds with their springs, mattresses, pillows, clean, white sheets and blankets felt luxurious after the last night in the open and our week in the pup tent. When I woke, I immediately checked Kath's evenly breathing form. This was not a dream: we were both *safe,* sound and back together. Shocked that my watch read 10:00, I raised it to my ear to make sure it was still ticking. My arm ached from this small movement.

I closed my eyes again. Of course Kath would be tired. She probably had a rougher time worrying than I did being lost. At least I knew I was safe. I wished we didn't have to leave the mountains. Belligerently, I wanted our whole week in the woods together, and we had been cheated out of a day. Still, the main reason for my coming to California was the conference. My brain began calculating our schedule, clicking ahead at professional pace: as soon as the mule team arrived with my backpack, we would be off. We could easily make it by 6:00 P.M., and I wasn't slotted to give my paper until 8:00. Damn, I hated to leave. Since our first day here, I had been counting the minutes left, like a death-row prisoner. This vacation had made me realize how much I missed Kath, how much I wanted her back in my life and, on balance, that understanding was a blessing.

Sun seeped through the white canvas, warming my back. I found myself reaching for the water bottle. I was so thirsty. Where had I put the damn thing? Better be still or I would wake Kath. I picked up her book and leafed through it quietly. She knew so much more about this place; I would never catch up.

"So are you planning to lie here for hours or are we going to see some country?" Kath sat up, pretending to be wide awake.

"Sleep well?" I asked.

"Fine. How about you, Annie Oakley?"

"Been waiting around for you to get your beauty sleep. In fact, I was bored about 6:00 A.M. and ran a couple of laps around the Meadows, then sneaked back in here." I smirked, swinging rubbery legs over the side of the bed. "Oh." I grabbed my lower back. "Guess my little vision quest has left some damage."

"You have to take it easy after an experience like that." Kath was frowning. "Sometimes I do think you live entirely in your head."

"I'll be fine," I declared, slowly pulling on my jeans. "But I could use a cup of strong coffee."

"They have a pot brewing at the lodge all day. I'm sure breakfast is over, but we can find some packaged cookies. Or drive over to the grill for eggs and pancakes."

"No, cookies are fine. I think reentry into the late twentieth century should be a gentle one. Gradual. Simple."

I waited for Kath at a picnic table by Miller Cascade. The morning sun relaxed me, made me realize further how tired I was. The campground was almost deserted now; most people had long since gone off hiking. Only a few mothers and small children remained. And an assembly of birds scavenging what the humans had left behind.

I laid out my arms on the table before me, letting sun penetrate the skin, muscles, bones. I had always dreamed about having a study that faced north, warmed by indirect morning sun. Funny, the things you put on your list of necessities when you're young: northern light, view over the garden, a lemon tree. And the last item impossible in the Northeast. Lately I had been thinking a lot about fragrant lemon blossoms: about shining yellow globes, miniature suns; the sweetness of soft, thin Meyer lemon rind and the smooth, erect bubbles of moist flavor inside. Iced tea. Lemonade. You could eat a Meyer lemon on its own, it was that sweet.

My arms were thoroughly warmed now. My skin changed this week, not so much tanned as exploded in tiny freckles. I inspected a few scratches, mementos of my wilderness overnight. And a good bruise in the soft flesh just beneath the right elbow. The arms were fairly firm. Hands were growing lined. Still, my long piano fingers remained kind of distinctive. Maybe I had thirty to thirty-five years left if I were lucky and ate well. I was definitely over the halfway point according to anyone's demographics. It was hard to fathom, really. In academia, you were always alert about what you hadn't accomplished, who had published better or received more grants. Still, there was so far to go that I cultivated an image of youthful potential, of almost having arrived. Likewise, with my family, I was less aware of what I did have than conscious of what we didn't own, how much we would have to save for the boys' college, how many years we'd have to wait to remodel the kitchen. These concerns also reminded me that I was almost there, almost satisfied. And that, in turn, caused me to invent new needs.

Perhaps I feared satisfaction as a kind of death. Too busy perfecting the art of wanting, I had never acquired a talent for appreciation. This was a serious character flaw. Still, I *wanted* my next book discussed in *The New York Review of Books.* Still, I hoped to get a Guggenheim and spend a year researching in London. Still, I ached for the room with northern light. And the lemon tree.

Kath set down the cardboard box of coffees and cookies. Regarding my arms, splayed on the table, she inquired, "Little early for a séance?"

I laughed, then accepted a cup, inhaling the strong, dark aroma. "Thanks."

"No problem." She pulled a road map from her parka pocket.

My heart sank. Sucking on a cookie, Kath began plotting with as much energy as she could summon. "They expect the mule train down from Vogelsang within an hour. So we should have our pack by 11:30. If we take off then, we can be —"

"I was hoping we could take a short walk to Lyell Fork, at least."

"Well, I guess." Kath unfolded the map. "I guess if we could turn off 880 at Hayward and take the Dunbarton Bridge, we could still do Lyell Fork and get to Palo Alto by six."

"Let's skip Palo Alto." It just came out.

"But isn't your paper tonight?" Kath asked cautiously.

"Don't worry, I haven't gone bonkers." I concentrated on not laughing, because I did feel giddy. "No conference is a fair trade for these mountains. I cheated us out of Sunday and Monday, so . . ."

"Adele, don't talk like that. I'm just grateful you're safe. I can come back here any time I want. It's only five hours from Oakland. I know how important that conference is to you. Don't make sacrifices for me."

I sipped my coffee thinking about sacrifice. I was beginning to understand which were the sacrifices, to honestly weigh certain gains and losses. While it's true I'd never failed to show up for a paper in my life, missing this one wouldn't be a grave sin. I had paid my own airfare, and there were three other people on the panel, who would probably feel delighted to have a few more minutes to speak. And getting stuck in the mountains was an excuse anyone could understand.

Closing my eyes and stretching my head back, I felt grateful for the caffeine, for the brilliant August day, for my beloved friend. "Well, we can talk about why sacrifices should be made for you later. Meanwhile, I'm doing this for me. For us. That is "— I was abashed by my insensitivity —"Unless *you* have something you need to get right back to."

Kath snickered and took another cookie. "Only the unemployment check."

"Are you sure?"

"Yes."

"Then, I can spend the extra day. Well, let me see if we can stay one more night here and I'll explain to the chair that I had a minor accident. No, that would get back to Lou. I'll tell them we have car trouble."

"Say it's the fan belt." Kath laughed. "Fan belts are always breaking on this model."

From a distance the meadow seemed a tranquil pool. But as we stepped into it and moved a dozen feet from the road, Kath and I were surrounded by life — by butterflies and dragonflies and salamanders, by the yawning creak of a branch about to crack and the soft, swirling blades of grass. She walked several paces ahead and I was happy to follow today. I thought about the two of us on the high school bus to the Asilomar Conference for Human Rights. Going down to the Monterey Peninsula to discuss poverty and racism and international politics with the visiting sages, William Sloan Coffin and Jay Rockefeller. All of us standing in that pretty Julia Morgan hall, holding hands, singing, "We Shall Overcome." Kath and I taking long strolls on the cold, foggy beach early in the mornings before the panels started, talking about how we were going to change the world.

Kath turned around to check on me. I waved cheerfully. Since my solitary outdoor slumber party, I found my mind darting into these odd, ruminative states, and now I let it run on again. . . . If we were naive in those youthful days, we were also right. Problem was — the ground shifted; the horizon kept moving; personal responsibilities escalated. Deaths of friends and family created fissures in your will-power. The gods of social change were revealed as human, and we lost our beacons. As our bodies aged, we grew more weary. As we learned to compromise, we made material gains, and those incremen-tally accumulated comforts eroded social commitment. Perhaps the remaining question was how to honor that young idealism, in fact how to recover some of it, while understanding the people we had become in the meantime. What would the Adele on that bus home from Asilo-mar have thought of me now? Would she be appalled at the accommo-dations I'd made? Would she be amazed I lived this long?

My attention returned to Kath, in the present. The grass had disas-sembled into a thousand jigsaw shades of green and yellow at this hec-tic site of insect reproduction and commerce.

I pointed to a young fir, its ends tipped a fragile, almost chartreuse, shade of green. "Looks as if it's holding painted fingernails out to dry in the sun."

"Nancy."

We both said her name at once.

"Yes," Kath declared. "We've got to call her tonight."

"Oh, I feel so bad."

"I think getting lost overnight at 10,000 feet is a good excuse."

"I guess you're right," I answered, unconvinced.

We ate lunch near Parsons Lodge, where rusty water had bubbled forth from Soda Springs for hundreds of years. As we stretched in the sun, Kath propped herself on an elbow and studied my face. "You know, you're really the same person."

"What do you mean?" I looked at her crossly.

"You haven't changed." She shrugged. "You're the same Adele I've al-ways known."

"I hate it when people say that to me." I sat up and regarded her ner-vously. "I've worked so hard to change."

She looked startled.

"To develop myself, to learn new things, to recover from my fam-ily" — my voice strained —"and after all this you tell me I haven't changed!"

"Well." She shrugged helplessly.

I felt terrible. I knew she meant it as some kind of compliment. "Lou always tells me I'm an earnest little self-improver. But improvement isn't the point. Maybe all these years in therapy were just invested in keeping me alive, in developing strategies for surviving."

"Maybe. Hey, lighten up."

"In surviving without too much self-destructiveness," I continued, as if she were my shrink, as if the point of this exchange were for me to achieve epiphany.

"And maybe when someone says you haven't changed, she just means she still recognizes a familiar light."

"Perhaps," I said.

"I didn't mean it as criticism," she tried.

"No, of course not."

"How about going back to camp for a rest now?" Kath suggested.

"I'm fine," I said, "really. Let's walk to Lyell Fork, instead."

"Actually, I'm feeling kind of wiped out, myself."

"Katherine Peterson!" I watched her face burn. "Don't patronize me. I know when I'm tired, when I've had enough." I wasn't sure whether I was more afraid of being fragile like Mother or being the object of concern for people who were afraid I was as fragile as Mother.

"OK," Kath said. "You win."

As we hiked out to the fork, I thought how much I missed California seasons. I loved the warm days of January that opened cherry and almond blossoms. Although I resisted the chilly spring storms, there was something mystical about swimming outdoors at the local pool in the March rain — the warmth of the pool beneath you, steam rising to the sky. I savored the dry passage of May into summer, the cloud-covered July mornings, the hot, arid wrap of August and September and the lingering warmth of October afternoons. In leaving California, in crossing these graceful mountains east and going so far from the valleys and the cold Pacific whitecaps, I felt as if I had diminished my capacity to imagine.

This midafternoon, Lyell Fork was also pulsing green and yellow, the rich heat of the day rising from earth. We passed several anglers, and a marmot played peekaboo for fifty yards. Sun ripened the day.

"How about a swim?" I suggested. The water in most of the fork was too rapid, but here near the sheets of granite, the current was gentle, almost still. And the afternoon sun would have warmed it enough for swimming.

"Be serious!"

"No, really. Forget your Nordic formality; really, our underwear is more modest than a lot of bathing suits."

Kath rolled her eyes. "It's one thing up at Vogelsang. But more people walk along Lyell Fork."

"And we could dry off here on the rocks." I patted a particularly smooth boulder.

"I don't think so."

"Spoilsport."

"No, I don't want to ruin your fun." Kath considered me carefully. "Go ahead, I'll sit right here."

"My lifeguard. No you don't. Come for a dip. What do you have to lose?"

"My clothes." Kath laughed.

"Your dignity!" I squinted into the sun toward her.

"You're the one with dignity, with class. Who am I in comparison?"

"Spare me, Miss Big Pride. Miss Always in Control."

"I have no idea what you're talking about."

I watched her resolve wearing down. I walked five yards. "See, over here, we'll be shaded from human curiosity." I pulled off one shoe and sock, then stuck my foot in the water.

"Good way to break your neck," Kath called. Never a diver, she slipped into the water carefully, as if opening bedsheets. Soon she surfaced, her hair sleeked back. "Brisk." The short word almost concealed her chattering teeth.

"You get used to it," I bluffed.

Kath ducked under the water, a river otter cruising the shoals. Suddenly she had my arm and was pulling, pulling me beneath the surface. We faced each other in the cool, gray underworld for a couple of seconds before popping up for air.

Then I caught hold of her ankle. She almost got away before I drew her, whoosh, under the water. We came up again at the same time, laughing, sputtering.

"Oh, that felt good." I sighed, doing an elementary backstroke to keep afloat. "I think I'm going to sunbathe for a while."

"See you in a minute. I hate to say it, but this actually feels good on my shoulders and neck."

Sitting forward, I watched Kath's strong, determined strokes, the solid brown shoulders, the certain, precise pivot of her arms. Kath had always had a lean, elegant body, and today she moved with effortless grace, alternating her laps with different strokes: crawl, breast, side. Only one day left and we still hadn't acknowledged any sexual feelings. Kath had felt something, I was sure. Was her silence — and mine — from wisdom or repression? Were we two stodgy matrons who had lost their candor? No, that wasn't it. We were understandably cautious about our fragile, renewed friendship. For my part, I didn't know how much of this strange, sensual connection was simply rediscovered pleasure in our close friendship. And Kath? One thing the last week — the last twenty years — had taught me is that I couldn't read her mind. I lay back, soaking up the hot, four o'clock sun. Ohhhh. I imagined a life where people lived in this glory all the time, where when you wanted to bathe, you slipped into cool, clean mountain water.

When I awoke, Kath was studying my face. Somewhere in the background: the strange sound of bells. Yesterday, there was something, yesterday. Her gaze was intense, worried?

"What is it?" I asked, alarmed, running a hand over my forehead.

"Nothing." Kath turned away and closed her eyes in embarrassment.

"Is something wrong?"

"No," Kath said, "nothing's wrong. I, well, I was just remembering what you said about changing. How are you different?"

I sat up. "A minute ago, I was inspecting my thighs; they've grown more lavish with the years."

Kath shook her head. "You've always had a beautiful body. You've always torn yourself up."

I blushed and noticed Kath's face was also red. "Well, it's a body that seems pretty comfortable in California."

Kath lowered her head against the rock, eyes closed, waiting. A ribbon of sunlight was draped across her body, then suddenly it was lifted away by a passing cloud.

I fell silent, damning my impetuousness, then became distracted by a small juniper bush growing out of a chunk of granite.

Kath persisted. "Comfortable in California. So that means you're glad you made the trip?"

I took in her worried countenance and the thumping of a pileated woodpecker in a tall sequoia.

I nodded. "Very glad."

Kath's shoulders relaxed against the warm rock. A breeze carried the scent of river water and her familiar sweat.

"And" — I was sitting up now — "and it means I'm coming back."

I didn't dare look in her face as my voice careened ahead. "I can always experiment for a year, get a leave from Wellesley. Lou and I can try commuting. He can look for something here. We can see what living apart feels like."

I listened to the air going in and out of my nostrils. I concentrated on the benign afternoon. On the smooth and pitted surface of the boulders. The faint aroma of lemongrass in the air. I was coming back home to the West. The world was bold and fragrant with August yellow-green.

"Of course I couldn't come home this year. I'm already booked for courses, and the boys are set up in their school. But next year, yes, I'm sure they'll jump at the adventure. I want Taylor and Simon to see my country: the California tulip trees, the almond blossoms, the hibiscus."

Kath looked at me, looked down. Then she uttered something inaudible.

"Pardon?"

She spoke more boldly, "I have a double-ruffled hibiscus in my backyard."

"Double-ruffled!" I laughed. "I'll have to see that."

"Yes." Kath nodded. "And a wall of bougainvillea."

25

Kath

DINNER AT TUOLUMNE LODGE was always substantial and usually late. I waited by the cold woodstove, saving a canvas chair for Adele as she ordered us each a glass of wine. While most people joined community-style at large, round tables, we had asked for a smaller table by ourselves off to the side. There was a lot to talk about. I felt agitated about her decision. Two miracles were enough: Adele rescued and our friendship restored. I'd ask for nothing more. Still, I could hope. Tentatively I touched the sunburn on my back.

Adele held the two glasses out in front of her, maneuvering around the stands of books and candies, squeezing past a young couple selecting perfect postcards. The complicated tensions of the last few days were beginning to register. I was shaky and exhausted.

My heart clenched as I saw the tall figure with a camera around his neck push open the screen door. Sleeves rolled up, a clean headband around his curly hair, Sandy was a handsome man. I considered disappearing out the kitchen door. After all, I'd witnessed this same scene too many times. He was greeting Adele now, giving her a chaste peck on the cheek, taking one of the drinks from her. I fantasized grabbing both glasses and pouring them over him. Even as my mind romped, I composed a mature greeting.

"Oh, Kath." Adele stood in front of me, grinning, delivering him as if he were a bouquet of flowers. "Sandy found us through that odd woman at the infirmary. He said he got back from searching too late to make the trip down here last night."

"Lucky we're still around," I said neutrally. I hated my stinginess. He *had* been a big help.

"Yeah." His voice seemed to fill the room. "I assumed it was hopeless, that you'd take off at the crack of dawn for the conference."

"What am I thinking about?" Adele said. "Here, Sandy, you take my wine and I'll get another."

"No, no thanks," Sandy said. "I don't drink. You go right ahead. It's great to see you looking so well." He beamed. "I mean, I don't want to be gruesome; yeah, I'll spare you my morbid worries."

Adele shifted. "I'm sorry I scared you — both of you — it must have been dreadful."

I sat watching the two of them, feeling twelve years old — timid, pouting, confused. I should have stood. It would have been more polite, but I felt weighted to the chair.

"Thanks for leaving the message on my backpack." Sandy turned to me. "I was so damned relieved to get it."

He smiled at Adele.

She blushed.

"Sure," I said, and experiencing genuine remorse, "sorry I couldn't wait for you."

"Oh, no." His face lit up at my friendliness. "You were right to go ahead. I stayed out searching till after dark."

I gulped, kicking myself for creating another platform for his heroism. Jesus, how could I be so petty?

"And I was overjoyed when I got back to camp, to your note." He grinned.

"You were a real help," I said, pleasantly surprised by my generosity. "A big support."

Adele looked from one of us to the other, smiling. "Well, here we all are." Then, maybe miscalculating my new appreciation for Sandy, she said, "Why don't you join us for supper?" She was sipping the wine. "I'm sure we'd both like that."

She turned to me.

Silence.

"Don't worry" — he intervened — "you've already made your reservations. They're hard to change here."

Adele stared at me. I looked down.

Eyes glued to my mud-streaked boots, I tried to lift my head, tried to sound cordial, but all I could manage was a grudging, "Sure" addressed to our collective shoelaces.

Sandy glanced at the floor, then at his watch. "No, better not. Should get back to the city tonight. "But, hey." He reached in his pocket and handed a card to Adele. "I put my home address on the other side. In case you get back to California. In case you take up that Berkeley offer or whatever."

"Yes," Adele answered warmly. "And here's my home phone. Unlisted." She scribbled the number on the wine receipt. "In case you get to Cambridge."

"May do." He snapped his headband in a wacky salute that even I found charming. "Take care. Both of you."

I stood to shake his hand but instead found myself drawn into the same kind of awkward hug he gave Adele.

Adele watched him stride across the room. He resembled those WASP male monologuists Spalding Gray and Garrison Keillor, who always made me wonder how people with such mundane lives had so much to say about themselves.

"That wasn't very nice," Adele said once the screen door had wheezed shut behind him.

"Pardon?"

"Not including him in dinner." She sipped her wine.

"What are you talking about?" I retorted in the grip of my old belligerence. "I said 'sure.'" Why did we have to keep interrupting our trip? What did I owe him? I didn't know if I should be proud of getting rid of him or contrite.

" 'Sure!' What kind of invitation is that?"

"I thought this dinner was supposed to be your welcome-back evening. We asked for a table for two. I didn't know we were adding people off the street." I collapsed in the chair.

She perched beside me. "Kath, be fair. He's hardly a person off the street."

"Off the trail, then."

"He's more than that and you know it."

"Well, I'm sure you can catch him. Go ahead. Maybe you'd rather eat with him than with me."

"I didn't say that."

"So what *is* he to you? How much of coming back to California is seeing Sandy again?"

"Kath." She glared at me. "Be serious. I hardly know the guy."

"Then why did you ask him to join us?"

Adele was also clearly pissed off. "How about he just spent the day wandering the wilderness looking for me?"

This anger gave me pleasure as we faced each other with nothing between us.

"Peterson, party of two." An aproned young man called from the dining room door.

We walked forward.

"And Dyson, party of six. All eight people at the far table."

I explained, "No, there must be some mistake. We had requested a table to ourselves when —"

"It's OK," Adele interrupted. "We'll join the others."

The harried waiter shrugged. "You can have a deuce in half an hour, but this is all we've got now."

Adele turned to me. "If we're going to call Nancy before it gets late, we better eat."

How could she use Nancy to manipulate me? I glowered. But of course she was right about the call. "OK." I recovered my indifferent tone.

Adele smiled cordially at Mr. and Mrs. Dyson, Grandma Dyson and the three little Dysons.

She sat at the opposite side of the round table from me, eagerly engaging our dinner companions in High Country conversation. The Dyson family was from San Francisco and had been coming to Tuolumne Meadows for three generations. Today all six of them had hiked to Cathedral Lake and back. I found Margie, the matriarch, particularly interesting as she described the mountains in the 1930s, when the roads were rougher and the trails less crowded. The children were tired and squirmy, but pretty good sports about eating with strangers. Adele started an academic conversation with the couple, who taught at San Francisco State.

"The road from Cathedral Creek to Tioga Pass wasn't paved until the fall of '37," Margie was explaining to me.

My attention had drifted across the table.

"So that's quite a choice," I heard him saying. Roger, I seemed to remember his name was Roger. "Berkeley or Wellesley."

"But commuting sounds tough," Jean Dyson declared. "Particularly with kids."

I held my breath and nodded distractedly as Margie recalled riding a mule to Tenaya Lake. Hadn't Adele already made her decision? Was she going back on it now?

"We'll be OK for a year," she said. "It will probably be good for us. For all of us."

"What draws you to California?" The man approved of this move more than the woman.

"The question is — what draws me back?" Adele intended me to hear and met my gaze. "This is home, I was born here, in Oakland."

The woman nodded.

"In fact, Kath and I first came to Tuolumne twenty-five years ago."

"Oh, so this is some kind of reunion."

"Yes." Adele smiled at her, at me.

"There's nothing like California geography," said Margie. "I was a nurse in Europe during the War and in Asia afterwards. As far as I've traveled, there's nothing like these mountains."

It was 8:00 P.M. by the time the Dysons said good night.

On the way out, I began to tell Adele my strange dream. "There was this bear. And you were in it —"

"Really? I had a bear dream. I hope it was a dream."

"You're kidding."

"Well, I never did find our water bottle again," she said vaguely. "Anyway, this bear was terrifying, but comforting, too, in an odd —"

Seeing the phone booths, I remembered Nancy. "God, we almost forgot again." I pointed to the phone. "Let's call her now."

But both booths were occupied. Three men stood waiting to make calls. While Adele held our place in line, I ran across the campground to the lavatory.

Floating through the starry night, I felt satisfied with what Adele had told the Dysons. Yes, she'd be coming back — for a time — I'd stop worrying. And she was right, a year apart from Lou would be healthy for them. I hoped the boys *would* come with her. I was good with my friends' kids. And I had a huge curiosity about Adele's children. Did they look like her? How much had they inherited from each parent? We'd have fun bringing the boys up to the mountains.

The lavatory was busy with females of assorted ages brushing, washing, creaming, spraying, conducting the pink-colored and peach-scented women's rituals that still made me uneasy. I was overcome with that sensation of strangeness I often felt when I walked into the high school bathroom and found the popular girls smoking and gossiping. Adele and I complained about these celebrity cheerleaders, but secretly we savored our marginality. For most of my life, I had an image of myself as a sideline person, but in recent years, I'd had to admit all people picture themselves on the sidelines. And, actually, most of us were located in some center. There were lots of centers. Even Adele and I were at one center in school — the hip girl brains. Our gang may not have been the richest or the best dressed, but we had a good time together cultivating our eccentricities.

The night had grown colder. My friend looked pale in the artificial light of the phone booth. I was surprised that she'd gotten the telephone so quickly. Maybe the men had been hanging out, not waiting in line at all. Adele was leaning forward into the receiver as if she had a bad connection. I stared at her firm, strong shoulders, remembering the concentrated gentleness of her walk.

I waved. Showing no sign of recognition, she rested back against the door and bent lower to the telephone. Worried, I quickened my pace. When I rapped on the glass, Adele turned away, hunching into the corner of the booth.

The Dysons ambled by, joking, laughing.

"Kath," Jean Dyson called, holding Roger's hand.

"Hi, there," I called back.

"Drive safely tomorrow."

"Yes." I waved. "You have a good hike to Young Lakes."

I turned back to the phone booth. Adele was collapsed against the corner; she had hung up the phone and seemed to be examining the thickness of the glass booth.

I rapped again. She didn't move.

Cautiously, I opened the door and touched her shoulder. It was smaller than I anticipated, and tight.

Slowly, Adele turned, her face streaked with tears. I gathered her in my arms.

"Tell me," I whispered. "Tell me."

Adele heaved great sobs, her body moving up and down like a riveter's, the wails rising from deep inside her.

"She's dead, Kath."

I couldn't breathe.

"When they operated, they found it'd spread. She died Wednesday. Right on the operating table. All that chemo and radiation and still it spread. She just died. Like that."

I buried my face in Adele's neck and cried with her.

She held me close, weeping, shaking her head.

Tears boiled up. Tears of grief. Anger. Guilt. Of course Nancy had told me not to call until after the surgery. Still, I felt if I'd reached out earlier, I could have done something. At least I could have said good-bye.

Eventually I stepped back. "Well, I suppose we better get out of here."

She tried to compose herself. "We're making quite a spectacle in this lighted phone booth."

"Yes." I nodded numbly.

"Performance art comes to Tuolumne." Adele sniffed, forcing irony into her voice. "Somehow, I think Nancy would approve."

We went to the Meadows because it was Nancy's favorite place. I spread out an old tartan blanket, and the two of us sat talking about the night of the iridescent nail polish. The afternoon we all cut school to see *Waiting for Godot* (what pitifully wholesome girls we were, even in rebellion). The slumber party where Nancy phoned our chemistry teacher, disguising her voice and informing him he had won a lifetime subscription to *Man and Molecule*. Crying and holding on to one another, we asked why Nancy's life had been so tough.

"It wasn't what she expected." I lay back on the blanket. "Remember the plans for New York and Paris? The fashion magazines? The singing career?"

"But she had her kids," Adele argued, "and laughs. A great sense of humor. That night at the reunion, she laughed more than anyone." Her voice trembled.

I sat up and held my friend. "Yes. And she was stronger than either of us."

"Yes," Adele said absently.

Then, "How do you mean?"

"She got us back here. Together."

We broke down sobbing.

The night was warm, still. Crickets hummed. We were surrounded by a wreath of minty pennyroyal.

"She had a great hunger, she kept trying," Adele mused as she lay on the blanket, and searched the sky, "she was always reaching forward, wanting more."

"So it's the wanting that counts?" I leaned on one elbow.

"That's all there is." Her voice was soft, determined.

"Yes," I said, because it would be a relief to believe this were true.

"Oh!" She pointed. "A shooting star."

"Where?" I demanded. "Damn, I missed it."

She pulled me down on the blanket. "Here. You'll see them if you lie here and keep your eyes open."

I studied the sky and thought how long it seemed since that first trip. Lifetimes. How long since Adele's lost night. Meanwhile, we had always been here, always, lying on this sweet wool blanket, tracking the stars.

"There!" Adele said.

I missed this one too.

Together we located Libra, Sagittarius, Scorpio.

The evening grew cooler and we moved closer for warmth.

"There!" Adele called again.

"Where?"

"Quick, by Mars."

"Oh, yes, there. I see it now."